THE TOTAL PACKAGE

ALSO BY STEPHANIE EVANOVICH

Big Girl Panties

The Sweet Spot

THE
total
PACKAGE

STEPHANIE EVANOVICH

WILLIAM MORROW
An Imprint of HarperCollins*Publishers*

APR 0 4 2016

HarperCollins books may be purchased for educational, business, or sales promotional use. For information please e-mail the Special Markets Department at SPsales@harpercollins.com.

FIRST EDITION

Title page and chapter opener art © by Roman Malyshev/Shutterstock, Inc.

Designed by Lisa Stokes

Library of Congress Cataloging-in-Publication Data has been applied for.

ISBN 978-0-06-223485-8 (hardcover)
ISBN 978-0-06-241120-4 (international edition)

16 17 18 19 20   OV/RRD   10 9 8 7 6 5 4 3 2 1

For Robert and Doris
a.k.a. Boris and Natasha
a.k.a. Dad and Mom

With all my love

THE TOTAL PACKAGE

CHAPTER 1

ALTHOUGH SMOKING HAD been outlawed inside public establishments more than a decade ago, the bar still had leftover smog. Invisible yet pungent, it hung like an indiscernible cloud. Adding to it were eons of postadolescent hormones and a corner that never could completely ditch the smell of vomit. Aptly named the Bunker in this particular rural Pennsylvania college town, it was where a college freshman managed to get served a few beers, and the owner could get away with it as long as neither acted like a jackass. The red-plastic-covered barstools and chairs were sometimes sticky from humidity and residual sweat from game-winning celebrations and defeat commiserations. When ordering pitchers of beer you didn't look too closely at the glasses, telling yourself that the alcohol would kill any germs, which was part of the general belief that one was invincible. Still, the Bunker inspired the kind of nostalgia that made it a must-stop whenever former students attended homecoming.

Everyone remembers their old college hangouts. But while Tyson Palmer sat alone at a table in the barf corner of his alma mater, he was grasping for memories. Maybe it was the weed that dulled his senses. Or maybe the Percocet. He still believed he could hold his liquor.

"I'll take another Jack Daniel's on the rocks." He jiggled the ice in his now-empty glass at the server making a pass across the room, his voice deceptively steady. "Make it a double." Some of the recollections were so clear. Not too long ago, around these parts people had described him as promising and gifted. Tyson had been the classic success story, raised in a hardworking, middle-class family that met all the American Dream criteria, even if those requirements were throwbacks from the '50s. There was one boy and one girl born to a mother who worked part-time when they were in school and dressed them up for church every Sunday. A dad who came home every night from his management job at a local building supply store at five fifteen on the dot to enjoy a cocktail with his loyal wife as she finished preparing dinner. Douglas Palmer was the kind of father who played poker once a month with the neighborhood fellas and never missed a peewee football or baseball game. Whose eyes lit up when he realized just how far and accurate his then-ten-year-old son could aim. He tried to downplay his pride as the accolades began rolling in and coaches took real notice. Then, slowly but surely, he became the father who vicariously began to live his own variation of football fantasy through that son. After acting as his agent when Tyson signed with the Boston Blitz, his dad divorced his mom and moved in with a twenty-three-year-old exotic dancer.

Within the last three years, the adjectives attached to Tyson Palmer's name slowly morphed into overrated, reprehensible. A real waste.

Wanting to stay in his father's good graces, Tyson had often joined him in his downhill slide. Douglas Palmer proved a bad example. Tyson took responsibility for his mother's heartbreak, stuffed all the hurt and pain deep down inside, and set the sequence on his time bomb to self-destruct.

Coming back here was supposed to be a kind of victory lap. But Tyson wasn't being followed by throngs of alumni or asked to attend any ceremonies, not even the ones taking place on the football field. He wasn't invited to any parties. Instead Tyson had been forced to retreat to the Bunker, where he was pointed at from a safe distance, like an animal in a zoo. Occasionally someone would approach him, politely engage him for a few moments, mostly about the weather, and be on their way. Nothing to see here—the phrase cops always used to move spectators along from a crime scene. His teammates and Blitz management had tried to be supportive . . . in the beginning. But it wasn't long before Tyson's shenanigans robbed him of his ability to lead, and they all had grown weary of him, even before he started racking up more interceptions than touchdowns on game day. He knew that within the next twenty-four hours his dirty drug test results would leave him jobless and probably tossed out of the league. The book they were getting ready to throw at him was heavy. *I sure won't miss those cold Massachusetts winters,* he thought to console himself.

"Tyson?"

Bloodshot eyes focused on a face that was vaguely familiar. It was a wisp of a ghost brushing by him. Someone insignificant, but at the same time, not—pretty, but low maintenance. Dark hair, hazel eyes with a glint of determination magnified through the lenses of her glasses. When he'd seen her last, she had something he needed. And something he'd wanted.

"Helen?" he tried to zero in. They had spent quality time together, at least for a while. He hadn't seen her naked, but it probably wasn't from lack of trying. Those whose pants he didn't get into were much more likely to stand out. "Ellen?"

"Ella," she said hopefully. "I was your English tutor, in your senior year?"

Now he remembered. A flash that was stark and vivid, from the predrug days, before those first few injuries that weren't so quick to heal. She had been one of several students handpicked by the administration when he fell short on his classes during football season. Hired for several hours a week to basically cram the exams into his skull and dictate his essays to him. He wasn't stupid, but he also didn't make it easy. Back then he thought about nothing but football and was easily distracted when it came to anything else. "Right." He smiled at her, feeling the warm nostalgic wave. Her last name was something Italian. "Ella Bella."

He had made up the cheesy nickname for her on a rainy afternoon four weeks into that semester, after they abandoned meeting at the library in favor of his dorm room. When he decided he would rather make out than recite the answers to an upcoming test. She was appealing enough, fresh faced and makeup free, a sophomore who had held on to her freshman fifteen. Not girlfriend material, but he wasn't looking for a girlfriend.

And after one delicious kiss, Ella Bella had shot him down. Not in cold blood, of course; she'd stammered through the willing-to-date-him speech, but he'd never asked her for a date, and casual sex was off the table. She told him that she was still a virgin and she planned on staying that way. Something about a virgin never failed to make a horny guy hum. Tyson jokingly asked her to bang him every time they were together after that, but he was hardly brokenhearted when she laughed him off. There was always someone else on the sidelines. It was more his way of telling her he was available if she ever wanted to change her mind. He began to view her more like a little sister, especially since she could talk football better than any other girl he knew at school, even better than some of his teammates.

"You remember?" She smiled back at him, and then giggled. He still had it. And clearly she knew nothing of what was happening in his world. These days he was on almost every woman's shit list.

The server dropped off his fresh drink, but Tyson kept at the remaining ice in his drained glass. Pheromones were producing an equally worthy rush. Ella with the Italian name had barely changed at all. She was still cute. The bar was starting to wind down. It was after 1:00 A.M. The music had stopped playing, but the other drinkers in the bar didn't seem to notice. Those in hushed conversations still were quiet, only now lip-reading was no longer required. Rowdy voices remained boisterous.

"Of course I remember. Thanks to you, I got a B." Not sure if that was true, but he had a knack for mixing his caddishness with boyish charm, even when he was half in the bag. "You're here for homecoming?"

"Yes, by default. I stayed here to continue on to my master's. I graduate this year."

"Congratulations," he said, straightening up, envious that she would soon be rewarded for having learned all her lessons, including the one about resisting temptation. Suddenly being the biggest partier in the room was a dubious distinction. "Have a seat, let me buy you a drink. We'll celebrate." He slid his fresh drink across the table in her direction.

"I'm not there yet." She took up his offer for a seat across from him and ignored the highball of whiskey. "I still have to make it through the year. How are you?"

A loaded question if ever there was one. And the first time he was asked it all night without the asker trying to quickly take it back. By the kindhearted look on her face, she really wanted to know. But how is anyone who's about to lose everything and become a social pariah? Who will have managed to fall from grace in such a spectacular fashion and in record time? Looking into the eyes of this innocent bookworm, who was still protected from the outside world by two square miles of college campus, he longed to answer honestly. To tell Ella Bella that he wanted to go home but couldn't remember his own address. And then confess that even if he did recall it, he couldn't go there anyway because the repo man was probably lying in wait to take back his Land Rover, the only thing he had left after his exceptionally beautiful trophy wife cleaned him out and left when the rumors started to surface and the police came calling. He wanted to admit that he couldn't tell the difference between stoned and tired anymore.

"I'm doing great," he replied, longing to pick up one of the conversations from his past. And if there was one thing he could never be accused of, it was being a whiner.

Her expression didn't change, and she continued to study him with the same gentle smile.

"You don't have to keep up appearances for me, Tyson."

At first it didn't register, and then he just didn't want it to. He had already attached himself to the fantasy that she was too busy being intelligent with her nose in a book to be bothered with television. Or the Internet, where his life seemed to play out as he lived it. A train wreck he couldn't stand watching even as he stood at the helm and drove. He resisted reaching into his pocket for another Percocet, opting instead to take back the Jack Daniel's he had previously offered her.

"Here's to the good old days," he toasted before taking a swallow. He quickly put his hand and the glass back on the table, a trick he'd learned to feel grounded. Now was the moment for her to take her leave and join the ranks of those repulsed by him. But sweet inexperienced Ella wasn't beating a hasty retreat. Instead she pulled her chair up closer and lowered her voice.

"I'd much rather toast to your future," she said, picking up his half empty drink and polishing it off.

He didn't want to pretend anymore. And he didn't have to carry on the charade. She still seemed to be looking at him with the wide-eyed adoration she had in the past, only now with a shadow of Jack-shooting tough girl.

"I don't have a future."

"Of course you do," she proclaimed, "and I want to help you get back on the field."

Tyson leaned back in his chair, stretching out his long legs to one side of the table. He crossed his arms over his chest and let out a single chuckle. Not the follow-up he'd expected. And she said it like he should've known.

"Just how do you propose to do that, Ella Bella?"

"By being a real friend for starters, the kind that wouldn't just sit idly by and watch you get hooked on drugs."

"Nobody got me hooked on anything," he said stubbornly, more defense mechanism than anything else. By the time the news broke that she was indeed correct, this conversation would be over and he'd never have to see her again. And he refused to blame anyone other than himself for his lousy choices.

"So it was just alcohol that influenced your decisions that night with Carla Dowe?" she asked, moving on to the next topic, sounding more like a sideline reporter than an old friend.

Tyson grimaced. That was one face he'd never forget. At least she got right to the point. Carla Dowe was the beauty he met in a nightclub outside of Houston. She had long hair, longer legs, and rode him like a cowgirl in his rental car in the parking lot where they shared a joint after drinking the night away. His other transgressions surfaced rapidly after she sent one too many selfies of them looking a little too cozy. Her tune changed altogether once her parents found out. In the lawsuits that followed and thanks to his expensive attorney, the bar that let her in and served her took the brunt of the fallout. The suspicion around him remained as the allegations intensified, and rightly so. Even he had trouble recollecting the events of that evening. His blackouts had become a frequent occurrence. Luckily, his own lawyer was ruthless enough to subpoena and systematically grill friend after friend of the girl's to testify about that night and Carla's delight at having landed herself the ultimate score, complete with all the smiles she snapped, captured, and sent. But it was a double-edged sword. She looked young and innocent. He looked like ten miles of bad road. Tyson was spared a jail sentence but convicted of being a total scumbag in the court of public opinion.

"I swear she told me she was twenty-one." He tried to make it sound like a joke, but the embarrassment reflected in his bloodshot eyes. "And she *was* eighteen." He added feebly. He wasn't sure why he bothered. There was still the issue that he was married at the time.

"Four days into eighteen. Easy to lose sight of that fact given she was still in high school," Ella replied, graciously making no reference to his now-ex-wife.

Tyson scowled defensively, before leaning his forearms down on the table between them. "Then I guess there really isn't any story left to tell. Sounds like you know it all." He was sorry he had offered her a seat, much less his drink.

"I told you, Tyson, I want to try to help you," she reiterated.

"Why?"

"Because I believe in you," Ella stated with conviction, as if that was enough to earn his trust. But Tyson Palmer was long past trusting anyone, including himself.

"Why?" he repeated, now angry.

Ella looked down at the table for a moment, then said quietly, "Because I remember the guy I tutored. Who was serious about his game and never had a problem taking no for an answer."

He wanted to laugh in her naïve face. To mockingly tell her at the time she hadn't been worth the pursuit, if for no other reason than to get her to leave him alone. He wanted her to stop looking at him in the way she was, like he was not a total disaster. But most of all, he no longer wanted to be reminded of when he was in control and held the world in the palm of his football-throwing hand.

"That kid doesn't exist anymore. When you graduate and join the real world, you'll realize that people change, usually not for the better," he spat out cynically.

"I refuse to believe that."

Tyson sighed and ran his hand through the shaggy brown hair that had outgrown his clean cut months ago. She was being way too persistent, but her sincerity was admirable, and part of him wanted to believe her.

"Okay. We're friends, now what?"

She brightened with his acquiescence. And she really did have a pretty smile. "Now you let me be a good friend and help take care of you. You look so tired. "

This time he didn't hold back the laugh, and while it wasn't exactly harsh, it still was hollow. She wasn't able to help him any more than he could help himself. And she made it sound so easy, like she could perform some sort of exorcism and all his demons would flee. The more likely story was she was trying to get close to him under the misguided impression that he had something left to offer.

"You're good, Mother Teresa. Why don't we go someplace quiet where I can confess my sins and you can absolve me? Make sure you turn your phone on to RECORD, so you don't miss the good stuff."

"You're wrong, but I understand you being leery," she patiently explained. "I . . . I always liked you, Tyson, and you were always so nice to me. You deserve to have someone on your side. I know this is all just your circumstances talking."

"Sorry, not interested." Tyson took back his now-empty glass and went back to sucking the last remnants of Gentleman Jack off the ice. Damn his mouth was dry, always so dry. As far as he was concerned, the conversation was closed. He wanted her to get out before he settled back into the dark side.

"What would it take for me to get you interested? For you to consider coming home with me, at least for a decent night's sleep?"

Maybe it was the way she asked it, completely oblivious to the fact that the question itself made her sound like a hooker. Maybe it was the pity or her dogged insistence that he see himself for something other than he was, which was a lost cause. And then, like a lighthouse shining through the fog in his brain, it dawned on him. His cute little virtuous tutor had joined the ranks of pleasure seekers and was trying to get him into bed. At least that explanation turned the exchange from ludicrous to one that made sense.

"You still a virgin, Ella Bella?" He answered her question with one of his own, accompanied by a smile of complete impropriety.

Finally she blinked. Her grip tightened around the handle of the purse in her lap, and she stared at it before looking back up at him and meeting his gaze head-on.

"Yes." She spoke her one-word answer unemotionally, even as the flush crept up to her cheeks.

Tyson sat back in his chair, the recesses of his drug-addled mind jarred. Wrong answer. She was supposed to have forsaken her outdated notion of chastity. She was supposed to have been tainted by now, like everyone he knew. As corrupted as he was.

"Hey Ella Bella, what do you say to you and me going someplace to get freaky?" Part of it was said in jest, trying to recover from just how badly she managed to throw him. Another part of him longed to engage in just a little bit of the same harmless banter from the days when she was a sweetheart and he was a hero.

"Your place or mine?" Her answer was so unexpected and sounded just as foreign to his ears.

She was supposed to have played along and let him down easy, as she had done a hundred times before.

Tyson shook his head, unsure if he'd heard her correctly. He took a moment to let it sink in. Perhaps she was just trying to be funny, to save them both from the awkwardness of his initial reaction. Or she was trying to show him she was all grown up.

"You shouldn't be so glib, Ella," he scolded her. "It could get you into trouble."

She seemed to enjoy watching the emotions that played across his face. "Maybe I'm looking for trouble."

Despite all his best intentions his body once again started to hum. She had upped the ante.

"Are you suggesting what I think you are?"

"I want you to be the first person I make love to." It sounded romantic, but romance wasn't what he was currently known for. Or what he wanted. He wanted dirty, sleazy, guilt-free hookup sex, at least until they lawyered up. It was what he was used to. But not what he wanted for her. He was surprised that he even cared at all.

"You don't know what you're saying."

Not only did she not appear chastised, but by the set of her jaw, she looked more determined. "I'm a grown woman, Tyson. I know what I'm doing."

The very idea was preposterous. They were little more than strangers. He knew better than anyone that strangers didn't have sex to forge relationships. They did it to avoid them. Who in their right mind would make such an offer after so many years? He gave her some time to come to her senses, but she continued to stare at him, waiting for his answer. "You do know what they're saying about me?"

He felt her foot clumsily begin to slide up his leg in response to the question. He gave a short laugh and then narrowed his eyes.

"You realize this ride has no refunds?"

"I do," she confirmed.

"And when it's over, I'm going to consider you just another whore?"

He fully expected her to stand up and slap his face. To see him for what he was. To finally abandon the notion that she was going to save him and leave him to his misery. But she only tilted her head and studied him, every bit the sophomore he remembered, only now with her foot finding the inside of his thigh.

"No you're not, Tyson. Quit trying to scare me away."

He finally stopped caring. The hum had gotten loud enough to be heard through the numb. Nostalgia was grossly overrated anyway. And her smile was positively naughty.

"Put your shoe back on. The room's on me," Tyson said ungallantly, pushing away from the table and standing up. "You're on."

He gave her two of the last five one-hundred-dollar bills he had, and they checked into the local Motel 6 under her name while he waited outside. It was a condition Tyson insisted on, and he did it automatically out of self-preservation. There would no confusion as to who was initiating what, should she end up having second thoughts after it was over.

He wasn't sure what to expect next from her and he had long forgotten how to properly execute foreplay. He half hoped she would chicken out and run screaming into the night. He wasn't even sure in his current state that he could adequately perform.

They took off their coats and Tyson sat on the edge of the bed. He thought about just lying down and dozing off. They could forget the whole thing. He watched Ella turn the television on and begin to surf, stopping on the motel's promotional channel, which was the closest she could get to mood music. Nothing said romantic interlude quite like a picture of a continental breakfast with Muzak playing in the background. Then she began to dim the lights.

After checking the dead bolt on the door, she went and stood between his legs. She wove her hand into his hair and then gently fisted it, to tilt his head up to her and hold it in place. The fingertips of her other hand stroked over his cheekbone and down his jaw, then up over the bridge of his slightly crooked nose, the result of him playing through two quarters before having it set during his rookie season with the Blitz. He had considered that bump a badge of courage, even if it was the injury that became the catalyst to launch him into his new normal, courtesy of that first bottle of Vicodin being slipped into his locker by a team doctor. She was mesmerized, like she was walking around in her own amorous fantasy, her movements deliberate and calculated. She looked down and pulled his hair slightly to make sure his eyes were looking into hers.

"You really are still so beautiful." She exhaled in awe before gently placing her mouth against his. She tasted him, then unhurriedly ran her tongue over his upper lip before nipping at it. Her breath was sweet, Tic Tacs with traces of the whiskey they'd shared.

Whatever Ella's teacher had been, whether book or movie, she had learned well, Tyson thought. His hands gripped around her waist and he roughly pulled her flush against him. His mouth opened wider as his hands drifted lower before coming to rest on her bottom, giving it a squeeze. Her response was to wiggle into his palms and draw his tongue into her mouth, teasing it with hers. This was no timid virgin, Tyson continued his inner justification, she was more like a vixen, and his body responded to it. Maybe she hadn't been truthful and had just told him what she thought he wanted to hear. She wasn't behaving like someone doing something she would regret. She was fully engrossed in her seduction. After that first kiss, he took off her glasses, placing them on the nightstand, and then stood. They took hasty turns stripping each other down, with kisses in between, beginning with Tyson and a sturdy tug at her cumbersome skirt. She pulled off his shirt in exchange for hers. What he uncovered was lush and curvy and a crime to keep hidden. She cooed words of encouragement as he unveiled her, becoming increasingly excited with each piece of clothing discarded, until there was only one thing left to remove. She wasn't shy or inhibited as his hands freely roamed her nakedness, concentrating on boldly raking her nails down his chest, over the speed bumps of his abs, hooking them into the waistband of his boxer briefs. He kicked the boxers to the side, and his sex sprang to attention. Her fingers curled around him and she carefully pulled and caressed, her eyes lighting up with her discovery at his size, though she had nothing to compare it to. If she kept at him, he would lose it right in her hand. He pulled her hand away and lifted her, landing them both back onto the bed, careful not to crush her. He squeezed ample breasts and sucked at taut nipples. Her touch was hot, her skin supple, and her behavior nothing short of aggressive.

Her lips moved to his neck, the beginning of a trail of kisses that slowly started making their way down his belly. She sighed in what he could only define as genuine pleasure, moving lower. It felt good, too good, and he stopped her before she reached her final destination, bringing her back up to him before pressing her back into the bed and covering her body with his own. She clutched him tightly, squirming beneath him in lust as his hand wedged between them to find her core. He toyed with her, using broad strokes from strong fingers until she was damp with wanting. She arched her back and began to whisper his name over and over, allowing herself the full pleasure of the sensation. He left her on the brink and abruptly pulled away, unwilling to admit that he questioned his own staying power.

"I have to have you," he groaned.

He pushed her back onto the bed, spread her legs with his own, and took her. He heard her sharp intake of breath at his penetration and his mouth captured hers again to avoid hearing her cry as he filled her. She was hot and tight and Tyson forced himself to remain still until her body relaxed. Her tongue found its way back into his mouth, and she wrapped a leg around his back. Then he began to slowly rock inside her. She wrapped her other leg and both her arms around him and found, then matched, his rhythm.

It seemed to be over before it began and despite all his efforts, he was soon shuddering above her, his release brought on prematurely by her enthusiasm and the lack of control over his own body. He couldn't be sure she had gotten hers, and then he realized, albeit callously, he didn't need to care. She had offered herself to him, on his terms. And by her own admission, she didn't have any real experience. Still, no man wants to be thought of as a lousy lover. Tyson rolled off her and onto the bed, now discomfited by the whole encounter.

The Muzak was still crooning from the television. An electronic instrumental symphonic take on the Bee Gees' "How Deep Is Your Love." Ella tentatively began to curl up next to him. And to his own surprise, he let her, going as far as to wrap an arm around her and settle her on his chest. He had forgotten how much he missed human contact, the kind that didn't end up giving him a bruise or a concussion. He had been caught up in his addiction for too long. He lightly stroked his hand up and down her back, appreciating her soft form molding against his muscles while he caught his breath. He fleetingly wondered if she was really as enchanting as she seemed. Booze and drugs had played tricks on him in the past. "Lady, you just blew my mind," he told her, in the effort to explain away his lackluster performance.

"Ditto." She smiled up at him, hugging him tighter. "I say we try that again."

Even if she meant that she wanted to do it again because she was now free to enjoy and explore her sexuality, all he heard was criticism. Like a coach sending him back to the field after an interception. In fact, her eagerness only reminded him of exactly what he'd done and how he wished he'd done it better. Tyson's hand stopped moving and his sense of afterglow quickly dissipated. "Once was enough."

"That's okay, then let's take a little nap," she said, snuggling up closer to him and sighing. "We'll have breakfast later, after we freshen up. And then I'll take you home."

Take him home? Was she serious? He began to feel cornered.

"There's not going to be any breakfast." His arm fell away from her shoulder.

She picked her head up, trying to get a read on him. "Are you mad at me? Did I do something wrong?"

"No, I'm not mad." But he was. When he had agreed to this idea, his plan was to sneak out after she'd fallen asleep. But she didn't look too sleepy, and it wasn't like he'd exhausted her, like he would have if he had done it right.

"I could totally fall in love with you, Tyson," she confessed, blurting it out before she saw the look on his face.

Those words had fed his ego before, but it had been a while. In this particular case, he'd never felt so undeserving. "You don't even know me."

His head was pounding, his ears were ringing, and the guilt was mounting. And his body was already starting to reach out for its next fix. He dislodged himself from under her and rose, beginning to search for his clothes.

"Tyson—what's wrong?"

Everything was wrong. Coming back to his old college as a last resort to escape from reality, letting her sit down and fill his head with memories with her sweet talk and then trap him. Tyson stormed around the room, hating her and himself, while trying to quickly redress. Not bothering with his socks, he stuck them in his pockets while sitting down in the room's only chair to jam his now-clammy feet into his shoes. Ella jumped up from the bed and scrambled to find her own clothes, which he had thrown all around the room. "Tyson, I don't understand . . ."

He reached into his jacket pocket and pulled out the vial that was his only friend, his Percocet. He threw two down his throat without any water. The mere action seemed to calm him. He put the bottle back in his jacket and reached for the doorknob, stopped momentarily by the sheer desperation in her voice.

"Tyson, please don't leave. You can trust me. I want to help you," she pleaded.

He looked back at her, standing in the middle of the room in nothing but her underwear, tears of bewilderment and humiliation brimming in her eyes.

"I don't want your help," he stated coldly.

She swallowed hard, trying to keep her voice from trembling and the tears from falling. "But you . . . I thought . . ."

"Welcome to the big time," Tyson told her cruelly before opening the door, then staggering back out into the darkness and his downfall.

CHAPTER 2

THE WEEKS THAT followed were nothing more than a blur. Tyson went back to his now-empty house and spent some quality time ignoring foreclosure notices and other bill collectors. Within days of getting the official word that he was suspended for the rest of the season and subsequently cut from the team, he packed up some of his clothes and cleaned out his medicine cabinet. He ended up in a fleabag motel near the now-deserted Blitz training camp. He just couldn't think of anywhere else to go. He wandered, mostly on foot, around the streets that were his old hangouts, where he no longer felt welcome. Every night was spent in local dives blathering randomly to anyone within earshot whenever football came on television. He celebrated Thanksgiving alone with a fifth of Wild Turkey and a ham sandwich from 7-Eleven. Not even Tyson's cell phone was invited to his pity party.

The one message from his new agent was, *Talk to you next year. Get your act together. Stay off social media*. He didn't want to hear from well-meaning friends either. In his mind, he had no friends and those trying to intervene were just trying to ruin the only good times he had left. His family back home was fractured and hurting, he couldn't add to that burden. He just wanted to do his own version of *Leaving Las Vegas* and be done with it.

That's when Tyson met the Goons.

There wasn't much of an introduction. They broke down the door to Tyson's room and hauled him off the floor by his armpits, then they dragged Tyson out to a waiting car and punched him when he started waking up on the tarmac of a small airport. The next time he awoke, it was with a splitting headache and in a comfortable bed in what looked to be someone's guest room. It was spacious and tastefully decorated, even the sunlight smelled fresh. The headache, though, was completely familiar.

"Where am I?" The words hurt his ears, and the dryness in his mouth and throat was ever present. He put a trembling hand up to his face, to shield his burnt-out retinas from the light streaming through the window.

A man sitting in a chair near the foot of the bed spoke up. 'You're in my home. If you're going to throw up, there's a bucket on the right of the bed." The Goon standing at the man's left shoulder took a step and pointed in the direction of the receptacle, to make sure they sufficiently had Tyson's attention.

"I need a drink." Tyson rasped out the same four words he had started every day with for the better part of a year.

"There's water next to you, on the nightstand," the man replied. He was soft-spoken with a country twang. "If you're looking for something stronger, I'm afraid that's not going to happen."

Tyson tried to focus on the man through his painful tunnel vision. He was someone Tyson felt like he knew, or at least knew of. He was sixtyish, trim, sporting a full head of silver hair and a weathered tan face all packaged neatly in a brown Hugo Boss suit.

"Who the hell are you?" Tyson asked irritably.

"I'm the man who's going to save your career." He had the nerve to sound nonchalant, even soothing, "And considering all the scuttlebutt surrounding your pathetic display around Blitz training camp, probably your life."

Hearing the words got under Tyson's already stretched skin. Making matters worse, the man was standing in the way of Tyson's hair of the dog.

"Let me guess." Tyson tried to sit up despite the hammering in his head that increased with movement. "You're my guardian angel and we're going to take a tour of what the world would be like without me."

The man smiled. "Yes, I'm the patron saint of party boys. Call me Saint Mercenary."

The Goons snorted in unison from their positions on either side of the chair and then went back to looking menacing. The man added, "Sorry, son, I'm not that noble. I'm just a businessman who enjoys a good challenge."

Tyson eyed the trio from the middle of the queen-size bed. Whoever this man was, he was able to pull off a kidnapping, had at least two vicious-looking henchmen, and a really nice bedroom. Tyson glanced down at the stained, grungy Blitz T-shirt he'd been wearing for five days straight. He could remember when the word *challenge* filled him with vision and determination. Currently, standing on his own two feet without falling over would be about all the challenge he could handle.

"I'm still waiting for you to tell me who you are," Tyson said, dropping his head into his hand and attempting to rub his eyes free of the double vision that, added to the smell of his shirt, was making his stomach churn. One of the Goons snorted again, this time in disgust. Apparently he took Tyson's lack of knowledge of the importance of his host personally.

"My name is Clinton Barrow," the man replied evenly. "I'm one of the owners of the Austin Mavericks."

Tyson knew the name. Barrow was one of those high-profile dudes whose family made their fortune in crude. Clint and his oil baron cronies started the Mavericks a decade ago after deciding that the fine people of Austin shouldn't have to choose between the Cowboys and the Texans when it came to professional football. He prided himself on being a hands-on guy who was loaded but classy. While he wasn't above the occasional spectacular stunt, he didn't drive a big Cadillac convertible with steer horns mounted on the grille.

"I didn't recognize you without the hat," Tyson said, referring to Barrow's signature ten-gallon Stetson.

"The missus doesn't like me to wear it in the house." Clint grinned. "But I didn't bring you here to talk about wives. I'm sure they're not on your list of favorite topics either."

Tyson rubbed his face again. Jessa Thompson, the former Mrs. Palmer, wasn't on any of his lists. Tyson really couldn't blame her. She had been one of his last attempts to make himself appear an upstanding citizen. It was a whirlwind romance that started when he met her after her failed Blitz Babes cheerleading audition. He swept her off her feet and provided her with a lavish and highly publicized wedding. She was beautiful and sweet and they made a lovely couple. Tyson tried to be a good husband at first, but he was already too far gone. And he never took into account just how shrewd his wife was. She remained unassuming and adoring, right up until the day TMZ broke the Carla Dowe story. By the time he rushed home, she had blocked his number from her cell phone and packed up all her belongings (plus some of his) and gone, leaving behind only a note with her lawyer's contact info. He had signed the papers that officially ended his marriage while in a stupor over a month ago.

It was clear that Clint Barrow had done his homework on him, but why?

"At this point, I would've thought there was something wrong with Jessa if she stayed," Tyson said, sighing, giving up and falling back onto the bed. "You still haven't told me what I'm doing here."

"I have a proposition for you," Clint said. "A one-time deal designed to mutually benefit both of us."

Tyson stared at the ceiling, trying to gather his bearings and sighed again. "I don't know anything about the Blitz that can be of any use to you."

Clinton Barrow shook his head. "I'm not looking for insider information. That would be cheating, and I abhor cheaters. What I have in mind is more of a long-term investment. This one is all about you, if you're man enough to accept the test."

Tyson steadied himself on his elbows to get a better look at his would-be benefactor. "Go on."

Clinton Barrow waited a moment. The smile was gone and he became all business. "I'm going to buy your contract at the fire sale, and you're going to win me a Super Bowl."

Despite the war raging between his stomach and his head, Tyson laughed. "You're out of your mind. I couldn't pay to play football now, even if I wasn't flat broke."

A general grumbling could be heard from the Goons at the perceived insult directed at Barrow. Clint didn't join in and instead leaned forward, resting his elbows on his knees. "You have a hell of an arm, Palmer. And I believe you have a good head on your shoulders, or at least you did, before you started spending all your time in the gutter. If it wasn't for your no-account daddy taking you out to the strip clubs instead of the woodshed, you wouldn't be in this mess. But here we are. And if you were any closer to thirty, we wouldn't even be having this conversation."

Barrow paused for full effect so that Tyson might recognize the gravity of the situation before he continued. "Now here are the terms I'm offering you. You're going to leave straight from here and go to an intensive rehab facility I've already lined up. You're going to be a model patient in every way and get yourself clean of whatever shit currently pollutes you. After they're satisfied you've completed their program with flying colors, I'm going to see to it you have the best training out there to get you back to playing form. I will supply all your housing, transportation, hell, even your clothes. There isn't going to be any fanfare, nobody is going to know what's going on. As far as the league is concerned, you will have gone down the drain with the rest of the sludge. With the exception of a phone call to your mother to tell her you're going on a retreat to clear your head, you're not going to have contact with anyone from your prior life. You won't have a phone. You may want to think about firing your agent. He's out of the loop. The only people with access to you will be the ones I've appointed, who will be reporting back to me on a regular basis. Your sole focus is going to be on getting yourself ready to get back on the field as soon as your suspension is up."

"Looks like I'm not the only one trippin'. You're never going to be able to make that happen," Tyson jeered, both skeptical and scared. What if he agreed and couldn't pull it off?

The Goons both began to lunge forward, probably to clock him again for disrespecting their boss, but Clinton Barrow straightened up, raising his hand to stay them. He sat back in his flowery upholstered chair, crossed one leg over the other, and picked at some imaginary lint on his slacks before rounding out the details of his proposal. "As soon as you're reinstated and eligible, my partners and I are then going to sign you to a three-year deal with that first year being paid at the league minimum. The following two years' salary will be determined by your performance, but you will not leave the Mavericks for any better offers unless we cut you loose. These terms are nonnegotiable, and if you don't agree to them, my associates here will be more than happy to return you to the dump we pulled you out of."

The only sounds that could be heard after Clint finished his speech were the four men breathing. Clinton Barrow had lost his mind, Tyson thought, probably the result of his team never making it past the first round of the playoffs. Or Tyson was the pawn in an extreme game of wealthy boys with toys who spent their free time making outlandish bets on the downtrodden.

Or maybe he had just been thrown a lifeline to get back into the game. "What if I can't do it?" Tyson broke the silence, giving voice to all the fear, doubt, and self-loathing that had plagued him for months.

Clinton Barrow rose from his chair and buttoned his suit jacket, seemingly satisfied that Tyson's question was his agreement. "Well, that's the risk now, isn't it? And it's a risk I'm willing to take, even if my partners think I've taken leave of my senses. All I'm asking for is that you participate in your treatment with the same gusto you used to give your game. And that you give a hundred and ten percent every day, even when you can't stand one more minute. I think you're going to do just fine and I'm looking forward to owning a championship ring.

Now get yourself cleaned up, you have a plane to catch. Welcome to the Maverick family."

Tyson sat up, only to quickly lie back down as the room began to spin around him. "Wait! Don't you want me to sign a contract or something?"

Clint started to make his way to the door but stopped short of exiting. He turned and gave Tyson a fatherly smile that belied his parting message. "This part of our deal is based on a gentlemen's agreement. Your word is considered our bond. I have faith in you, son, but if you try to double-cross me once you're back on your feet, it'll be my pleasure to have you killed."

Clinton Barrow strolled out of the room, leaving the Goons behind. They pounded their respective meaty fists into equally imposing palms.

"Now *that* sounds like a party, right, Pilly Bob Thornton?" the bigger of the two said.

Tyson might have been more intimidated, but he was busy making use of the bucket by the bed.

CHAPTER 3

THE GOONS WERE uncommunicative on the ride back to the airport, where Barrow's private jet waited to take Tyson to his new, as yet undisclosed, location. Before they confiscated his phone, they demanded Tyson call his mother, per the boss's instructions. Too ashamed to admit that hearing his worried mother and trying to sound optimistic was a conversation he couldn't pull off, he texted her instead. Without waiting for her to answer back, one of them took his phone and fiddled with it a bit.

"Your agent just got his walking papers," Tyson was informed with a sneer. He could only imagine how that text must have read.

Then the Goons removed the phone from its protective case and took turns stomping on it. After that, any of Tyson's attempts at garnering information were met with various grunted versions of "shut up."

They were the hard-core disciplined Neanderthal types. Both taller than Barrow, who was already six feet, they were all muscle and had sunglasses they didn't remove. One had a crew cut, squared off and sharp enough to etch glass. The other was one earring, a white T-shirt, and a grin short of looking exactly like Mr. Clean. Tyson measured up physically, but he was too strung out. And they were the kind that would never be found facedown in a bar. It was obvious they viewed him as a lower life-form. Tyson gave up saying anything once he began to shake uncontrollably. His bucket had been replaced by a bag that he gripped tightly in his hand and occasionally used although he had nothing left to deposit. He spent most of his ride to the airport floating in and out of consciousness and retching. He refused to groan or complain to the monsters, although on more than one occasion, his eyes filled with tears of self-pity and despair. After showering and changing into fresh basketball shorts and a plain T-shirt and hoodie, supplied by Barrow, he thought he might be starting to come around, but as the day wore on, the feelings only intensified. Or maybe he had just begun to feel again, period, after months of near blacked-out haze.

Tyson had just agreed to something he didn't think he could deliver. Surely Barrow had to have known what a clusterfuck he was setting them both up for when he made his offer. How was he, as one man, supposed to guarantee a championship season for a team, even if he was at the top of his game and in peak condition? It was by sheer luck and maybe even divine intervention that Tyson was alive at all. But all he'd really been asked for was his participation. Go back to being a football machine, even if it was football that had ruined his life. And he was getting three years to make good on it from his end. Clinton Barrow had made him feel worthy. Barrow had called him "son" in a way that struck Tyson at a primitive level, and he responded like a child who once again would do anything to please the father.

Of course, it was probably just coincidence that his real father had also threatened to kill him. Right after Tyson fired him, a drunken argument over his mother came to fisticuffs. Now all that remained was a long road ahead, and a very unpleasant one.

Tyson continued to shake after he and the Goons took off in the luxury jet. They sat as far away from him as possible, alternating between snickering and snarling, all the while making disgusted faces in his direction. Tyson finally fell back into a tormented sleep. When they landed and one of the Goons shook him awake, it was almost dark. Tyson had lost all sense of time or space. All he could do was go with it. They unceremoniously tossed him and a small duffle bag out the plane's door and onto the tarmac with a contemptuous "Go get 'em, dipshit."

A black sedan was waiting. Standing outside the car were a man and a woman, dressed more casually, businesslike. The man retrieved the duffle and Tyson stumbled, still groggy, into the backseat of the car through the door the woman held open for him. She went around to the other side and joined him while the driver put the bag in the trunk, then took his position behind the wheel and they left the airport. From the backseat of the car, the woman introduced herself as Wanda. Withholding her last name, she identified herself as a doctor and after a quick inspection of the bruises on his face, began to take his vital signs. She was gentle in her approach, plump and motherly, her black hair streaked with gray contained in a loose bun. She had a very proper British accent. She handed him a bottle of water and asked him what substances he'd been using, heroin and cocaine in particular.

"I'm a weed-smoking, pill-popping alcoholic. No crack or smack. I had to draw the line somewhere." Tyson replied with feigned indignation, earning a small grin from Wanda, who looked up from the file she was writing in.

"We're very glad you did. What are you currently taking, starting with prescriptions?"

She stopped his recital of pain meds somewhere between Adderall and OxyContin. "Do you know how long you've been on them?"

"As long as I can remember," Tyson answered flippantly in an attempt to hide his true misery. This time, her face remained expressionless. She no longer appreciated his jokes. But bad jokes were all he had. He felt like the very definition of a bad joke himself. "About three years. I didn't think my withdrawal symptoms would start so soon. I could use a cigarette right about now, and I don't even smoke. Am I still in the United States?"

"You're in California, Mr. Palmer, Southern California. You're starting your new life where the weather is always sunny. And we're very happy to have you. Every person's physical withdrawal pattern is different, and we're here to help you through it. You are on the road to recovery. It's not going to be easy. But I promise you that it's going to be worth it. You're worth it."

"I played in California," he mumbled. Then he remembered the terms handed down by the man footing the bill, with that first condition being *You will be a model patient*. Tell the lady what she wants to hear. "That's great. I'm ready to get to work."

Wanda resumed her questions about his background and history, and as he answered honestly, he began to feel the weight and scope of what exactly he had done to himself and those closest to him. He added completely emotionally overwhelmed to dizzy and nauseated. Wanda took note and, after giving him a reassuring pat on the hand, stopped talking. Tyson leaned his head back against the seat and closed his eyes to combat it, but there was no escape. His self-loathing was unrelenting. By the time they turned onto a hidden driveway that ended in front of the sprawling ranch that would become his new residence, he felt like bawling. As soon as they settled him into his private room with its magnificent view, he did just that. Surrounded by people who were there to support him, he'd never felt more helpless and alone. He kept repeating that he could handle it all, as long as nobody saw him break. He spent the night curled up in the fetal position, trying to keep from sobbing.

The first week was akin to one long dry heave. As the chemicals started making their way out of his system, his addiction screaming to be satisfied, Tyson shook, hurled, and had manic, vivid dreams that bordered on hallucinations. Any food he put in his mouth tasted like it had been poisoned, and it was all he could do to keep it down. And while going through it all, he was expected to keep a very scheduled routine, which the staff monitored closely. Like a robot, he went through the motions and showed up on time without any fuss, even when fighting off wide-ranging mood swings. He made an effort not to come off as surly, while trying to make deals with God to end his suffering. He was quiet, contributed when asked, but never volunteered. There were five other patients, three women and two men, all ranging in age and in different stages of recovery. Some were having a harder time than others, but they were all respectful of one another and if there was any serious drama, he made a conscious effort to keep his distance from it. One man, a celebrity, had been through the program before. If anyone knew who he was, they made no mention of it. The facility itself, which sat on several acres, was beautiful, with amenities more in keeping with a five-star resort. There was a pool and a hot tub and several waterfalls leading to babbling brooks. Koi ponds were the view from the cardio equipment in a gym that also had a Universal and free weights. He was scheduled for an hour of exercise twice daily. It felt like someone was watching him constantly, always leaving just enough room to keep him from getting completely paranoid, but there if he wanted some company. When he wasn't being led from one therapy activity to another, he spent all his free time sleeping or staring off into space, trying to reconcile who he once was with who he had become.

And then something happened. Without knowing it, Tyson embraced his program. On the first day he woke up without a headache, he got on a treadmill and ran. Originally, he thought he was doing it just to fulfill his exercise requirement. As days passed and his endurance built back up, it became something he looked forward to, and then turned into something he couldn't stop himself from doing, like a new addiction. With the pounding of his feet against the belt, he felt his focus coming back. Then it started to resemble a pointless effort to run away from the disgrace of his past, much of which was foggy at best. Most of it was a complete blank, but he knew deep in his gut that whether he remembered it or not, all of it was bad. What he did remember was a good indicator of just how low he had plummeted. It made him run faster, longer, as he struggled to fill in the missing pieces of the time he had spent in a fog. As soon as he was allowed, he began taking his runs outside, where he felt free to yell at himself with only the flora and fauna to hear. He berated himself for miles. Christmas came and went without his celebrating. On a subdued New Year's Eve, he drank coffee around a fire pit with the staff and clients before turning in well before midnight.

He preferred to listen rather than talk in the group sessions, which were twice a week, and because he was attentive, no one pressed him for his story. Through their confessions, he discovered that he really didn't have the market cornered on addiction, or despair. Though every story was different, the struggle was still the same. But in the safety of the psychiatrist's office Tyson began to open up. About his family and the destruction brought on by his wealth and fame. About the frustration over the chunks of time he couldn't account for. In doing so, he learned that he didn't have any control over his father, or his mother and sister for that matter. He could empathize and support, but he couldn't take responsibility for their broken hearts or control how they handled their pain. He was allowed to stop punishing himself for the mistakes made by those around him. Eventually he might forgive his father, but when he did, it would be for himself, and it didn't have to be today. He could only manage his own actions, and now it was time to forgive Tyson Palmer. Even for the things he couldn't remember. He owed it to himself to live fully, complete with all the feelings that sometimes bring grief, but his self-medicating days were over. He would learn the skills to cope, then make amends. The first step was to take each moment at a time. And that's what he set out to do.

Tyson started to meditate, which fueled an interest in learning yoga, when weight lifting and running no longer seemed like enough. When Wanda suggested acupuncture as a pain management alternative, he willingly let them stick him with needles. He began to read for knowledge and pleasure and took long walks, sometimes with others, occasionally Wanda, forsaking his solitude. And when he was alone, his self-talk turned from critical to introspective. After forty-five days, when he looked in the mirror, the reflection staring back was not only one he recognized, but also one he could bear to look at. He was finally beginning to feel some peace. The last time he'd looked in the mirror and truly liked what he saw, he'd been a boy. Now he was a man.

Within days of that revelation, after breakfast and his morning run, it was Wanda who joined him on the patio.

"Good morning, Tyson, what are you reading?" she asked, sitting down on a neighboring chair.

He looked up and smiled, showing her the cover. "*The Alchemist.* I'm almost finished."

"Ah. Paulo Coelho and his shepherd Santiago, one of my favorites. How do you like it?"

"It's an easy enough read," Tyson replied truthfully, "and I get what old Paulo is trying to say, but I'm not sure I agree with all of it."

"Which parts do you take issue with?"

"I agree it's important to follow your dreams, but I don't think the universe necessarily opens up to help make them happen," he told her, reluctant to pan a book he knew she favored. "If anything, I think the opposite is true, the universe sets up roadblocks to test you on how badly you really want them."

"I can see where you might come to that conclusion." Wanda nodded in the customary neutral way that all the rehab staff practiced. There wasn't anyone at the facility that Tyson found fault with, but out of everyone, he'd come the closest to bonding with Wanda. She seemed to get him, never preached, and was good at imparting words of wisdom. It was something about that accent, all proper and British. It made everything she said sound very matter-of-fact, like she was merely confirming something he'd already thought of.

"And I don't think there's anything really wrong with looking forward to the future." He added with a chuckle, "Please don't tell anyone I said that. I know I'm supposed to be taking it all one minute at a time."

Wanda took her finger and made a crisscross over her heart, with her standard proper smirk. "You have my word. In your case, it's probably a very good sign and the reason I searched you out. Dr. Mayfair has spoken to Mr. Barrow and told him that he's thrilled with your progress."

"That is good news." Tyson felt a tiny surge of gratification with the thought that Barrow was getting his money's worth.

"Both are impressed with the way you checked your ego at the door, and the level of your dedication. They think you're ready to tackle the next leg of your journey."

"You used the word *tackle*. I see what you did there," he teased. And then he fought a wave of apprehension. When he left the ranch, he'd be leaving the forgiveness that came with it. Thanks to his celebrity status, all the evidence of his bad behavior, which he'd been shielded from, was still out there. Little land mines that might trigger some of the memories he was convinced didn't bear remembering. "Do you really think I'm ready?"

Wanda patted his hand the exact same way she did when they first met. "I don't know if you remember the day you came here, but I do. Maybe that's why I wanted to be the one to tell you the news. I've watched you make good strides, seen firsthand the way you've wrestled your demons. You didn't rush the process, you let it take root. Everybody understood your need for caution when it came to your interactions, since you won't be returning to any sort of anonymity, quite the opposite. You can't do anything about those who are determined to judge you. We've equipped you with how to handle post–acute withdrawal. You're ready."

"If you say so," Tyson said, not completely convinced. "I hope you're right."

"I don't need to be right, you do," Wanda told him. She stood up and turned to go back inside. "Better finish up your book, you leave tomorrow. Remember, stay humble. One day at a time."

"Wanda?" Tyson called after her. "Is this it, or am I going to get one more chance to make you say 'pip-pip-cheerio'?"

She turned back around and gave him one last reassuring smile.

"Mr. Palmer," she said as professionally as possible, her best imitation of a member of the royal family. "We are taught in this business not to become chummy for the sake of our patients. It's been a real pleasure getting to know you. I look forward to watching you from my couch next season."

It was the only time anyone other than his therapist had made any reference to football, and the first time anyone mentioned his playing again. Tyson knew it was her way of saying good-bye. "Do you know where I'm going next?"

Wanda called over her shoulder to him: "New Jersey. Don't forget a jacket. I hear it's cold there."

THE GOONS WERE WAITING OUTSIDE Barrow's jet when the same black sedan dropped Tyson off before dawn the next day. They were a little less hostile and a little more cautious in their approach this time, but he didn't need them to take their sunglasses off to see they were still unimpressed by him.

"Get a haircut, douchebag," one of them said from behind him as they boarded.

"Can't argue with that," Tyson replied easily as he took his seat on the opposite side of the plane. He'd thought about shaving his head free of the now-shoulder-length mane the night before. It might have made the Goon that looked like Mr. Clean a little more sympathetic. Then he remembered Wanda's warning about the cold and decided against it. It was going to take more than a haircut to win either one of those two over.

A Mavericks cap landed in his lap, thrown at him by a Goon. Wedged inside the hat and held within the dome by a single piece of Scotch tape was a bank envelope. He opened up the envelope and found a single one-hundred-dollar bill and his driver's license, another small step forward into his new reality. He pulled back his hair and put the cap on with a sense of pride, something that had long been unfamiliar to him. He knew any expression of appreciation would be wasted on his companions.

"Thanks, man." Tyson smiled anyway.

"Shut your pie hole, maggot." It was the sort of response he expected he would get and got.

Tyson could feel them watching him for most of the flight, waiting for him to get jittery or show some other sign of weakness no doubt, but they were robbed of the satisfaction. He spent the entire six hours reading sports magazines and meditating. He was too nervous to sleep, wondering what was waiting for him when he landed. He switched out the word *nervous* for *excited*, a positive reinforcement trick he'd learned in group. And, anyway, he had slept enough in rehab for a lifetime.

They landed in New Jersey, and Tyson was greeted by the all the chilly February dreariness that came with it.

"Good luck, skid mark," Goon Number One said from the plane after tossing out a different, slightly larger duffle bag from the hatchway door. Goon Two didn't trouble himself with getting out of his seat.

This time a white BMW convertible, canvas top up, was waiting for him on the tarmac.

The woman who got out was the polar opposite of Doctor Wanda. Tyson could tell with one glance that the petite thirtysomething redhead was a brick house in a leather bomber jacket and jeans. He picked his duffle bag off the ground and carried it over to meet her. She opened the trunk of the car, giving him a bright smile.

"Hi, Tyson, I'm Holly." She extended a firm hand in introduction.

Tyson shook her hand and dropped the duffle in the trunk. He got into the passenger seat of the toasty running car thinking that Clinton Barrow was either a genius or a moron. Holly was busty and solid, quite a looker, a sight for his sore estrogen-deprived eyes. If Barrow was trying to make a statement by having him train with a woman to help clean up his reputation, he wasn't sure it was the right move or how it would play out. And she didn't look like his first choice to ready him for a return to football. But his job was to show up and shut up. He contemplated this new turn of events as she shifted the car into gear and they sped away from the airport.

"How was your flight?" Holly asked politely after a few minutes of silence.

"Uneventful." *I didn't get punched out or puke this time. Now it's up for grabs.*

"Always the best-case scenario." She gave a half-laugh. "Logan wanted me to apologize for not meeting your plane himself, but he had a couple last-minute details to see to before your arrival."

"Logan?" Tyson repeated, realizing that being in the dark was becoming less and less appealing the farther he got away from the comfort and safety of the ranch. "You have to forgive me, I don't mean to sound stupid. I've been on a need-to-know-basis."

Holly took her eyes off the road for second to give him a quick look. "No need to apologize. Logan told me this operation was on the covert side. I just didn't think he was serious. You're in New Jersey."

"That much I do know." Tyson chuckled before adding, "But that's about it. You're not my trainer?"

"Hell no!" Holly laughed. "I'm just your pickup. And my vast knowledge of football pretty much ends with whatever color team uniforms are."

Tyson asked tentatively. "You don't follow football?"

"Watch it all the time," she said with a sly grin and didn't elaborate.

So she knew who he was and why he was there. And she wasn't treating him like a leper, which he looked at as a good sign. He wondered just how many questions she could answer. "Can you tell me where I'm going?"

"We're going to meet Logan at the gym. He wants to get right to work."

"Does this guy Logan have a last name?"

"Montgomery."

Tyson looked out the window and took a deep breath. Clinton Barrow wasn't kidding when he said he was getting Tyson the best. On the list of athletes currently destined for the Hall of Fame, from nearly every sport, there was a common denominator—they all trained with Logan Montgomery.

CHAPTER 4

HOLLY PULLED UP the Beemer behind an average two-story structure in downtown Englewood and popped the trunk. After Tyson removed his duffle bag, they walked around to the entrance at the front of the building and took a set of stairs to the second floor. Once inside, Holly went into the small office in the back while Tyson took in his new surroundings.

What surrounded him was a complete state-of-the-art training facility. It took up the entire floor and was completely disguised within the walls of your run-of-the-mill office building. Any lingering questions on how Barrow would keep Tyson's training from being leaked were laid to rest. Whoever wanted to get to this gym had to already know its location. The few windows in the space were high and ran along the ceiling. Logan Montgomery was good at protecting his clients' privacy. What he wasn't good at was choosing music. The place sounded more like a disco, with bubblegum-like tunes reverberating through hidden speakers. Tyson would be pumping iron to Taylor Swift, not his first choice for producing adrenaline. He had spent the last two months in a serene, picturesque environment. If he was going to forsake all that and live in a gym, he wanted the deafening kind of music that would send him into beast mode, with pulsing bass lines and frenzied drumming to drown out any extraneous thoughts. He needed old school angry: Megadeth, Ozzy Osbourne, and Audioslave. Instead he was going to get Maroon 5 and Ed Sheeran. Good grief.

Holly came out of the office, gave Tyson another winning smile, said her good-byes, and left. A minute later, his new trainer came out of the office to join him. Tyson did a double take.

Tyson was no stranger to the term "man candy." But there were pretty boys and then there was this guy, with his perfectly chiseled features, staggering physique, and swagger that oozed out of every pore.

Was this really the fitness guru to the sports world or a male supermodel? Logan gave him a curt nod and a brief introduction, which didn't include a handshake.

"Palmer, I'm Logan Montgomery. There's a shower room in the back. Change up and let's get to work."

Tyson took the duffle bag into the changing room without comment, thinking that Logan sounded more like a five-star diva than the Ariana Grande currently grating his nerves. What he came in wearing underneath his hoodie—basketball shorts and a T-shirt—was certainly sufficient to work out in, but he had no desire to start this association off on the wrong foot. He could always just take off the sweatshirt and make it look like he'd changed if there was nothing he could use in the new bag. There was no way he was taking off his new cap.

He found that, along with several pairs of blue jeans and new cross-training sneakers, the bag was full of shorts, T-shirts, sweats, hats, and gloves, all with the Mavericks logo on them. He felt an embarrassingly giddy rush that was hard to contain. There was even a sideline jacket. Tyson was part of a team again. He changed quickly, excited to get started.

The excitement was short-lived. When he came back out Logan was waiting for him, hands on his hips and his face anything but welcoming.

"Before we get started, Palmer, let's get a few things straight. Whether you succeed or fail, I'm getting paid. I personally don't give a crap which you choose. I'm not here to coddle you. I have no interest in following you around like some sort of spy to make sure you keep yourself clean. I'm here to train you, and I expect you to fall in line. My word is law. If you blow this, it's on you. All I'm going to do is report back to the person who's writing my big fat checks."

"I accomplished my rehab without incident . . ." Tyson began defensively.

"Good for you," Logan said, his voice dripping with sarcasm. "You successfully completed a stint at Club Med. Way to go. From here on out, when I want your opinion on something, I'll ask you."

Tyson was getting an unprovoked dressing-down that rivaled what he'd gotten from any coach he'd ever had, only without all the swearing and arm waving that usually accompanied such things. It only made him more insecure. It was hard to match up all he had heard about the legendary training authority with the bitchy Adonis who sounded like he listened to the likes of Britney Spears.

"I understand," Tyson said, more determined than ever.

And that was how their relationship began. Tyson worked hard and Logan worked him harder. They went from interval training to power lifting as Logan Montgomery took assessment of Tyson's strengths and weaknesses. There was no small talk. In between their two sessions that day, Logan retreated into his office and shut the door with a "Be back in an hour," leaving Tyson alone and to his own devices. Tyson was so fatigued that he spent the time meditating in the corner Logan used to stretch him out.

It was already dark when Logan gruffly told him to get his duffle bag. They drove silently together to Logan's high-rise condo. *Nice digs,* Tyson thought as Logan led him to one of two bedrooms and told him that's where he'd be staying. Then Logan showered, leaving Tyson to acclimate to his new accommodations. Everything seemed to have a place and was in it. It was just like the gym, where as soon as Tyson was done with a free weight, Logan immediately reracked it. It was exceedingly tidy for a bachelor. Tyson added *anal retentive* to the list of adjectives he had started to compile about his host. Logan reappeared, grabbed his keys, and left with a "I'm not your babysitter. Make sure you're here at midnight."

Where was he supposed to go? He didn't have a key and wasn't even sure where exactly he was. Disoriented, Tyson sat on the imported leather couch in Logan's living room until he felt strong enough to take a shower. Framed autographed jerseys and pictures of Logan with all of his famous clients decorated the hallway. His room was also full of carefully preserved memorabilia, so much athletic greatness reminding him to be inspired. He showered, then changed into fresh Mavericks gear. It rejuvenated him. He was also starving. Still feeling like an unwelcome guest afraid to touch anything, he wearily ventured into the kitchen to have a look around. Both the cupboards and the refrigerator were completely stocked with healthy, nutritious foods, way more than enough for one man. In the fridge was a stack of containers that held premade meals, mainly grilled chicken with vegetables and brown rice. He pulled two out, heated them in the microwave, and proceeded to devour them. He followed that up with some grapes while watching television. Not yet ready to dive back into reality full force, he kept away from sports and the news, and put on the History Channel, where he could watch the long line of people before him who'd messed up their lives and, in some cases, the world. His jet lag kicked in and he fell asleep watching a program about the Manhattan Project.

It was Logan who shook him awake early the next morning. He was also wearing the same clothes he'd had on when he left the night before. They ate breakfast with minimal conversation, both showered in separate bathrooms, and left to head back to the gym, where they resumed the grueling workouts. That was the pattern the two followed: working Tyson out until he nearly dropped, usually with Justin Timberlake making him think about getting it on and One Direction boring the life out of him, then going back to the condo, eating, and falling asleep alone. He was too exhausted to be depressed or give any real thought to the food that seemed to replenish itself as he ate it.

Logan had an intensity that at first Tyson understood and appreciated. But within two weeks, Tyson was longing for the warmth and compassion of the Goons. He was expecting a mentor; what he got was more along the lines of a tormentor. Logan was relentless with no sign of letting up, no matter how many challenges Tyson faced and conquered. His grim perseverance seemed to only aggravate Logan further. They never took a day off, and Tyson began to lose all track of time. There was only one bright spot in his routine, and it was the presence of Holly, who arrived around the same time every afternoon. She was unobtrusive and kept in the background, never contributing to conversation or getting in the way, instead slipping on the headphones to the iPod she brought with her and using an elliptical machine for an hour. That was the only time Logan actually took a break from his bombardment of animosity long enough to act somewhat human. Tyson tried to keep a respectable distance, but if "SexyBack" happened to come on during her visits, his testosterone would begin to flow whether he wanted it to or not. Add Jay Z with a little "Suit & Tie," and unless he was willing to poke out his own eyes, there was no way to keep from noticing her.

"She's my bookkeeper," Logan snapped when Tyson innocently asked about Holly.

"Damn, what kind of tyrant are you?" Tyson couldn't refrain from commenting in her defense. "Does her job depend on a weekly weigh-in?"

Logan floored him with the beginning of a grin. "Would you feel better if I told you she was my girlfriend?"

"No, not really," Tyson replied, and Logan actually laughed. The first laugh Tyson heard from the man. And Tyson gained some insight on where Logan was spending his nights.

That glimpse of comradery was short-lived, however, and the acrimony returned, now overshadowed with jealousy whenever Tyson so much as glanced in Holly's direction. Tyson thought he must be imagining it, since Holly had never been anything other than courteous in her comings and goings. He was hardly a threat. But the more they smiled at each other in passing, the more Logan would bark "Focus!" and some sort of borderline torture was sure to follow. Any admiration Tyson held on to based on Logan's reputation quickly soured. The two were on a collision course. Less than a week later, Tyson finally surrendered and gave Logan the fight he wanted.

It started when Holly came in and took her place on her elliptical machine, and before putting on the headphones and starting it up, shared a small joke about there being no pain, no gain. Logan broke up the conversation from going any further, and as soon as he caught Tyson looking over in her direction, he growled.

"Are you flirting with my girlfriend?"

"No way!" Tyson replied quickly and hated that he sounded more and more like a wuss every day. 5 Seconds of Summer started blaring bubblegum pop from the speakers, grating him further. He resented the accusation that held a ring of truth and muttered under his breath, "But I would if I could get her to give up her iPod and save me from this asinine junior prom music."

It wasn't really about music anymore. It was about the abuse of power.

"Say what?" Logan taunted him. "If you're going to insult me, why don't you be a man and speak up?"

Tyson took the bait and dropped the barbell he was curling, which shook the floor's foundation. "Your music stinks, and you're a glorified prima donna. I can't believe anyone would write a check and willingly subject themselves to you. Why don't you go and report that back to the boss?"

"And deprive myself of the pleasure of riding your sorry ass? Not likely, at least not yet. Good to know you're worried about that though."

Tyson began to back up, his peaceful, easy feeling of self-control hanging by a perilous thread. "Maybe I'll be the one who reports in, and tell Barrow all about the cash he's throwing away on a little prick who's more worried about his girlfriend than his client." The threat was a total paper tiger. He didn't know how to reach Barrow.

"Go ahead, crybaby. My reputation precedes me, as does yours. You might want to remember that."

"Fuck you, man. I didn't go to rehab to end up the whipping boy of a spoiled egomaniac. There aren't enough drugs in the world to make it worth putting up with you." Tyson started heading for door, momentarily forgetting that he had no place to go and everything he owned was in Logan's condo.

"I think there's a crack house a few blocks down," Logan replied casually.

He stuck out his middle finger behind his head during his exodus with a resounding "Peace!"

Logan called from across the room, "Hey, Palmer, listen up! You're not the first athlete that ever fell flat on his face after being given too much too soon. The only difference with you is somebody actually gave enough of a shit for you to get a second chance."

Tyson stopped, had a nano-second debate in his mind, and walked purposefully back to where Logan was standing.

"And if you weren't such a tool, you'd see I'm trying to make the most of it!" Tyson shouted in his face before forcefully giving Logan a two-handed shove against his chest, sending him reeling backward.

It might have turned into a full-on scuffle, but both men were stopped by the shriek-like gasp coming from the one other person in the room. They turned to look at Holly, Tyson heaving and Logan getting up off the floor. She was still on her elliptical, but it was no longer in motion. Her headphones were still on but her green eyes were wide. Then her eyes narrowed as she glared from one man to the other and she slowly shook her head. Saying nothing, she got off the machine and began to reach for her purse, intent on leaving. But Tyson beat her to the door and was gone ahead of her.

Once on the street, wearing sweaty, inappropriate clothes for a lion-like day in early March, Tyson did the only thing he could think of. He began to run. Knowing nothing of the area, he took the only path that was remotely familiar, the one from the gym back to Logan's. After a couple wrong turns and through the course of several miles, some of them along a highway, his feet began to drum in time with the single thought that pounded through his head.

You blew it.

He viewed the attack on his trainer in the same light he would an attack on a coach. It was totally unacceptable, by any standards. It was probably too late to apologize. In all likelihood the first thing Logan did was call Barrow and inform him the project was a failure. And no doubt, he did it with pleasure. He could collect his salary and spend the rest of the winter in Tahiti. Once again, Tyson was a man with nothing, not even his identity, since his license was still at the apartment. With the one-hundred-dollar bill he hadn't been given the time to spend. Tyson wanted that money back, after what he'd dealt with in the last month, he'd earned it. Then he pondered if Barrow would actually have him murdered or simply make sure he never threw a football professionally again. After all, Tyson hadn't backstabbed Barrow, merely botched up the plan.

"Mavericks SUCK!" someone shouted at him from a passing car. The remnants of a Big Gulp hit him with such force, most of its contents splashed up his shirt and ricocheted onto his face. He licked his lips: Mountain Dew. Tyson continued on, only now trudging more than running. He was inclined to agree.

But of all the things Tyson was unsure of, there was one ideal that wouldn't be shaken. No matter what happened from here on out, he'd be handling it with all his faculties. He would not go back to using.

Almost two hours later he arrived at the high-rise, prepared to at least try to get his stuff back, even if it did all really belong to the Mavericks. That task would be easy in comparison to what would come after it. He would be forced to make a collect call to his mother, the only person he could count on to bail him without conditions and his last resort. She would wire him the rest of the money to get him home. He couldn't worry beyond that. He was back to taking it one minute at a time, only now his heart was heavy, and he was disappointed in himself.

He stormed into the building, ready to take on the doorman.

"I'm here to see Logan Montgomery," he announced with as much dignity as his now-sticky attire and sweat-soaked hair would allow. He hoped the shivering looked more like he was vibrating in anger.

But the man behind the front desk didn't buzz up to the apartment. Instead he reached into a drawer, retrieved an envelope, and handed it to him.

"Mr. Palmer," the doorman said cordially, "Mr. Montgomery asked me to give you this."

Inside the envelope were Logan's keys to both the condo and his car with a note that read:

The address to the gym is in the GPS. Be there 8:00 A.M. sharp.

Tyson was stunned. He had started an altercation with the person who held the keys to his future, and it appeared he was being rewarded for it. With keys no less, that gave him more easy access to the outside world. Puzzled, he thanked the doorman and proceeded to the elevator to follow his usual routine. He showered and went to the fridge, which was magically restocked once a week. But on this night there was one major difference. While nuking his food, instead of meditating on his gratitude for having made it through another day, he reflected on how if he'd had any inkling as to what the end result would be, he would've knocked Logan Montgomery on his ass weeks ago.

CHAPTER 5

TYSON DROVE TO the gym the next morning with a new sense of purpose. He owed Logan an apology, and it didn't matter to him if he got one in return. He took into consideration that being offered use of Logan's pricey Navigator and finally getting a key to his home might be the best he could hope for. It was enough. He was eager to get back to work. And he'd forgotten how much he liked to drive.

The first thing Tyson noticed as he climbed the stairs was the thumping bass line. When he walked into the gym, he was greeted by the aggressive head-banging sounds of AC/DC. If Logan never said another word about the incident the night before, Tyson still considered them square.

Logan came out of his office looking more relaxed than Tyson had ever seen him. He grinned. "Better?"

"Much," Tyson replied, not sure if Logan was talking about the music or his fit of temper from the day before. He got right to the heart of the matter. "Logan, about yesterday . . ."

Logan held up his hand. "Don't. It's not necessary. You were supposed to have done it long before you actually did, although I wasn't expecting it to get physical. Nice push, by the way."

"Thanks. But I don't get it." Tyson frowned in confusion.

"At first I needed to see whether or not you were going to go straight back to your bad habits," Logan explained with another rueful grin. "Then I realized I had a much bigger problem."

"Now I'm really lost."

"All the Zen inner peace stuff makes for a great human interest story, but a crummy top-shelf quarterback. You're not going to be facing a bunch of Buddhists on game day. But it's essential for your recovery, and it'll come in handy when you go up against your critics. You're not the first athlete I've seen through a scandal. But it's up to me to make sure you get your edge back. You're a big guy. They like to hit you hard, you can't be afraid of them coming. Recovery is about surrender and stepping back, football is about anything but. Now we just have to strike the balance."

"You could've just told me"—Tyson quirked an eyebrow—"or was it always your plan to use me as an experiment?"

Logan gave a semiapologetic shrug. "I had to learn as much as I could about you in a short time. And while working with you was an offer I couldn't refuse, I still had six months' worth of clients to blow off. I didn't want all your first impressions on me based on hearing one side of phone calls where I basically had to kiss some ass for turning them down. It's worth it if I manage to keep some of them."

"You gave up all your other clients to train me?" Tyson asked in amazement.

Logan responded with a knowing smile. "You should know better than anyone, when Clinton Barrow asks you to do something, you do it. And you can't half-ass it."

Tyson seriously doubted he and Logan had similar conversations with their mutual boss. Logan didn't look like he responded well to threats.

Logan continued, "It was interesting to watch you slowly build up some steam. I'm not sure if it was Holly or the music that was really behind it."

"I would never poach on another guy's girl. Trust me, it was the music," Tyson replied dryly. "It's hard to find the eye of the tiger to Justin Bieber."

Logan looked thoughtful for a moment. "You're not the first to complain."

"I want to know if you actually would've forced her to flirt on demand. She seems way too nice to be so shallow."

Logan threw back his head with a laugh. "Don't be fooled. She's one of the toughest girls I've ever met. I'm not going to lie, it was not among the best ideas I ever came up with, and she wasn't overjoyed about being the bait. The longer you held out once I started pushing, the more she let me know it. But she's another part in your current challenge. Mr. Barrow has emphasized his desire for secrecy. If he had his way, we would be on some desert island and he would fly people in blindfolded. I think that sort of isolation is way too drastic if you're going to have any hope of functioning in the real world once you're thrown back into it. We need to come to a meeting of the minds about Holly. My girl is the only girl in town, so to speak. She wants to be able to be your friend and support you, but not if it's going to send a mixed message."

"I take it that this isn't your way of inviting me into a sexy three-some?"

"It's my way of telling you that you ain't getting any for a while."

"My record with women is sketchy at best," Tyson reminded him. "I don't mind taking a break."

They got to work, and it was different. Logan was still supremely focused, but now actively encouraging. In between sets, he began to slowly fill Tyson in on the details of his plan. Within the next week, they'd be adding a massage therapist to the mix and shortly after that, a retired offensive coach and the late-night use of an actual football facility. Clinton Barrow's plan had been well thought out.

Just before lunch, Logan ducked into his office and came back flipping a football in his hand. He threw it halfway across the room. Tyson caught it and felt a jolt of electricity course through him. Never did holding a football in his hand have so much meaning.

"Have you ever heard of the Marine Corps Rifleman's Creed?" Logan asked.

Tyson shook his head, feeling the leather secure within his palm. He couldn't resist mimicking a few forward passes to imaginary receivers across the room as Logan explained.

"The Rifleman's Creed is about always having your gun with you, becoming one with it. Never letting it leave your side. That's what you're going to do, but with that football. Carry it with you as much as you can, play with it, study it. It's a part of you already. Your talent is the proof."

"Thanks, Logan," Tyson said, grateful for the compliment as well as the gift.

"It's also my hope that it's going to help you get through trials you haven't had to face yet. You're not going to stay hidden forever. Eventually, it's going to come down to temptations and triggers. And you're going to be alone when they pop up. There are going to be times when it's about nothing but the choice to use or keep clean. I'd like to believe that as long as you can touch something that reminds you of where you are you'll make the right decision. If you can do something to keep you grounded and your mind occupied for the few minutes it will take for the urge to pass, it could make all the difference."

Logan quit before it turned to a sermon and went to go pick up lunch. Tyson played with the football as he waited. He aligned his fingers with the white stitches to judge the best grip and then he did it again from a different spot. He balanced it by one of its pointed ends on his finger. It was like he was looking at a football for the first time, and he fully appreciated the spirit of the gift as well as the message behind it. It was easy to follow his program to the letter when the only people in his circle were dedicated to his success. Eventually the day would come when he would be casually invited out for a beer. He squeezed the football tight in his large hand. He could do it. He would just never touch another drop.

Logan returned with what he labeled a celebratory meal. Tyson couldn't remember the last time a cheeseburger and fries tasted so good. By the time they finished, Holly had arrived, looking very relieved that she wasn't entering into a war zone. Logan took a minute to check his messages while Holly grabbed a bottle of water and got ready for her daily grind.

"I think I owe you one," Tyson said as she started climbing onto her usual elliptical machine.

"You do?" she asked with a giggle.

"Rumor has it you went to bat for me," Tyson said.

She glanced over at Logan, still in his office, and laughed. "Not me.

I would never critique the way Logan does business. He's the best there is. I thought you were talking about the food."

Tyson chucked in response. "So you're the elf that's been restocking my fridge?"

"Yeah," she confirmed. "I was worried at first when Logan asked for my help. I'm not known for my cooking skills. I'm so glad I didn't inadvertently poison you."

"I was pretty much just eating to stay alive at that point. But thanks for doing it. It was delicious."

"No, a pizza is delicious," Holly corrected him with a wide smile. "Grilled chicken and brown rice is the stuff athletes are made of. Please don't tell Logan how much you enjoyed it. I don't want him getting any ideas."

"Don't worry, it wasn't *that* good," Tyson told her, adding a wink.

Her face scrunched up. "Please don't tell him that either. He'll make me keep doing it until it is."

"You sound like you know this from experience," he hedged.

"I'm not only his fan club president, I'm also a client," Holly told him teasingly before turning on her iPod and starting the moving of her feet. "Why do you think I have these headphones? I love him and all, but hey, every now and then, you need some 'Enter Sandman.' "

WINTER GAVE WAY TO SPRING and Tyson didn't miss the symbolism of rebirth. Under Logan's watchful eye, the threesome embarked on a friendship, and Tyson thrived. With the sun now warming his skin, his confidence began to shine through. At the end of the day, instead of feeling exhausted and on the verge of collapse, he was excited. Thanks to Logan's knowledge and support—both in the gym and out of it—Tyson was starting to get his game back on. Every movement of his workout was specifically designed, through drilled repetition, to make his body leaner and stronger. As Tyson got stronger and faster, so did Logan's enthusiasm. It was obvious the man practiced what he preached. They stopped spending all their time in the gym and began taking early morning runs outside, before the sun came up. They would jog to a local high school and race each other up and down the bleachers. They'd sprint from goal post to goal post. Three nights a week, they took a ride down the much more scenic Garden State Parkway to the shore and a sports complex that had a "bubble": a football-size field contained within a dome. Used mostly for birthday parties and by various soccer, lacrosse, and flag football leagues, it closed at midnight to the general public. Logan and Tyson met the Barrow-appointed coach there at 2:00 A.M. and they would work on his passing until 4:00 before going home and taking their run. They'd resume their workouts around noon, back at the gym.

"Can't we get some other guys here for me to throw to, maybe run some plays?" Tyson asked Logan and the coach hopefully, both of whom shook their heads and told him no, Barrow hadn't authorized it for fear of someone spotting them and blowing their cover.

Still, within a week of that conversation, three men began to show up at the assigned time in the middle of the night for Tyson to throw to. Tyson was introduced to them by Logan as "Palms," and that was all they ever called him. Little did any of them know, the nickname would stick.

"Coach called Barrow and told him he was missing a golden opportunity to get a head start on his playbook," was all Logan gave him by way of explanation, adding with a smile, "and you were wearing me out."

Aside from Logan's condo, Holly set up a room for Tyson in her beautiful four-bedroom Colonial in a neighboring town. That was where Logan kept most of his clothes and spent most of his time, so Tyson began spending time there as well, at first hesitantly, afraid of feeling like a third wheel. But Holly wouldn't have any of it, and her invitations became insistent. She considered him part of the family. It wasn't long before the three spent their free nights and weekends holed up watching movies or playing video games, with Holly wrinkling her nose in distaste and leaving the room to do something else whenever the choice was Grand Theft Auto.

"Boys." She'd sigh under her breath as she made her escape. Both Tyson and Logan knew that a chick flick of her choosing would be in their future.

Tyson would watch Holly and Logan in action. They were playful and affectionate, clearly connected, but without too many public displays. It was all so very intriguing. Logan had the kind of looks and magnetism that could draw a dozen supermodels, yet he genuinely appeared to be head over heels for the feisty, buxom spitfire who could get his attention with little more than a look. That forced Tyson to think about the women from his own life. The beautiful party girls, their names long forgotten, who he always knew deep down were using him for one thing or another. Much as it pained him to admit it, that was probably true of his marriage as well. Now he saw how hollow those relationships had been, and that made him cautious. He still had too much work to do on his own. He wanted sex, but now he wanted it to be meaningful too.

"TURNABOUT IS FAIR PLAY," HOLLY told him one night in late July when Tyson asked her about how she and Logan had met as they watched TV and Logan snoozed on the couch next to her. "I did my time on Planet Logan."

They had been seated next to each other on a flight from Toronto to Newark three years earlier, she explained. Holly had been recently widowed and was lost and afraid, using food as her main coping mechanism. By the time that flight landed, Holly had made an impression and Logan threw down a gauntlet.

"He offered to train me, more as a challenge to himself disguised as an attempt to save me," Holly said, lovingly running her fingers through the black hair on the sleeping head that rested in her lap. "He's a good man, but he needed to be reminded the whole world isn't gorgeous and ripped like him."

"Please tell me you made him suffer"—Tyson chuckled—"just a little bit."

"He wanted a challenge. He got one."

"What I wouldn't give to have seen it."

"I heard that," Logan mumbled sleepily, with his eyes still closed. "All you would've witnessed was that I can take a punch better than Rocky."

"That sounds way more like the beginning of a story than an ending."

"Let's just leave it with we both learned a lot. We should turn in. Tomorrow's a big day. You're going out to get a little exposure."

"Like for a haircut?" Tyson asked, reaching his hand back for a grab at the thick ponytail that he'd grown tired of.

"If you want," Logan replied, sitting up and then standing. "But first, we take our run in broad daylight. Around the reservoir in Manasquan I think, then maybe hit the beach."

"I love the reservoir!" Holly exclaimed.

"Then come with us," Logan said, leaning down to give her a quick kiss and extending a hand to help her up after rising off the couch. "I'd like to be on the road by seven."

"I don't know what I'm more excited about," she said as all three of them began to shut off the television and the lights to make their way to bed, "the road trip or seeing Tyson without that raggedy mop."

"Don't be jealous," Logan said, giving her a swat as he followed behind her while they climbed the stairs. "You wish you had that hair."

"No comment," was all she said in reply.

When Tyson bounded down the stairs the following morning, Logan and Holly were already in the kitchen, packing up a cooler with snacks and bottles of water.

"I was thinking that since we're going to be down by the shore, maybe we'll spend the rest of the day at the beach," Logan said.

"You weren't kidding about putting me out there," Tyson said, excited about the prospect of giving up his vampire-like secrecy and letting the sun really shine on his face. But a guy that looked like Logan was bound to draw some attention, especially if you stick him half naked on a beach in the middle of summer. "What if people recognize me?"

Logan gave him an indifferent shrug. "Then they recognize you. Come on, help me load this stuff into the car."

The Manasquan Reservoir was also a county park, a beautiful twelve hundred acres complete with a playground, fishing areas, and hiking trails. It was still early when they arrived, but there was a sizable number of people taking advantage of the cooler morning hours to get their exercise done before the already oppressive humidity really kicked in. They all got out of the car and did some quick stretching as they made their way to the five-mile trail that surrounded the perimeter of the main attraction, the large serene body of water.

"You going to run with us?" Tyson asked Holly as they made the trek from the parking lot, already aware of the occasional looks being cast in the trio's direction.

"No thanks." Holly shook her head as they approached the path. "Gravity already has one eye on my rack. I don't see the need for all that gratuitous bouncing and jiggling. I'll be here, doing the slow and steady behind you."

Logan snickered and rolled his eyes but didn't press her, instead starting a slow jog. Tyson followed his lead, and they left Holly behind to stroll along the trail. They ran for a while in virtual silence, the only words coming from Logan being the friendly "good mornings" with casual nods to people they encountered as they passed. The more Logan did it, the more conscious Tyson became of the people around them. He kept his head down, hidden underneath the brim of his now-faded Mavericks cap.

"Head up," Logan would tell him every time he caught Tyson doing it. "There's no oxygen down there."

After three miles, they began to slow down until they were walking.

"How you feeling?" Logan took several deep breaths to start his cooldown.

"Fine." Tyson matched Logan's more relaxed pace. "We do three miles with our eyes closed."

"That's not what I mean."

"I know." They continued to walk along the manicured path together until they were alone and the only sounds were the water lapping against the sides of the dam that contained it and some children laughing in the distance.

"I heard from Barrow. The mother ship is calling you home," Logan announced as he stared out over the water.

"Already?"

Logan nodded. "I guess you and I did our jobs well. They want you down in Austin for training camp to start running drills with the team. Barrow is holding a news conference August first, the day your suspension is up."

A wave of mixed feelings washed over Tyson. He knew he was ready physically. It was what he'd been training for. He had been having dreams of making Hail Mary passes and running the ball in for touchdowns on his own. But he'd felt like he'd been watching it all from a distance. It was easy to succeed with all the safety nets that had been put into place around him. Once he landed in Austin, all those nets would disappear, starting with the most comfortable one, his anonymity.

"We knew this day was coming. We've done all we can, and you're ready to get back to the game." Logan broke the silence, reading Tyson's mind at the same time.

"I've never felt stronger," Tyson said confidently.

"There's nothing left for me to teach you, except for one thing. From here on out, you will never avert your eyes or hang your head in front of another man again. Ever. No matter what they say or any comparisons they make to your past, you've earned the right to be back on the field. You are not the same person or player you were a year ago. You have to be able to win the stare-down against any critics and cynics. And you might be surprised to find just how short the public's memory is. It may be rough at first, but in the end, the world loves a good redemption story. I'll make sure you have my number if you need it."

If it was any other man who said it, Tyson might have viewed it as a lecture. And if it had been a year ago, he would've taken offense. All the new Tyson did was reply, "I can do that."

"I've got a reputation to uphold," Logan told him jokingly, then said seriously, "and you have one to tear down. Remember—fake it till you make it. And ice, lots and lots of ice."

CHAPTER 6

Four years later

Tyson pulled up in front of the Barrow Building in downtown Austin and got out of his Bentley, handing his keys over to a doorman. He stopped inside the lobby to sign in with security, shook a few hands, and then took the elevator up to the high-rise's top floor. He told Barrow's secretary not to bother getting up and strolled down the hall to knock on the closed office door at the end.

The door swung open before he reached it. Theo and Sal, who Tyson had stopped calling the Goons several years ago, both gave him a friendly nod as they walked past him out of the office.

"How's it going, rock star?" Theo said. He had yet to run out of alternates to Tyson's name, only now they had more positive connotations.

"What's up, Palms?" Sal asked, using his nickname and adding a fist bump.

Clinton Barrow brought up the rear, happy to see his all-star quarterback. "Tyson, thanks for stopping by."

"We are having lunch in two hours. You only call people to the office when you don't want business talk to spoil it," Tyson pointed out.

Clint laughed before patting Tyson heartily on the back. "You caught me. Come on in, have a seat."

Clint closed the door behind them, leaving the two men in private. He went back behind his large mahogany desk while Tyson settled into a leather wingback chair across from him. Barrow studied Tyson for a minute. Hard to believe he was the same man who had woken up groggy and disheveled in his house nearly five years ago. The Tyson Palmer before him now was clear-eyed, level-headed, and one of the best quarterbacks in the league. It had been a long, sometimes bumpy journey to redemption. When it was originally announced who the Mavericks had signed as their new quarterback, there was palpable surprise followed closely by universal condemnation. Even the Mavericks' coaching staff and players were caught off guard. That first year, both Tyson and the Mavericks were the laughingstock of the NFL. But the critics were silenced after Tyson appeared on the field in top physical condition and proceeded to take charge. His nickname "Palms" spoke to his talent for keeping his hands on the football, no matter what was happening around him.

"You know we've been through a lot together. I'm proud of you, Tyson. You surpassed all my expectations. Our agreement turned out better than I could've ever imagined, if I do say so myself."

"You never got your ring," Tyson replied, with a twinge of guilt.

"*We* never got our rings," Barrow corrected him firmly, "and that's not your fault. Thanks to you, we made the playoffs. If it wasn't for damn injuries, I think we would've taken the whole enchilada last year."

"That really was awful timing," Tyson readily agreed.

Silence lingered and Barrow leaned back in his chair with an uncharacteristic sigh.

"I know you didn't bring me here to rehash last season," Tyson said, cutting to the chase.

"Ty, I need you to play one more year," Clint told him bluntly.

It was the last thing Tyson expected to hear. They both knew the beating Tyson's body took on the field had started taking its toll. He had put in his three years without complaint, plus another one for good measure. It was Barrow himself who had used his influence to get Tyson the audition with the national broadcasting group, telling them that Tyson was a good fit for television. He was handsome and good-natured, had poise and a quick wit, not to mention a thorough under-standing of the game. Now Clint wanted to take it all back, reneging on their deal.

"Clint, I don't think you really know what you're asking of me. I'm grateful to you, you know that. I gave you everything I had. I'd take a bullet for you. But I've been getting knocked around with nothing stronger than Tylenol, ice, and cortisone shots for going on five years now. I'm no complainer, but when I got word I was going to get the opportunity to move into broadcasting, I didn't lie to you about how excited I was and why."

"Agreed. You've done everything I've ever asked of you and more. I think of you as a son. And there's no question that you've been serious about your sobriety and what you've had to sacrifice to keep it. I'm ashamed to say it was the one thing I didn't consider when I made my offer. It's out of respect that I wanted to see you taken care of. I wouldn't be asking you this if it wasn't important to me, to the team."

Tyson tried not to whine. "What's wrong with CJ Bradford? He's a third-round draft pick. We've been prepping him all season. He's more than ready to lead the Mavs."

"Two words, Marcus LaRue."

The name hung in the air. Tyson and LaRue had a history. They had faced each other six times in two years, and every damn time their teams played, Marcus could be counted on to intercept him, often more than once. Adding insult to injury, it was only part of what made LaRue the absolute best. Most of those interceptions Marcus ran in for touchdowns, he was just that fast. And he did it in a Boston Blitz jersey, racking up the score for Tyson's former team.

"Are you just throwing that name up in my face to motivate me?"

"He's thinking about making a change. A couple of them." Barrow broke into a sly grin.

"So the rumors are true," Tyson said flatly. There had been rumblings that Marcus was thinking of making the switch from defense to offense. "The kid is cocky enough to think he can play the whole field. I don't know what that has to do with me."

"Every team wants him, and they are willing to sell the farm to get him. He wants to come here."

Tyson was more baffled than enlightened. "That's great. Go get him. Not having my salary to burden you frees that money right up."

Barrow laughed at another one of their inside jokes. Tyson had never been one of the league's top salaried players, but this last year Barrow had forced him to accept a salary more in keeping with his superstar status, stating that he no longer looked like a savvy business-man, but more like he was taking advantage of his outstanding quarterback. This time, Tyson invested wisely. After his rehab, Tyson had started living simply, and it suited him. The trappings of his previous life no longer held any appeal. He was choosier about where he spent his money. When his mother mentioned wanting to move out of the family home, he bought her a lovely maintenance-free town house. When his sister got married last year, he paid for her wedding, and his gift to her was substantial. Douglas Palmer couldn't be found to invite. Tyson still did enjoy a nice car though, and every now and then he liked dressing to impress. When he became enlightened, his priorities changed. Gone from his now-uncomplicated life were multiple houses and jet-set vacations. If it didn't involve some sort of greater good, it was easy to talk himself out of doing it. Most of his endorsement deals were donated to charity. It was only recently Tyson considered marrying again, maybe starting a family. Neither of those scenarios included going back to the gridiron until he was too crippled to make a good run at either.

"The Mavericks have enough to afford you both, plus the backup it would take to prevent you from feeling the sack. I'm willing to pay you double what the television deal is worth."

"I don't think this is about money."

Clinton Barrow leaned way back in his executive chair, no longer mincing words. "You're clever, Tyson. I know what I promised, and it seems like I'm pulling the rug out from under you. But LaRue has several conditions on coming to the Mavericks. The main one is he wants you to be the one who throws to him."

"Why me?" Tyson asked, caught by surprise.

"We haven't gotten that far. I wanted to make sure we were all on the same page," Barrow hedged, making it seem as if Tyson actually had a choice.

It felt like pouring salt in an open wound. No matter how friendly or fatherly, Clinton Barrow was still going to do what he had to do to get what he wanted. The TV gig wasn't going to wait another year, even if Tyson was the perfect fit. The guy up for retiring was not only old enough to have given Moses directions, he was a pigskin warhorse who had begun to prattle aimlessly about the glory days of football. It left everyone in the production control room uneasy that a seven-second delay wouldn't be enough and his next diatribe would land them all on the wrong side of some controversy. A strange irony, given Tyson's own past was embroiled in scandal.

"Won't you at least meet him? See what's making him tick?" Clint asked.

"I get the feeling there is no way to gracefully decline without you taking it personally."

"It would end our relationship on a sour note. And I'd owe you a favor, a big one, the offensive coordinator kind of favor, if you can wait a year or two. You'd still be the youngest in the league."

Even if Clinton Barrow threw the morsel out on the spur of the moment, they both knew he would make good on it. Tyson would've never put it on the table, but a coaching job would keep him on the field, the best of all worlds. It was also testament to just what length Barrow would go to make this deal with LaRue happen.

"When can you set up the meeting?" Tyson caved.

"In about an hour, I thought it'd be nice if he joined us for lunch."

Tyson shook his head, wondering why he should be surprised. Clint was a man of action.

"There is one other thing you should probably know about Marcus, if you didn't already. He wants to come with baggage."

Tyson began to grit his teeth. Marcus had achieved the level of stardom that made a great deal of his whims reality.

"You know he's not what you would call media-friendly," Clint said with full-on twang.

"That's one way to put it," Tyson responded.

"We frown on those things here in Austin. Once he puts on that uniform, he's part of a team. To that end, we've told him we're willing to meet him halfway to make everyone happy. His concession is that he have his own reporter, a handler, if you will, who will be the only person who ever gets his comments before or after games."

Geez, LaRue was smart, Tyson thought. Pompous, but brilliant. He waited patiently for Barrow to drop the bomb.

"He wants that reporter to be Dani Carr."

Tyson shook his head. Now he saw the reason behind Clint's advance warning. But he was also intrigued, and it made his pulse quicken. This might not be so bad after all.

Dani Carr represented so many things. Not only was Marcus LaRue's choice for personal correspondent the league's current broadcast darling, but she also happened to be the most current test of his humility.

TYSON AND CLINT WENT TO a steakhouse that was one of their favorites. Within minutes of being seated, Marcus arrived alone. No agent, no entourage, no fanfare. Without being led over by the maître d', he seemed to appear out of nowhere and suddenly was standing beside them at the table.

If nothing else, the young buck is prompt, Tyson thought as they shook hands and Marcus took his seat. He had a firm handshake, but not a long one, as if he disliked the contact.

Tyson studied Marcus as they made polite small talk with Barrow. He was shorter than Tyson, maybe as much as six inches, lean and compact but with too much muscle to be considered wiry. Wisps of platinum blond hair occasionally fell into his eyes. Eyes that were bright blue, like a robin's egg. There was a hardness to them, as unreadable as the man himself, who at twenty-four had only recently become a full-blown adult. He was detached, responding to questions with little more than one-word answers even while his eyes seemed to be looking everywhere at once, already bored with the conversation. No actual smile, but a permanent half-grin, the kind that a wise guy wears as he's getting over on you.

Arrogant, was Tyson's final analysis, not that arrogant football players were anything new. And why wouldn't he be? Marcus was a hot property who kept his nose clean, which only added to his mystery. But there was something else—it was the completely disinterested look that Marcus wore that translated into he couldn't care less, about football or much of anything else.

As they dined, Barrow's conversation slowly began to segue into all the wonderful things Austin had to offer, leading up to the Mavericks in particular. He didn't press Marcus in any way, and Tyson couldn't help but compare the difference in the way he was trying to finesse Marcus to join the team to the way he had invited Tyson.

After they ordered coffee, Clint rose from the table. Giving Tyson a little wink he said, "I'm going to leave you two to get better acquainted. Tyson, my car will be waiting for you to take you back. The check is settled. See you at the office."

The two were left alone, and from their opposite sides of the table, they engaged in a brief stare-down, the veteran and the rookie.

"I expected to see a coach or two here, maybe a marching band. If nothing else, an accountant," Marcus commented drolly.

"Let's cut the bullshit, LaRue. What's your angle here?"

Marcus maintained his careless expression. "I want to win a Super Bowl. Don't you?"

If this punk was trying to intimidate him, he was barking up the wrong tree. Tyson had been intimidated by the best. "We all do. But this smells like a stunt. I don't do outrageous grabs for the limelight anymore."

Marcus shook his head slightly and exhaled loudly. "And I never did them. You know how I feel about my right to privacy."

"Then why am I sitting here as the only thing contingent on you signing with the Mavericks?"

Marcus looked like he might start to laugh but didn't. "There are a lot of reasons I want to play here. You're only one of them. The rest are my business."

"I couldn't care less about your other reasons," Tyson replied, "but I will get to the bottom of the one that concerns me."

Marcus tilted his head and stared at him before saying, "Don't you see it, dude? You gotta know I'm reading your mind out there."

Tyson looked at him skeptically from across the table. For all the times he wished there was some paranormal force to explain away Marcus's uncanny ability to intercept his passes, it sounded absurd.

"That's a bit farfetched," Tyson said. "And I don't believe in voodoo."

Marcus leaned back in his chair. "This has nothing to do with voodoo, which is a real religion back where I'm from, by the way. What I'm talking about is more like telepathy. Didn't you ever wonder how I always manage to be right where you're throwing, even when I don't make the steal?"

Tyson could feel his jaw tightening. He not only wondered how Marcus did it, but he often agonized over it. But when push came to shove, there was no logical explanation for the sixth sense Marcus claimed to possess. "I'm not the only quarterback you've run the score up on."

"That's true," Marcus replied, neither humble nor conceited. "And there are times I do get it right with others. But with you it's consistently the strongest."

"I don't believe this," Tyson scoffed, one step closer to pushing away from the table and going back to Barrow as the bearer of bad news.

"You don't have to believe it, although it would help. But can you imagine how much damage we could do with that sort of advantage?"

"Why haven't you shared this with anyone else?"

"Why would I? I don't like to waste time. Or breath."

Marcus sounded like he had a clear understanding of the politics of the game and his value as a commodity. He also had an advantage that he wanted to capitalize on, but he needed Tyson's help to do it. A strange, cosmic advantage, the very thing Tyson had learned to stop questioning. There was no need to let LaRue in on the fact that Tyson was at a disadvantage and really couldn't say no. He itched to tell Marcus that Dani Carr would have to go, to give it the appearance of a true negotiation, but he didn't want to reveal just how much that woman managed to get under his skin. It looked like there would be plenty of time to pursue that subject. If Marcus was speaking the truth, it would be like having two quarterbacks on the field. And if he was right about it, it'd be like having an extra receiver as well. Tyson had nothing to lose and everything to gain. He would fulfill every obligation he ever felt to Barrow and if all went well, would be able to go out on top in the process.

"The only way a secret weapon works is to keep it a secret," Marcus added with his half-grin becoming close to a full one. "We both know you excel at those."

"Keeping secrets is exhausting, Marcus," Tyson said, trying to keep from sounding like he was doling out unwanted advice.

"So is having to placate a bunch of greedy assholes."

The man had a point, even if Tyson didn't completely agree. He had always viewed Barrow as a mentor if not his savior. But even now all Barrow thought about was a championship, and he was more than willing to let Tyson take another year of pounding for a shot at it.

"It can never work if we're suspicious of each other," Tyson said.

Marcus actually smiled, but it looked unnatural, like it pained him to do so. "If you're willing to trust me, I might begin to trust you. Starting with what we've just discussed and what you do with that information."

Tyson smiled back. "You get one year."

Marcus crossed his arms and narrowed his eyes. He sounded almost insulted. "That's all we're going to need."

CHAPTER 7

DANI CARR STOOD in front of her closet and carefully considered her shoes. Did she want to make a fashion statement or show that she was ready for action? The heels would give her height, and she loved the way they made her legs look, but if she had to move quickly, there was a real chance that she could trip and make a spectacle of herself. She had done that once already and didn't want to repeat the experience, even if the payoff that first time had been huge. Then she took into account the height of who she'd be standing next to. It wouldn't make much of a difference. She prudently chose a pair of flats.

"Mommy, Mommy, Mommy!"

The chant could be heard starting from in all likelihood the top of the stairs and then coming down the hall from the second story of the house Dani had grown up in. Not a distress call, but more of a demand.

It stopped periodically, then would start up again until she could see the little cherub behind the ruckus.

"Mommy!" Brendon Carrino stormed into the room like the four-year-old powerhouse he was, barreling up to Dani and grabbing her tight around the legs, nearly knocking her over.

"You found me!" she exclaimed proudly, regaining her balance. She shuffled over to the bed, with him still hanging on, and sat down on it to give him a proper hug.

"This time you stay," he stated with conviction. His arms tightened around her neck.

She buried her nose into his golden mop of hair. It still had remnants of that baby smell, but it had begun to get darker. It was getting closer to her natural color, before she started spending quality time every four to six weeks in salon chairs with double processing highlight foils. Another sacrifice in the long list of modifications she endured in the pursuit of her ambition.

His blue eyes were also starting to tone down and become more indigo. That was courtesy of his father.

"Don't you have fun with Papa and Danza?"

Papa was the name they called her father. Danza was the shortened version of the name her father affectionately called her mother. Originally Abbondanza, it represented everything her father loved about his wife, abundance. From her fondness for children and opera that she was terrible at singing to her pear shape that her father still couldn't resist pinching whenever she passed him. Most importantly her nickname was derived from her insistence that from sunup to sundown, there had to be a pot of something always cooking on the stove. Demetri Carrino moved his bride out of South Philly after the birth of their oldest, Dominic. Now, over thirty-five years later, there probably wasn't anyone in Ardmore, Pennsylvania, who could tell you that her real name was Doreen.

"Danza!" Brendon yelled joyfully and ran off to find her, already on to the next thing. It spared her from having to comfort him, something she wasn't sure she was up to right now. And it was confirmation that her son was in good hands, not that she didn't know it already. There were people whom children were naturally drawn to. And then there were people who were genuinely fond of children. Then there was Danza. The woman clearly had a gift. She was a veritable Pied Piper, specializing in small children, with a penchant for infants in particular. From the time Dani was little, Danza ran a day care out of their home. Dani couldn't remember a time when she didn't come home from school to find at least one, if not several, children of varying ages free-ranging around the first floor of the Carrino house, where they were efficiently corralled from wandering upstairs and into the bedrooms. Danza could often be found on the floor, surrounded by either playing or sleeping babies, all while still keeping the pots on the stove simmering. But it was also another painful reminder that Dani was not the center of Brendon's world. She shook it off with the thought that she wasn't alone. Throughout the years, lots of working mommies and daddies had been thrown over by kiddies who were over-the-moon excited to see Danza. What parent doesn't feel slighted by their toddler eagerly outstretching their little arms wanting to be held by someone else? *Separation anxiety* was not a term in Danza's vocabulary.

"Whoa whoa whoa JAILBREAK!" Dante's voice boomed as he threw himself against a wall in the hall in dramatic fashion as Brendon tore by him. Dante was the Carrinos' third child and maintained he would have been the last had he been born a girl. He still occasionally teased Dani about how she should be grateful, because if it weren't for him, she wouldn't exist. They all knew there wasn't any truth to it. Danza would've happily given birth to a dozen children, but it wasn't in the cards. And no child within Danza's reach could ever claim to feel neglected. The three Carrino boys were all fiercely protective of their little sister, a mandate handed down by Papa when he was still called Daddy.

"How's it going, Daniella?" Dante said when he appeared in the doorway to her room, drawing out the pronunciation of her name, fully aware that it annoyed her.

Dani shrugged, and went back to packing her suitcase.

"He's going to be fine," Dante said, trying to be reassuring.

"I know." She sighed. After all the inner debate, Dani grabbed a pair of heels anyway and threw them into her suitcase. Better safe than sorry. She wished all her decisions were so easy.

"For someone who's breaking all the rules, you sure don't seem too happy." He leaned against the doorway.

"I'm about to become the indentured servant of a temperamental jock who doesn't like to communicate. It wasn't quite what I had in mind."

"Yeah, but look on the bright side, you're nearing a hundred million hits on YouTube," he said with a mixture of pride and envy. "Not bad for a girl who was doing the sidelines for a fourth-level broadcasting team two years ago."

Dani briefly closed her eyes and then bit her tongue. She wanted to be known for her intelligence and her skill, not for being a viral sensation. She tried to look at the whole scenario as another opportunity, mainly because she had no other choice. Sometimes you just have to make the best of what you have.

Dani's unexpected notoriety had just celebrated its first birthday and in some ways it was like having a prayer answered. In others, it was like being sent to purgatory. Today she could feel the flames beginning to lick at her feet.

"Dante, could you go check on Brendon and make sure he's not coloring on Papa while he naps?" she asked, desperate for a minute alone.

"Sure, sis." Her brother nodded and left, but not before forcefully grabbing her head in both his hands and slamming a sloppy kiss into her forehead. "And don't worry. We all got your back."

After Dante left, Dani sat down on her bed and shook her head.

Thanks to her three brothers, Dani genuinely liked male company. She had learned to think like the boys, or at least be able to guess what they were thinking. Her mother had wanted a princess and what she got was a tomboy. Frilly dresses and barrettes felt more like costumes than clothing. Much to her mother's chagrin, in her young years she refused to be told she couldn't climb as high, run as fast, or throw as far. Her protective older brothers indulged her. But then she began to blossom, her brothers' friends began to notice, and everything changed. They stopped allowing her to follow. She would catch the tail ends of arguments between her brothers and their friends that included the words *hands off*. She became acutely aware of those same friends as their gazes all began to drift downward to her chest when they talked to her. The day she got her first period at thirteen, she cried with the injustice of it. It could no longer be denied that she was viewed as different, and she resented it. To distance herself from the *D* theme her parents had created for her brothers Dominic, Damian, and Dante, she insisted on being called Ella. She endured countless lectures on what boys were really looking for, which led to advice on how and where to kick those boys when they stepped over the line. Of course, the few girlfriends she had held very different opinions, and there were times she was certain those girls were only friendly to get to the dark and handsome Carrino boys. She listened to them pine with adolescent longing and watched them make fools of themselves to get her brothers' attention, often heartbroken as the reward for their efforts. By the time she was fifteen, she had determined that hormones and boys in general were not worth the trouble. She had too much firsthand knowledge about the species to be blindsided by romantic notions. And her parents instilled in her that she should never settle for a man who was only interested in her body. If he loved her for her mind, he would always love her. Beauty fades, they told her.

All that changed the day she laid eyes on Tyson Palmer.

She had been trying to earn some extra money while in college. Even with her scholarships and her parents picking up the slack with her tuition, there was nothing left to spare. She wasn't eligible for the RA program until her junior year, and it seemed impossible to find a job off campus that would fall in line with her classes and leave her weekends free. She was already working for the school paper in the hope of earning the coveted football team reporter spot by the time she was a senior. When she applied for a position in the tutor pool, it seemed like a logical choice. When she got the call that she was going to be tutoring the team's star quarterback, it was impossible to not look at it as a sign from the universe that she was on the right path. Now she would have someone to talk football with, someone with the ability to put in a good word for her with the newspaper's sports editor.

The first time Dani met Tyson, her breath unexpectedly left her in a rush. It wasn't just that he was handsome, although he certainly was. It wasn't that he looked like he was wearing shoulder pads, even when he wasn't, or the way his jeans were held up by his sexy backside. It wasn't the swagger in his walk. It was the mischievous twinkle in his deep blue eyes, his playful sincerity. And the way his face would light up whenever she mentioned his most recent game, which she always attended. He remained kind and respectful even after she was sure her crush became obvious. Her heart thumped so loudly around him, she was certain he had to have heard it. The more time she spent in his presence, the more all her old beliefs became challenges. Her heart would race when he talked to her and she would feel tingly all over.

Even when people were kissing his arse and she was an ignorant underclassman, he took the time to make her feel . . . special. He always gave her a quick wave, like he was genuinely happy to see her, shouting out hello sometimes from across a courtyard on campus, even when he was busy dashing from one task to another, which he usually was.

Dani had convinced herself that his flirting was all in her imagination, until the kiss.

It had been right out of every schoolgirl's dream. It was soft and romantic, and he was embarrassed for a minute after she broke the bad news that she wasn't that kind of girl.

But when it came to Tyson Palmer, she wanted to be that kind of girl. She wanted to be uninhibited and sexy, like the women who always seemed to follow him around. But she also wanted so much more. She wanted to be the one girl, out of all the others, that he remembered. But she knew it was too much to ask. She just wasn't that extraordinary, didn't devote her life to being pretty. She soon became another face in the crowd. Everyone knew he was destined for greatness, and they were rooting for him, as was she. The semester ended and her services were no longer required. Without having booty call status, her number was dropped from his phone.

But instead of watching his rising star shine, she bore witness to his steady decline and eventual breakdown. Her heart ached for him on a weekly basis, even as her brothers joked about how, thanks to her, at least he knew sentence structure. But she had already seen firsthand a taste of what his life was like and the kind of pressure he was under, even back in school, when he had to mix his education in with a grueling schedule. It wasn't a question of if but when the constant stress would take down his devil-may-care, happy demeanor. Dani never outgrew the crush and continued to love him with her nineteen-year-old heart.

She would fantasize about him, concocting elaborate scenarios of a chance meeting, where he would recognize her and they would reconnect. He would confide in her, and she would listen. She would be his rock and he would gather and regain his strength from her.

And in her dreams, she would do all the things to him that she wanted to after that first kiss. She would love him so much that he couldn't imagine a life without her.

And in a moment of serendipity, Dani got that chance. She never expected to see him at homecoming. She had never gotten the job to report from the sidelines either. She swallowed that bitter pill and watched another dude rattle off stats and high-five players all season. Word had come down from the alumni office that Tyson hadn't been invited. They didn't need to voice the reasons why. He had become an embarrassment. While waiting for the elevator at her dorm, she overheard students talking to each other about having sighted Tyson at the Bunker. The more they laughed at what a hot mess he was, the more resolved she felt.

Dani believed she had manifested her own fate. This was her chance to be Tyson's rock—to pick him up, dust him off, and show him how much he deserved her. But sometimes fate is fickle.

In the months that followed, when she could no longer hide her expanding belly, she began her career in deceit and told her first lie. She tearfully told her parents about a party she went to and after having one too many, she made a bad decision with a handsome nameless stranger. They only had one question: Had it genuinely been her decision? After assuring them she hadn't been assaulted, they were nothing but supportive. Her parents laughed and sang while they converted Damian's old room into a nursery. They all showed up and clapped with pride as she waddled up to receive her master's diploma in media and communications, telling her that she could be anything she wanted to be. She thought about Tyson every day, worried about where he was and reflecting on how it was probably for the best that her baby never know his father as a drugged-out mess. On the very day she woke up and promised herself she would spend this day and every day thinking of nothing but how to be the best mother possible, Clinton Barrow held a news conference. The kind designed to set the football world on fire. From the press room at Maverick Field, and with all the frenzied pomp and circumstance he could manage, Barrow made the announcement.

Tyson Palmer was making his return.

It only took hearing his name spoken out loud for Dani's heart to start racing. She watched from her parents' couch with her feet up to minimize the swelling in her ankles as Barrow trumpeted his new acquisition, flanked by stone-faced coaches doing their best to look optimistic. Sitting in the middle, next to his new boss, was the man himself.

Tyson was back, bigger, stronger, and hotter than ever. Gone was the rambunctious loudmouth, replaced by a subdued, clear-eyed version who spoke humbly about how grateful he was to the Mavericks organization for giving him the opportunity to play again.

Clinton Barrow was smart. He made it short and sweet, and they all left the room before any questions could be asked. It wasn't until it was over that Dani was able to draw a decent breath. Five minutes after that, her water broke.

DANI FINISHED PACKING AND WENT downstairs. Her stomach growled, tempted by the smell of sausage and peppers. Danza and Brendon were at the big kitchen table working on a SpongeBob jigsaw puzzle. She crouched down next to her favorite boy.

"Hey, you. Kiss me," she said. He looked up from what he was doing and complied. Then he showed her a piece of the big chunky puzzle.

"It's Mr. Crab's foot," he told her proudly.

Dani looked at the little stub of red surrounded in blue. "I'll take your word on that."

Then Brendon gifted her with an adorable, bubble-filled, raspberry-like laugh. "Real crabs don't wear pants," he pshawed, shaking his head.

Her mother stopped humming the SpongeBob theme song and asked, "You staying for dinner? Now that you got this new job, I see you've started eating again."

Her mother wasn't trying to give her a hard time. She hated to see good food underappreciated. It was really the only time she criticized her daughter.

"Of course I'm staying for dinner," Dani was quick to reply. If there was ever a time to incorporate stress eating and comfort foods, it was now. "Who knows when I'll get cooking this good again?"

Danza took a moment to look up from the puzzle.

"Sometimes the things we want most come with the most sacrifice," Danza reminded her while getting up to stir a pot of sauce.

Dani bit back the joke about wanting to get her out of the house so she could have the baby to herself. Not only wasn't it true, but of all the people in her corner, her mother had said the least about her transformation. At times, she helped with the planning and execution.

"Yeah." Dante came into the room to grab a couple beers for himself and Papa while they watched some baseball. It provided an opportunity to bust her chops. "Come on, by now you have to be getting tired of grilled chicken breast."

But Dani hadn't heard him, she was busy staring at Brendon and still reminiscing.

Not long after Brendon was born, during a middle-of-the-night feeding, they sat together in the nursery. Whenever Danza heard him cry, she would put on her robe and slippers and pad down the hall to see if Dani needed any help. She never interfered, but on that night Dani was feeling especially tired and hormonal. After one look at Dani's exhausted face, Danza asked if she could join her. They sat for a few minutes to the sound of Brendon sucking on his bottle and the occasional creak from their rocking chairs.

"You've been blessed," Danza said gently.

"He is beautiful, isn't he?" Dani sniffed with emotion. There were times she longed to tell someone, anyone, about her unrequited love. In the quiet times when it was nothing but her newborn and a night-light, she could hear the sound of her heart aching.

"He certainly is. But that's not what I mean. You've been blessed in many ways. Not many people have your brains. Or your gonads. Or your support system."

They exchanged small smiles, Dani's one of relief, Danza's one of belief.

"All women should be able to do what they love," Danza stated from her chair. "When we were young, your dad used to tell me that a woman who feels fulfilled will remain beautiful her entire life. I loved being a mother and homemaker. He worked hard so I could be the best one."

"Daddy's a smart man." Dani felt her eyes welling up, grateful for the relative darkness.

"And a good one," Danza said.

"I wonder if he's the last one."

Danza's toned-down chuckle filled the room, and Brendon's eyes opened for a moment. He cooed slightly in response to it before closing them and resuming his feeding.

"He's not the first, last, or only good man out there. He just needed minimal training," Danza teased before asking, "What would you love to be?"

"I would love to be a good mother. Like you." Not only did she want it to be true, but she also thought it was what her mother wanted to hear.

"And you can be, if you feel fulfilled as a woman."

"All I feel like right now is a bloated, weepy wreck." Dani laughed weakly.

"That will pass. And when it does you're going to want to be ready. Ready to get back to your dream and your calling."

Her calling had always been to break into broadcasting, and not just any broadcasting. She had never gotten over being passed up for her time on the sidelines.

Her dream had been the same for years. She had never shared it, and even while sniffling in the dark, she still didn't want to.

The knowing smile from her mother made her want to have both. And strangely enough, they did go hand in hand. But was she willing to give fate another chance?

"Give me that baby," Danza whispered while reaching out for him. Brendon fussed briefly while Dani handed him over, followed by his bottle. Danza expertly cradled him in her arms and he stilled. "Go get some sleep, you have plans to make. Remember, you don't win by playing men at their own game, you win by outsmarting them."

It began with a gym membership to lose the baby weight and rock her bod in general. She didn't become discouraged as her figure struggled to bounce back to her prebaby days. She refused to hate herself for having put her body through the ultimate endurance test, one that resulted in a miracle. She changed the color of her hair from chestnut to highlighted blond. Next to go was her wardrobe. She studied the girls who were already in the biz and piece by piece started buying similar clothes. She gave up the glasses in favor of contact lenses. And her mother cheered her on as she did so. She even shushed her father when he bemoaned his disapproval after she changed her name to Dani Carr.

"But she's a Carrino," he said, pouting.

"Demo," Danza chided her husband. "She wants to compete in a man's world. She thinks a more masculine name gives her an advantage. It's like a stage name. She'll always be a Carrino."

"She sure doesn't look like a man. Some of those sweaters are pretty tight," Papa grumped in fatherly fashion.

By the time she submitted her first application, Dani had come to several conclusions. She didn't just want to make it in a man's world. She wanted to infiltrate what she decided was more of a misogynistic boys' club.

After her first interview with the Philadelphia affiliate of CBS, she was sure of it.

The timing was perfect. Women were being hired at an alarming rate to satisfy the now-public outcry for less sexism in sports broadcasting roles.

She got a job as the fourth-level sideline reporter. It was really more of a glorified internship. Her responsibilities would mostly entail feeding stats to the woman who had already paid her dues and the boys in the booth. It didn't even guarantee her airtime.

But Dani Carr had arrived. The job fueled the dream of once again meeting up with Tyson Palmer. But she couldn't spend too much time dreaming; she still had lots of work to do. Most of it was an uphill battle.

Dani learned to ignore blatant sexist remarks and catcalls. She stiffened her spine when people insinuated that she didn't know a damn thing about football because she'd never played. She got good at judging whose stupid jokes she needed to laugh at, even when her first instinct would be to introduce her knee to their inseam. By Brendon's second birthday she was being courted by an agent and offered a second-level position.

The Mavericks had become a hot ticket, thanks in part to their recently redeemed quarterback. Dani had moved up the ranks and now had the privilege of being fed live to the "good ole boys" in the studio. It was one step closer to her final objective, breaking up the all-male posse that sat in the comfort of the studio discussing matchups and sharing well-calculated predictions. She knew what she wanted to accomplish was daunting at best, but she was also willing to put in the time. The boys back in the studio, unaware of her final goal, actually had begun to respect her knowledge. When broadcasting was ahead of schedule and there was airtime to spare, it wasn't uncommon for them to engage her for several minutes about her interpretation of the game's high and low points, which in and of itself was a major coup. It was then Dani started thinking that maybe, just maybe, she might be able to have it all.

Three weeks later, she was told she was going to Boston to cover the Blitz-Mavericks game. As soon as she found out, her heart started to pitter-patter in an all too familiar way. She worked herself up with the fantasy that after his initial shock, Tyson would apologize for his behavior that fateful night. She would forgive him because that's what people did when they loved someone. And then, once she knew he was truly healthy and worthy, Dani would tell him about their son.

By the time the Blitz-Mavericks game was in the fourth quarter, she was practically dancing with excitement. It was clear that nothing short of a miracle would hand over a win to the Mavericks. The wait was excruciating, and she was anxious to set her plan into motion.

She would go right up to him, with her microphone off, and ask him, "Tyson, the Blitz defense was really all over you today. Were you starting to think the only way to keep you safe would be to stick you in a 'bunker'?" She'd make sure to add a little wink. She would come clean as soon as he gave her the "Do I know you? You seem familiar."

Dani kept her eyes on him after time ran out with the Blitz's win and field began to flood with players and press. She jockeyed her crew into position to make sure he couldn't get past her.

It had all gone according to plan. Until he got close enough and every single feeling she ever had about him hit her full force. It was worse than when she had seen him last. Her feet were the first to betray her and walked her right up to him, microphone ready to thrust in his face. As soon as she caught his eye, all her words failed her and her mouth refused to open.

She didn't really expect him to recognize her right away, but deep down, she had always been sure he would. But Tyson looked right through her. He gave her a dazzling smile, but there was no hint of any recognition whatsoever. That was bad enough, but even worse, she was suddenly, painfully tongue-tied and to her horror, could only stare up at him and blink.

"Darlin', you're supposed to wanna talk to the winner," Tyson quipped. He winked at her before taking off to the locker room.

He was correct, of course. The losers wanted to make like good sports and get off the field fast. Professional courtesy dictated that you allow them to go back to the locker room and lick their wounds a bit before putting on their brave faces in postgame press conferences. Sometimes a reporter wanted to try and make a splash and sneak a question in there, usually trapping the more emotional and volatile players, but it was generally considered bush league.

Dani knew going in that the odds were slim he would recognize her. Part of her held out hope that the night they spent together had stayed with him in some fashion. But apparently not. He was polite, but it was clear he had no idea who she was. Worse than that, he had winked at her in a way that suggested if they were in a different setting, he would hit on her. Now that he was back on top, he was as cocky as ever. She felt so foolish. Once again, he had successfully humiliated her, this time without even trying.

Dani got the nudge from her crew that the studio wanted her feed and she hustled to find another player, preferably from the winning side. She was too late, though. All the worthy playmakers of the day were already occupied with other reporters.

Still, even in defeat Dani found victory. She managed to score eight words from Marcus LaRue, the rookie phenom who hated reporters. At first she wasn't even going to bother. Getting snubbed twice in one day would make her look like a total amateur. But something about the way his icy blue eyes connected with hers made her take the risk. She stuck out the mic and asked him the stupidest thing she could, figuring he was just going to walk by her anyway.

"How do you feel, Marcus?"

He stopped right in front of her and bent his head to her microphone long enough to say, "Like I got Palmer's number on speed dial."

He looked at her so hard it was like a slap. Her mouth dropped open, and Marcus LaRue went back to trotting off the field with a dozen other correspondents running after him. Her crew was already feeding the exchange to the booth, ecstatic at the feat she had managed to accomplish and wanting to beat to the punch anyone else who might have caught the sound bite.

But Dani was still shaken from the encounter. And while there wasn't a station that wouldn't rush to run such a rare comment from LaRue, there was still going to be time to fill.

She quickly managed to conjure up what she remembered of the game and added some commentary. She must have made some seriously spot-on points because the booth threw her a follow-up, one that made her already preoccupied mind overcompensate and become overconfident.

The announcer in the booth asked about the chances of the Tyson Palmer–led Mavericks finally getting their Super Bowl. A legitimate follow-up, with an eye-rolling snort when Dani replied live:

"I'm not sure the Mavericks have what it takes to win the trophy. It appears they're still reeling from the losses of Macey and Stillman, so the protection just isn't there and it shows every time they try to rally. Lots of missed opportunities for the Mavericks today, from late throws and hesitation on some key plays by the offense. Maybe it's a communication breakdown, but from here it looks like Tyson's chicken."

It was bad enough she broke her first rule of sports reporting: when talking to a player, address them by their first name; when referring to them, use only their last name. It created a clear boundary of professionalism. But Dani couldn't resist the not-so-subtle dig at Tyson.

And then, out of nowhere, a large black fly went barreling into her mouth. Startled and grossed out, Dani waved her arms and made what sounded like a loud accompanying squawk, complete with bulging eyes. Once again, her timing had been perfect. A pretty, blond girl had just called one of the league's finest quarterbacks a chicken and then did a perfect chicken impression, flapping and squawking for the camera. The capper being that Tyson was an actual, well-known chicken brand.

The cameraman couldn't cut away fast enough, and everyone in the studio, including the boys at the big desk, guffawed about it on air for nearly two minutes. It completely eclipsed Dani's coup of getting the LaRue comment. By the end of the day, her squawk had been replayed on every major network at least a dozen times. Within twenty-four hours, there wasn't anyone in broadcasting who didn't know Dani Carr's name.

Dani tried to look on the bright side of the whole experience. She'd gotten a little payback for Tyson blowing her off. When he played away, loud clucking jeers began whenever Palmer took the field. Even Mavericks fans at the home stadium were known to start squawking when his performance was less than stellar. Tyson Palmer tried to play it off, but after it stuck, his easy smile began to get tighter and tighter.

And Dani was strangely okay with that.

CHAPTER 8

DANI HAD DINNER with her family before heading to the airport to begin what she tried to view as an adventure. She indulged in sausage and peppers and ignored all the jokes Dante made about Brendon's preference for chicken nuggets.

"His father must be some sorta Swede," Dante said.

Both Papa and Danza gave him a stern look, with Danza adding a very chastising shake of her head. They all knew the day would come when Brendon would fully understand that despite all the people around him, he had only one parent. Not a crime by any means, but they all felt sad for him nonetheless.

No one felt worse about it than Dani. She pretended she was going to steal a nugget from Brendon and when he held out his chubby little hand to feed it to her, she thought about calling the whole thing off and going back to Carrino's Plumbing and Supply.

Dani had only shared the same stadium with Palmer one other time since that day. Keeping her distance had been easy. She was now considered a media darling, and she took a tiny bit of license with it. She didn't care if anyone thought she was ducking him. Her newfound celebrity meant she now had her choice of which games to report, which kept it simple.

Until the day she got the offer she couldn't refuse, presented to her in such a way that she would not only be crazy to turn it down, but to do so would also be career suicide. It had started with a phone call at home from her boss two weeks earlier. He had sounded equal parts confounded and amused.

"Sorry, Carr, I have to fire you. You're going to work for Marcus LaRue."

"As what?" She laughed, waiting for the punch line. Sure, everyone knew Marcus was an odd sort. And Dani was the only person he'd talked to all season. The one sentence he gave her were the final words before the total media withdrawal that had started with the death of his mother. After that he started giving mostly one-word answers and would turn his back completely when pressed for more. But even then, he was leveling them with his aloof stare. He drove the league crazy with his refusal to cooperate. It was quite comical really. Reporters followed Marcus, screaming questions at him while he went about his business as if they weren't there. There was nothing they could say to shake him, and it wasn't long before they started to complain. The league fined him and he still remained silent, seemingly willing to lose money in return for what he deemed his right to privacy. They stopped short of threatening him with suspension, mainly because they wouldn't have the nerve to actually do it if he called their bluff. Nobody wanted Marcus off the field, not the owners of his team, not the fans, not the league. If anything, his reticence only added to his allure, and many began to sympathize with his plight. By strange coincidence, his withdrawal occurred simultaneously with Dani's rise.

"LaRue struck a deal with the league. He's willing to go back to giving interviews. But he wants his own correspondent, the only person who gets his time. That person is you."

"Me?" Dani said, shocked.

"We're just as surprised as you are," her soon-to-be-ex-boss confirmed. "Half of us think it's just his way of making fun of everyone, wanting to use the 'chicken girl.' My vote was for he has a crush on you, but we all know the odds of *that*. We all tried to find out the real skinny, but in case you haven't heard, you're the only one he'll talk to."

"That's not funny, Brad."

"What a coincidence, I'm not laughing," he responded dryly.

"I don't want any part of this," Dani snapped.

"Why the hell not?"

"Because it's not in line with my ultimate goal. I don't want to be some player's handler." Dani thought fast but not quite fast enough. She had never told her boss about her goals when it came to broadcasting, mostly because he didn't ask or care. As far as bosses went, he wasn't awful. To his credit, he usually looked her in the eye when he spoke to her. But through the conversations they had, it didn't take long for Dani to figure out that while Brad appreciated her intelligence, both of them knew that once she got old, or gained weight, or lost her looks, her job would be given to the next twentysomething in line. Every woman currently on the sidelines knew their clocks were ticking, in one way or another.

Unless Dani did something spectacular, something that would set her apart permanently from the rest, and Dani knew just what she wanted that something to be: she wanted to sit with the "boys." Her rise in popularity had been steady, thanks to the video, and they were getting ready to bounce the oldest member of the current pregame crew on one of the major networks. Her agent agreed that while it was a long shot, Dani's iron was hot, and it was time to strike. The last time they spoke, she was all but guaranteed an interview for the broadcast job.

"I don't think you get it. This is your ultimate goal."

"I'll call you back. I'm going to call my agent."

She called her agent, who not only knew about her current job offer, but was also the bearer of bad, if not infuriating, news.

"When I called to schedule your interview, I got the blow off. They told me Tyson Palmer is being outfitted for the position behind the desk."

Once again, she was back at square one. Her agent told her what the Marcus offer was in terms of a salary. Then she called Brad back.

"I really don't want to do this."

"And at the risk of repeating myself, why not?" Brad said in all seriousness. "It's already creating the most delicious buzz. The pay is more than *my* boss makes. It'll cement you in the industry from a publicity standpoint alone."

"Funny you would put it that way. That's what the job description sounds like. I don't do PR. Why does he want me for a publicist?"

"Who cares if he wants you to be his chief cook and bottle washer? There's not a woman in broadcasting who wouldn't kill for that kind of exposure. Someone created this job just for you. Take it, Dani."

She really couldn't explain why not without sounding like a nut. It was the creepy look Marcus had given her that day. The only way she could've described it was it felt like he had opened up her skull and looked inside.

"I don't want to move my son away from the family. They watch him while I work," Dani said. It was a righteous argument, and it was definitely at least part of the reason.

"Wait, you have a kid?" Brad really knew how to hit her where it hurt. "So hire a nanny. Hell, hire ten nannies."

"A nanny isn't family."

Brad sighed so loud Dani could hear it reverberate through the phone. "Move your family with you. I don't think you understand, Dani, if you turn this thing down, you're sunk. There are higher forces at work here."

She knew Brad was referring to the tight-knit community of puppet master billionaires that controlled the league. But what Brad didn't know was that Dani was up to her highlights in higher forces, and it had started to freak her out.

"I guess it's been nice working with you." She crossed herself and surrendered to the inevitable.

"You start in two weeks. We're sending you out the paperwork. May the force be with you."

"Let me know if and when you're rolling through Boston," she said sarcastically. It wasn't like she was in any danger of getting fired now. "I'll be sure to shut off my phone."

She heard him snort through the receiver. "You must be slipping. Or now that you've gotten celebrity status you're getting lazy. You better start watching some ESPN and do your homework. You're not going to Boston. LaRue just signed with the Austin Mavericks."

A chill went down her spine. Dani took a series of deep breaths, like they had taught her in Lamaze. On each inhale she thought, *Austin is fine, he won't be there.* With each exhale she breathed out, *He got the job behind the desk.* The worst thing that was going to happen was she was going to feel irked most of the time because she would have to hear his name constantly being dropped. She could live with that.

After sufficiently calming herself she went downstairs to share the new development with her family. She thought that with two weeks to call her own and a new ridiculously high salary, she would offer to take them all to Disney World. Brad's genuinely surprised comment about not knowing she was a mother left a really rotten taste in her mouth.

As the family celebrated her good fortune, beginning with a vote on where they should stay in Disney, her eye caught something on the ESPN ticker feed as it ran across the bottom of the TV screen. It was the blurb about Marcus signing with the Mavericks.

"Look! That's my new job." *This is going to be okay,* she thought. *We'll be able to come back and visit whenever we want.*

The family resumed celebrating and making plans without noticing when Dani's face turned from excited to horrified.

The following story in the ticker feed was also about the Mavericks. It was announcing the one-year, very lucrative deal securing the services of Tyson Palmer.

DANI SPENT THE REST OF those two weeks trying not to think about it. They weren't able to pull off Disney on such short notice but settled for a long weekend in Hersheypark. Dani ate her weight in chocolate and thought about Tyson anyway. She couldn't take Brendon with her. She was going to be in uncomfortably close quarters, and the more he saw her, the higher the odds would rise that he might recognize her. Even if they managed to get past any lingering animosity, Dani had made up her mind that it was in the best interest of Brendon that he never find out the identity of his father. Her father and brothers were all the positive male role models he'd ever need.

After making her decision she concentrated on Brendon. Dani didn't want to waste a minute of being with him. As the days drew closer to her departure, she alternated between terror she wouldn't be able to pull it off and the depression that she knew she would.

She was busy taking some cell phone video of Brendon when Dante announced her ride had arrived. She held back tears and hugged her baby tight. Her parents assured her that they would take good care of him and she'd be back before she knew it. They promised to figure out the Skype thing. Dante promised he would stop by the house for lunch every day to check up on things and hang out with Brendon, which they all knew he would do because he lived a few blocks over and was a mooch who loved his mom's cooking.

"Be good, baby," Dani whispered into Brendon's tiny ear before kissing his cheek. "Mommy loves you."

CHAPTER 9

MARCUS "HONEYDEW" LARUE was discovered quite by accident at the age of seventeen by a recruiter for Tulane. While in New Orleans on business, he witnessed young Marcus swipe a large honeydew melon from an open-air market. So did the proprietor of the fruit stand, who gave chase. From his car at a red light, the recruiter watched Marcus dodge a cyclist, weave in and out of traffic, and jump over a large aggressive dog, all while protecting the melon. The exhausted owner gave up quickly, but the recruiter followed a hunch and the thief. Both were good moves. He tracked Marcus down to a run-down apartment on the outskirts of town. Marcus had earned an A in street smarts by the age of twelve, life lessons taught, most of the time unintentionally, by the various men who drifted in and out of his mother's life. Some of those teachers had been nice, some not so nice. The recruiter talked

Marcus into getting his GED, got him a spot on the team at Tulane, and the rest, as they say, was history. In Marcus's rookie year with the Boston Blitz, bragging that her son had "hit the jackpot," his mother died of an accidental heroin overdose.

He was stealing the melon for his mother, and it was the saddest coincidence that his mother used to call him Honeydew too, because she said he was as sweet as her favorite fruit.

Intellectually Marcus knew his mother's death wasn't his fault. He'd spent a long time readying himself for what he figured would be the eventual outcome of her addiction. He just never figured anyone else would care. No one gave a crap about his mom while she was alive. But as the media descended during what was supposed to be his time to grieve, the self-protective shell that Marcus had already formed became harder. His reaction was to do what he had always done: keep control. Only he was no longer a stray dog, scurrying from one place to another in the name of survival. He didn't need to worry about where his next meal was coming from. He also discovered as he watched the sometimes frenzied attempts to uncover his story, that he enjoyed the game.

Marcus was a loner who would always show up at the exact time he was expected, fulfill his contractual obligations, and then slip back out into mist. There wasn't anyone who could get a solid read on him and what he did during his off time. It fueled speculation that he had something to hide, and everyone wanted to know exactly what that was. His criminal record, such as it was, consisted of one shoplifting offense when he was ten. He never took a dirty drug test. There were no random baby mammas. With the exception of his mother, there was nobody from his past willing to lend insight. The lesson he learned was that when he thwarted those who thought they had the right to know something, they would resort to anything to get the story. If that failed, the proper media response was to go ahead and muddy the waters, careful not to cross the line into slander. Maybe the media did it in the hopes of making him talk, maybe just to screw with him. It eventually led to the widespread rumor that he was secretly gay, because he had to be hiding some kind of big secret, even if no one had ever discovered exactly what it was.

Marcus remained unaffected by that rumor and every other one that swirled around him. He perfected a nonchalant and distant stare. On game day, he didn't just bring it, he brought it all. He collected interceptions like a kid collected prize tickets at a county fair. When he refused to re-sign with the Blitz and went into free agency as an offensive player without any explanation, it put Marcus LaRue into a class all his own. There wasn't a team in the league that wasn't willing to take the risk in handing him the ball.

Now it appeared Dani was going to be the recipient of that thousand-yard stare on a permanent basis, with the added bonus of having to donate equal time to dodging the team's quarterback.

The longer Dani sat in the Mavericks Human Resources office and got the details of her new gig, the clearer it became that her job would be extremely cushy in some ways. No longer would she need extensive research on all the teams in the league. She wouldn't have to keep countless stats on quick recall. Her home base would be a room in a swanky hotel near the stadium, plus she'd get a company car nicer than any she'd ever driven before. The director was in the process of telling her about her camera crew when there was a light rap on the office door.

Both Dani and the HR director stood up out of their chairs simultaneously as Clinton Barrow entered the room. Between the ten-gallon hat and his outsize presence, he seemed to fill it.

"Dani." He smiled, extending his hand. "I wanted to personally welcome you aboard team Maverick."

Barrow and the director made small talk for a minute before the woman seemed to make up some excuse and took her leave, telling Dani she'd be right back. Dani and Barrow were left alone.

"How are you settling in?" he asked politely, taking a seat in the chair next to hers.

"Austin is a beautiful city," Dani replied. "I don't know how to thank you for this great opportunity, Mr. Barrow."

Barrow smiled. "I'm sure you've been getting your share of job offers since your sudden rise in popularity with the networks."

None stranger than this, Dani thought, *or as perilous.* "There's always plenty of exciting stuff going on in the world of broadcasting."

"I'm thrilled you used the word *exciting.* And that you were willing to let us lure you away from the network to join our team as we embark on this new adventure. We've wanted to try our hand at in-house broadcasting for a while now."

He had a very nice way of putting things, especially since Dani had already been made aware that she didn't really have a choice in the matter.

Barrow crossed one leg over the other and shifted, as if he was trying to get comfortable in a chair he was too big to fit in. "I'd like to think you've been in the business long enough to know that I pride this team on being innovative."

His voice had changed ever so slightly. It was still cordial, but with each word, it became less friendly and more authoritative. Dani could visualize the elephant lumbering into the room and plopping down between them.

"I look forward to being part of it." Dani sat up straighter. It felt like she was in the principal's office. She had always been a good student, a rule follower. Suddenly she could relate to how the rebels and troublemakers must've felt. Maybe she was just projecting her own paranoia. Maybe Clinton Barrow sat down and personally greeted all his new employees.

"There's another thing we pride ourselves on here in Maverick country. And that's loyalty, to our great city, to our state, and above all, to our team. The only grandstanding around here, be it unintentional or not, is done by me."

He was amazing, and if she wasn't so intimidated, she might have taken a moment to fully appreciate it. The man was able to perfectly convey his underlying threat without touching directly on the subject. Dani wasn't being paranoid. She was being put in her place. And despite the cushy perks of the job, it was the last place she wanted to be.

CHAPTER 10

THREE GAMES INTO the season, Dani fidgeted on the sidelines while Stan, her cameraman, took a few handheld shots of the field and the warm-ups. She had gotten good at keeping one eye out for Palmer at all times. Since his first snub and ultimately the "fowling," she had only seen him when Marcus was his opposition. Now that they were on the same team, she had to get cagey. She would scope out wherever Tyson was, and then keep a safe distance, making sure she set up her shots as far away as possible, something that Marcus seemed willing to accommodate and never questioned. Then it was get the footage and get out. But sometimes a field length wasn't enough and she would catch herself watching him from afar, because old habits die hard. Adding another layer of discomfort, there were times when she stole her glances and would find him already looking at her. At first it was with a lopsided grin of amusement, then fascination, and more recently, determination. Those times were becoming more frequent, and his look was getting more intense. But if he took even one step in her direction, she would vanish before he reached her. It became a contest, spoiling his attempt at confrontation. But this time she didn't hear him sidle up next to her. She only saw a huge shadow slowly being cast over hers.

"Good afternoon, Dani."

His voice was deep but the three words had a teasing singsong quality to them. She looked over at Stan in the hopes he was at least facing her so that she could make a quick getaway. But her cameraman was fully engrossed chatting with one of the officials. She turned her head briefly and glanced at Tyson. He was uniformed, clean and crisp, ready to take the field, holding his helmet in his hand, and to avoid looking suspicious he began to stretch by bringing one knee to his chest and then the other.

"It's *Ms.* Carr," she told him haughtily, returning her focus to the field. She double-checked that her microphone was off.

He stopped flexing and cocked a hip. It gave the appearance of casual conversation.

"You're right, we haven't been properly introduced. You look like I caught you by surprise. The clucking hasn't started yet, so it gave me a chance to sneak up on you."

He was acting way too self-deprecating for someone with an ax to grind. Before it had been about getting him to notice her. Now it was all about him never making the connection. Her hopes of a happy reunion had been foolish, she realized, and now they were dashed for good. Her plan B was to never let him get any closer.

"I'm here to work, not socialize."

Tyson laughed, which was all the more exasperating. It was as if he knew her intentions all along. "We can talk shop then. I tried to get a real introduction, but you're like a unicorn, Ms. Carr. Mysterious and always one step ahead of me. If I didn't know better, I'd say you were trying to avoid me."

He'd adopted this occasional twang, like a Texas native, even though he was from Ohio. Also a new development was a perfectly groomed permanent five o'clock shadow that Dani could easily picture running up and down her bare leg. She knew this time there wasn't going to be any sort of easy getaway.

"I *am* avoiding you. But you win, now's your chance. Would you like to extract revenge for something that was completely out of my control? I did have a fly go down my windpipe."

"So you *are* avoiding me. In the beginning I thought you were embarrassed, and you're right, it was awkward. But now I think you protest too much. You have a chip on your shoulder about me, and I'd like to know why. Chances are if you're hating on me that hard, our paths may have crossed. Maybe not in a good way. I'm sorry if I never called again. Trust me, if that's the case I did you a favor."

He had changed her life in the most profound way and he still hadn't recognized her. But he had gotten one step closer. Relief switched off her disappointment. It's what she needed, but she didn't want his apology. Tyson had inadvertently given her and her family the best gift they would ever receive. And his cavalier attitude about the trail of broken hearts reminded her to not be fooled. He was her only one, but she was one of many, too many to keep track of. Dani knew she should bite her tongue, but the words spilled out shrewishly. "Not every woman you come in contact with finds you irresistible, Palmer."

"Of course not. And thanks for using my last name, by the way. Whenever I hear you say 'Tyson,' I die a little inside."

"You'll never have to worry about me making that mistake again."

"I'm allowed my shot at redemption, Ms. Carr."

"Oh yeah, and why's that? Because you're so damn special?"

"No. Because we all are."

"Then go forth and sin no more." She waved her hand in sarcastic absolution.

Tyson shook his head and exhaled dramatically, still smiling. Damn, watching her blush and bluster was adorable. There was something about her that lit him up just looking at her. She had grit and spunk, not to mention curves that went on for miles. He had known all along it was impossible to stay mad at her, even if he'd wanted to. "You're a hard sell, Dani Carr. And I would never question your principles. But if you think I don't see you watching me, you're dead wrong. Maybe you'd like to further discuss my shortcomings over dinner?"

His stare was fixed on her. He was seriously asking her out. Dani wasn't sure her nerves would hold up. Too many things were coming at her at once. He was just so formidable, and sexy. Way too sexy that close up. Part of her wanted so much to say yes, but her head knew it would only end in disaster.

Dani knew her face burned red as she sputtered the lamest comeback ever. "Don't hold your breath."

"And don't waste yours." He took a giant step and stood directly in front of her, using his free hand to make sure the small towel he used to wipe his hands during the game was properly tucked into the front of his pants. From his towering height, he looked down at her. He said it quietly, but distinctly. "One day, and that day is coming soon, you won't have the protection of a camera crew. There won't be a stadium full of people standing between me and what I want to do to you."

And what he wanted to do was shake her until she admitted she really was attracted to him, and then kiss all the other confessions right out of her mouth. He knew he was being antagonistic. There was something familiar about her that he couldn't put his finger on, something that he found endearing, even when she was lashing him with her sharp tongue.

"Is that some kind of threat?" She smiled at him through clenched teeth and asked the question with the same tone she would've used asking him about the weather. But both were well aware there were too many pairs of eyes out there that were already interested in the interaction. He had been a complete gentleman when the incident first occurred, agreed the video was funny, and poked fun of himself on late night television. That was before it turned into a cluck fest and his universal cheer.

Tyson laughed in a casual way, as if they'd just exchanged pleasantries. He shook his head and turned, loping a few long strides out to the fifty-yard line. Dani took a quick scan around to see if anyone was looking before allowing herself a peek at him running away, his perfect buns snug within the confines of his deliciously tight spandex. She was still staring when he stopped, turned, and had to wait for her to look him in the eye. She was stone-cold busted. He flashed a wicked smile.

"Promise!" he called out to her, loud enough for everyone to hear, before putting in his mouth guard and strapping on his helmet. Dani didn't want to make it look like he had the last word, so she didn't storm off. She checked that her microphone was still off for the hundredth time and took one more glimpse at his backside at midfield.

"Well now." Clinton Barrow's deep Texas drawl could be heard behind her. "I don't think Ty was saying that to me, because I haven't asked him for anything. But if there's one thing I do know, it's when that man makes a promise, you can count on him keeping it."

Dani could feel her shoulders tense up into her neck. Now she would have to call a truce. Being considered anything short of a consummate professional didn't sit well with Dani. Once again, her best-laid plans had backfired. The team began to head back to the locker room after warm-ups for their pregame pep talk. Marcus looked at her curiously and gave her a nod as he passed. She avoided meeting Tyson's gaze directly but caught him looking as he neared her. Despite her best efforts, Dani couldn't stop the tears of frustration building. Her chin began to tremble and her eyelids started to burn.

And Tyson didn't miss it.

CHAPTER 11

TWO NIGHTS LATER Tyson woke up drenched in sweat. It came to him like a horrific epiphany, in those few foggy moments before falling into deep sleep.

It was those eyes, even if everything else was different. From the color of her hair to the way she was dressed and how she carried herself, it all had changed. But not those tear-filled eyes. Those eyes would've brought him back from the dead.

One minute he was on the verge of blissful slumber, and the next Tyson was sent back in time on a lightning bolt. Back to a seedy motel on the outskirts of a Pennsylvania town, and the last evil deed he perpetrated on a cute little girl, before he landed in hell. Sometimes flashbacks from the bad old days came to him, and he would accept them, try to process them, and move on. This one he wasn't prepared for, triggered by the last time she had looked at him with the same heartbroken disappointment. He threw an arm across his forehead and heaved, thunderstruck by the force of the memory. A lot of it was hazy, but one part was crystal clear. He had banged his virtuous tutor and left her crying.

"Ella," Tyson whispered, still in disbelief. It was impossible. There was no way he was going to get any rest without solving at least part of the mystery. He got out of bed and pulled out his iPad, doing a quick search on his college's alumni website. Ella Bella with the Italian last name . . . Daniella Carrino. There wasn't a picture, or any information about what she did after graduating, but it was Dani Carr enough for him.

And that placed Dani Carr into what every recovery program labeled the "people, places, and things" category.

From the moment he had woken up what seemed like a lifetime ago in one of Clinton Barrow's guest rooms, Tyson knew his approach to a life of sobriety would be unorthodox. He was never going to be one of those people who checked in with a sponsor like he would a parole officer. Fitting AA meetings into his schedule would not be part of his playbook. But he understood the basic principles he would have to follow if he was to have any hope of success. He would have to cut out all the people who made it easy to slip back into his old ways of thinking. The enablers, who would soon lead him back down the dark lonely path he'd once traveled. Barrow knew it when he yanked every-thing and everyone Tyson knew out from under him. The vast majority of people Barrow replaced them with were good, clean-living folks, so it was easy to make the principle stick. And mercifully, Tyson's career as a practicing addict had been relatively short. Some actually viewed him as obsessed with his rigid dedication to abstention, and he was fine with that. There were still many blank spaces and unfamiliar faces from those dismal days, but when someone said they knew him at his worst, Tyson made his amends and moved on.

But it didn't feel right placing Dani into that group, and he didn't want to. She was from the part of his past that he cherished, when he was still living a completely charmed life. Memories of the time they shared in the campus library and then his dorm room were clear, and even as he lay in bed, Tyson began smiling. She hadn't identified herself, which meant she was holding a grudge if not waging a full-on vendetta. Now he just had to figure out exactly why. He fought back a wave of nausea at the thought he might have raped her. But even on the darkest day of his life, he was never a predator. He had always harmed himself instead of others.

Tyson stayed awake for several hours after making the discovery, painstakingly piecing back together the events of that night as best he could, followed by everything that had gone on since then, those eyes haunting him the entire time. He should've been furious, but he wasn't. It was the complete opposite. There wasn't anything about her that he didn't admire. He finally fell back to sleep after making two important decisions. One—he would find out for sure what he'd done to earn her wrath and why she wanted nothing to do with him. And two—he would apologize and finally get their relationship back on track. He couldn't help hoping that that track would end with her back in his bed. Only this time, he was going to get it right. When it came to Dani Carr, he wanted them both to get a second chance.

TYSON SEARCHED FOR HER EVERY day for the rest of the week without any luck. By Sunday he showed up for game day and asked everyone if they had seen Dani Carr. It ended with him shaking down Marcus, who at first seemed hesitant but finally told him where he could find her. She was in the media room getting her pregame assignment. Tyson marched right up to her, in front of her crew and several other reporters.

"I need to talk to you. Now," Tyson ordered with his gaze fixed solely on her, unconcerned with who was around and what they might hear.

"I'm working here, Palmer," she began brusquely, taking a quick look around. Several people had stopped what they were doing to observe, alerted by the tone of his voice. "And you should be suiting up."

"You sure you want to do this in front of other people?" He brought his voice down to a whisper, but there was still an unmistakable under-current. He looked perfectly capable of causing a scene. She gave him a curt nod and left the room with him following closely behind, much to the interest of everyone watching. They found an empty room, and as he closed the door behind them, she rounded on him, clearly miffed.

"You made your point the other day, okay? I'm playing nice," Dani told him peevishly.

"I just have a few questions," he replied, angrier than he intended, but it had been building all week. And when it came to her, he often found himself displaying more emotion than he normally would. "Starting with when exactly did Dani Carr kill Ella Bella?"

The sentence sucked up all the air in the room. She hated the way both the names rolled off his tongue. It made her momentarily forget all the potential ramifications of his discovery.

"Dani Carr didn't kill her, Tyson Palmer did," she spat, on the verge of blurting out more than she wanted. "So now you know. It took you long enough."

"Why didn't you tell me?"

"Because I've had sneezes that lasted longer," she replied. "And I didn't see the need to bring up old history."

She wanted to hurt him, but she also needed to send the message that his attention was unwelcome. She needed him to leave her alone. Because she was powerless when it came to him, she knew that now. After their last altercation, she had spent the night in her hotel room crying it out, alternately cursing him and then herself. She had created this quagmire, and every solution she tried to come up with only pulled her deeper. She couldn't let him get close to her on any level.

Nothing good could come from them becoming friends or, worse yet, lovers. Whenever she looked at Tyson, she saw the grown-up version of the child they shared, which brought nothing but guilt. Guilt over how there might come a day when Brendon felt shortchanged by not having a father. Guilt that the more she interacted with Tyson, the more he showed that he had put his past behind him and deserved to know the truth. Every missed opportunity to confess was another stab at her conscience.

"I deserve that," Tyson said without a single ounce of hostility. "I wish I could take that night back."

Her righteous anger drained away. Now that he had made a full apology, she could no longer pretend he was still a lowlife lothario. But the closer she allowed him to get, the harder it was to deny that she still felt all the longing for him that had tormented her since the first time she met him.

"I'll bet you've had a lot of those nights." Being unkind wasn't in her nature, but it was vital now that he back off.

"You're right." This time he chuckled, succeeding in making her feel awful. "There are a lot of days and nights I would take back if I could. But that's one I really wish I could do over, for a whole bunch of reasons. Maybe if I hadn't been such a jerk, you wouldn't have spent all this time thinking the worst of me and maybe we'd be in a different place right now."

He was sincere and contrite, and it was getting harder to stand her ground.

"But mostly, I wish I could do it over so that when you looked back on it, it made you feel as special as you are," Tyson added.

Dani's mouth fell open. He had put it more eloquently in reality than it sounded in her dreams, where she had chosen the words herself. No matter what else he may or may not have remembered about that night, he remembered that he was her first. She began to blush, heat creeping up her neck to her cheeks.

That made him smile all the more, because she looked so adorable when she did it, and when she tried to fight it.

"It wasn't that big a deal, Tyson," she mumbled, trying to get the conversation over with. "From what I hear it's not special for anyone."

"Still, it's the kind of behavior that warrants an apology and I'd really like to say I'm sorry, Dani. If it makes you feel any better, over the last couple years I've had to issue a lot of apologies. They told me in rehab it would make me feel better, and it usually does."

He didn't tell her that in this particular case, in many ways, it made him feel worse. He had gotten used to grappling with true regret. This went so much deeper. The more she tried to make it sound like it wasn't a defining moment, the more clearly it translated to just how much it was.

She started over, trying to keep it simple. "I accept your apology, Tyson."

"And don't worry about me going back to my old ways. Trying to be the life of the party all the time was tedious. Plus I like being able to look at myself in the mirror." He gave her a little nod and a wink.

I would certainly drink to that, she thought. She had always liked looking at him too. But why did he feel the need to explain his ways? Seconds ticked by and Dani wondered if he was waiting for an apology from her. Just how much of their night together did he truly remember? Was he taking all the responsibility because he was being chivalrous or because he really had no recollection of her throwing herself at him?

"It's nice to see you back on the field," Dani finally said, keeping it as noncommittal as possible.

Tyson took a deep breath. "How do you feel about new beginnings?"

"Like I get one every day," she teased, even though she knew encouraging him was the wrong thing to do.

"Can I get in on that?" he bantered back. "Starting with dinner after today's game?"

Dani sadly shook her head. She had to stop this now. There were only so many scenarios dinner with him could lead to, and all of them were treacherous. "That's probably not a good idea. I don't mix business with pleasure."

He nodded and blinked. When his eyes settled back on her, the brightness that was present just a minute ago was significantly dimmed. "Sure, of course. That's good policy. Thanks for hearing me out and letting me make my amends. I should probably go get ready for the game."

He turned on his heel and left. And for his own self-preservation, he filed her under "people, places, and things."

CHAPTER 12

THE HOLIDAYS WERE rough on Dani. Not even the exhilaration of the team having yet to be handed a loss could put a dent in her doldrums. The Mavericks played the Thanksgiving game against Dallas, so there would be no going home to Danza's feast, and she missed Brendon's excitement at kicking off the Christmas season. On the day after Thanksgiving, as they had for decades, the Carrinos transformed the house into a holiday wonderland.

"I don't work nine to five," Danza always said, scoffing at Black Friday sales. "I can shop anytime."

Back home in Ardmore, they were dedicating the entire weekend to putting up the tree and the village and the wreaths. There were craft projects from when Dani and her brothers were little, carefully preserved. Brendon would help and maybe add his own masterpiece to the craft mix. There would be Santas and snowmen and reindeer galore.

By the time Dani got home, she would pretty much have to turn around and head back. It just wasn't going to be worth it. So she stayed in Austin, and rather than sitting around her hotel room moping, when the request came to film a segment on Saturday with Marcus, she jumped at the chance to keep occupied.

Dani met Marcus in the hotel lobby, right on time, and offered to drive. Cameraman Stan met them in the parking lot and led the way in his company van to the location, which according to Google Maps was an empty lot close to the airport off Capital of Texas Highway.

Working with Marcus, even with its ups and downs, had been better than Dani expected. Upon getting what he wanted, his own correspondent, he began to give everyone what they wanted, his time. At first their interviews were stilted and awkward, and it was barely enough to create a news snippet. Nobody trusted either of them to go live. But as the weeks wore on, he and Dani began to develop their own rapport. Because they respected each other's space, it was easy for them to develop a comfortable exchange. They both had a dry, quick wit and played the little nuances of the game off each other nicely. It wasn't long before everyone was looking forward to the postgame to see what they would say to each other. All the national outlets picked up their feed to broadcast. Soon after that, jealous minds started whispering that the two of them were canoodling on their off days. It was a conclusion that was easy to draw. Marcus was rarely seen in public, and Dani kept to herself too, spending most of her off time in her hotel room, either Skyping with her family or watching TV and wishing she was home. Room service had most of her orders committed to memory. She had no problem ignoring the misconception, and she could tell Marcus appreciated her silence. It spared her having to confess that the rumors had an added bonus. If Tyson believed

Dani and Marcus were hooking up, it was sure to keep him at bay. But by the look on his face whenever she encountered him in passing, she wasn't so sure it did. She continued to watch him from afar, knowing it was the right thing and hating every minute of it.

But soon the pair's rumored relationship was quickly twisted until it was back to the same old story about Marcus being gay, only now Dani was his beard. On the few occasions she dared speak of it, Dani got the distinct impression Marcus thought that was hilarious.

The truth was she didn't know any more about Marcus by midseason than she did when she was hired to cover him. She could count on him to be where he said he would be at the exact time he said he would be there. He made no demands on her time other than an occasional stall tactic if someone pushed to get too close to him. But beyond that, he didn't volunteer a shred of information about anything else.

There was one other thing she couldn't help noticing. In most of their postgame interviews, Marcus would slip in a mention of his quarterback, practically forcing Dani to say something nice about Tyson. She always did, smiling, and making it sound like they were a pair of football superheroes, often with Clinton Barrow standing no more than a few yards away.

But now being alone in a car with Marcus was nothing short of nerve-wracking. They drove the first twenty minutes in silence while he looked out his window and she pondered just how one makes small talk with a clam.

"I can't believe I said yes to this assignment without even knowing the details." Dani tried opening the conversation with a half laugh.

"At our boss's request, I'm going to decorate a Christmas tree," Marcus said in response. "You're going to ask me some random questions about it, maybe talk a little football."

Dani couldn't tell if he was serious. "Decorate a tree. *You're* going to decorate a tree?"

"Okay, I'm going to spend a minute looking like I'm decorating a tree," Marcus clarified, before pointing out his window at the side of the road. "Like that."

Dani followed the direction of Marcus's finger. The sight was as peculiar as it was heartwarming. People had begun to decorate random cedar trees that dotted the countryside and ran along the miles of highway. Some were elaborate, others clearly decorated by children with ornaments made of construction paper and sequins that hung no higher than the middle of the tree. There were sections where there were multiple trees in a row and spots where single, lonely-looking dressed-up cedars stood. Fully immersed in her own conundrums, she doubted she would've noticed them if he hadn't pointed them out.

"Who decorates all these trees?" Dani wondered out loud after passing a dozen of them.

"Texans full of the Christmas spirit, I imagine," Marcus said.

"And where do you factor in with all this holiday spiriting? You don't strike me as the Christmassy type."

Dani wished she could take the words back as soon as they were out of her mouth. No matter how many secrets Marcus kept, the common knowledge of his family history was enough to conclude his holidays probably weren't very festive. Just when he had said more than three words to her in a more social setting, the first thing she did was slight him.

"We weren't the religious type, that's for sure." If he sensed her discomfort, he didn't let on. But he didn't answer her question either, asking instead, "What about you?"

"I hail from a close, progressive Italian Catholic family."

"What does that even mean?" Marcus queried, and Dani figured he knew even less about faith than he did family.

"It basically means that while we had crosses in every room, my parents refrained from hanging the ones of Jesus sadly looking down at us to remind us of all his suffering. They're just big believers in the Resurrection and all the redemption that came with it."

There were several long beats of silence before Marcus said, "That's pretty profound, considering how hard you are on my man Tyson."

"What are you talking about?" Dani mentally cursed his straying to her least favorite topic.

"At first I thought it was funny the way you two act around each other," Marcus continued, "and I thought it would create an edgy dynamic that would yield great results on the field. But now I think there's something much more personal going on."

"There's nothing personal about it," Dani denied, a little too vehemently. "But you're right, I don't like him. Five years ago he was screwing everything in sight and could've opened his own pharmacy. Now he's suddenly smooth and suave and all zenned out. I don't think so."

"There are a lot of questionable characters in this game. He's not the first player who ever fell down. It strikes me as odd because you're usually so nonjudgmental. You never pass up the opportunity to rag on him when the camera's off. He really rubs you the wrong way. Like there's a history there and you're trying to convince yourself of something. I was curious as to what that might be."

Curious? No, Marcus wasn't the curious type. Perceptive was a different story. She thought she had been careful to remain cool when it came to Tyson, especially around Marcus. She still hadn't gotten over the way Marcus seemingly peered into her soul that first day on the field. Apparently she came up short and her little tirade was only more ammunition for him.

Dani was spared having to directly answer him because Stan turned off the highway and down a small hill. She followed the van down to a strip mall at the bottom of the ravine. They drove past the parking lot, which was already full, and found a couple of spots on the side of the road past it. Stan grabbed his camera, and with his assistant, who carried Dani's microphone and the spare battery pack, the four of them followed a small group of people back toward the strip mall, which housed about a dozen small storefronts.

To Dani's surprise, nobody noticed her or Marcus. All eyes were on the cluster of trees at the far end of the parking lot, closest to the highway. As they neared, Dani could make out people decorating some of the trees, but the majority were gathered around a box truck that opened from the side. Inside the truck were neatly organized boxes of everything from plastic ball ornaments to solar-powered lights, to garland and tinsel. Christmas music floated from a portable sound system set up somewhere on the property.

At the center of the group near the truck, standing head and shoulders above the crowd of mostly small children and teenagers, was Tyson Palmer. Dani felt all her breath leave her in a rush.

Oh, hell no.

Which was really comical, considering that the expression on Tyson's face when he saw them approach screamed the same thing. He finished what he was saying, which Dani was still too far away to catch, and then wended his way through the circle to greet them.

"Happy holidays. Guess my secret's out." He smiled as he broke away from the crowd and joined them. But it was a stiff, tight smile reminiscent of when he realized the clucking wasn't going to go away.

None of it stopped him from looking positively scrumptious.

"I got a call from the boss's office," Marcus explained without acknowledging any discomfort on Tyson's end. "He thought this was the kind of thing that makes the Mavs look good."

"And if Marcus is willing to come out of hiding, it must be a pretty big deal," Dani quipped in the effort to ease the tension. "Do you mind if we take a few minutes to get some footage?"

"Sure, but is it okay if we make it quick? I've got kids to play with and Christmas trees to rock around," Tyson replied easily, turning the baseball cap he was wearing so that the bill was facing backward.

Dani and Stan had a quick conversation about where they should set up the shot. She placed Tyson and Marcus on opposite sides of the chosen tree and pulled a couple of kids out of the crowd who were willing to join them. She took only a few seconds of live action footage of them hanging a few ornaments on the tree. Stan suggested they ask Tyson a few questions, but Dani decided against it. The whole thing felt wrong, like they had intruded on something that was genuine and personal. As soon as Dani told Tyson she was done, he promptly excused himself and walked back over to a tree that was being decorated by what looked like three young kids and their grandfather. She asked Marcus and the kids to remain by their tree, asked a few questions of a general nature, and wrapped the whole thing up as quickly as she could. She dismissed Stan and his assistant, telling them they would add sound bites later back at the studio.

"I'm going to hang around awhile," Dani told Marcus after Stan began hoofing back. "I need to at least find out what the real deal with this is. Clearly there's a story behind it."

"That's cool. I'm going to go ahead and hitch a ride back with the guys and the van. See you later," Marcus said, not waiting for her response. He took off out of the parking lot in pursuit of Stan and his assistant, leaving her alone.

Dani lingered in the background and observed as Tyson went from tree to tree, interacting and helping each group decorate. Many of the grown-ups and nearly all of the children hugged him at one point or another. He posed for pictures with anyone who asked, but oddly enough, not many people did. Smartphones were conspicuously absent. Eventually Tyson noticed Dani and smiled. This time his grin was much more real, and he made his way over to her.

"You're still here. I thought you'd left."

"I could tell the crew wasn't particularly welcome and wanted to get them out of here. But I still need some idea on just what I was filming today."

"Was I that obvious?" Tyson laughed but didn't deny it. "Want to decorate a tree?"

"Maybe later," Dani replied. "Want to fill me in with what is going on here?"

"Sure. Come on. Let's go get some hot chocolate."

It was still warm in Austin; whether it was unseasonably so, Dani couldn't be sure. Back home, temperatures this high called for Slurpees, not hot chocolate. But this was one little break from reality she was more than willing to embrace. She let Tyson lead her over to a different truck that was closer to the building, with him high-fiving, fist-bumping, or patting the shoulder of every man, woman, and child as they passed them. This one was a food truck that provided the revelers with not only hot chocolate but also coffee, cider, water, and a vast array of snacks from doughnuts to popcorn, hot dogs, and caramel apples. The Christmas tunes were still cranking.

He had created an atmosphere so festive she could swear there was a nip in the air and a smell of pine that came with it. They sipped their drinks in silence for a few minutes while surveying the scene of dozens of cedars transforming into Christmas trees before them.

"I'm sorry we intruded," Dani finally said. "But this is really incredible."

"Thanks," he said with pride.

"Why would you want to keep something so wonderful a secret?"

"Because not everything is about drawing attention. Some of these kids have had a rough start and already feel exploited. I wanted to give them a break from that. I'm not trying to save the world here, just spread a little cheer."

"Right. Sorry," Dani repeated, looking down at her cup. She felt chastised, though technically she'd done nothing wrong.

Tyson took note and softened his tone. He could tell by the look on her face she had no clue about what she had signed up for. But it had a boomerang effect when she hadn't boned up on her assignment and was caught unaware. And she handled it not like a reporter, but a lady. Suddenly he didn't mind telling the story. "When I first came to Austin, I'd been off the grid for quite a while. I had gotten used to being alone. Thrust in the middle of it, I felt out of place, didn't know exactly what to do with myself. Right around the holidays it got unbearable. I knew I couldn't participate in all the festivities the way I used to, and I was afraid if I got into social situations, I'd get pressured to do so. I don't think I trusted myself. And I didn't see my solitude as a barrier. My chiropractor is in this strip mall, and when I sort of confided in him about it, he jokingly called me a Grinch. And something he said after really drove his point home, only I didn't know it at the time. When I walked out of his office that day, I saw this kid dragging all these crappy decorations out to one of the trees, paper plates with pinecones, construction paper rings to look like rope, stuff like that. I gave him a hand, and we started chatting it up. He told me about the whole tradition of the trees here. I spent a couple hours with him until it got dark, helping him decorate his tree. He was a nice kid and I'd seen him here before. Turned out, his mother worked at the coffee shop on the other end of the strip. His neighborhood was in a bad part of town and he was constantly being bullied. To keep safe, whenever he wasn't in school he would come here to the mall until his mother got off work. He'd hang out in her car and do his homework, try to keep out of her way. He hadn't seen his dad in years. He kept repeating he couldn't believe he was talking to me. I made this kid's day just by spending some time with him, even when I was in a rotten mood."

Dani didn't know whether to laugh or cry. She sipped her hot chocolate to prevent herself from doing either and hoped that this particular reason—boys without dads—wasn't the sole focus of his endeavor.

Tyson continued. "When my chiropractor called me the Grinch, it was because by keeping myself isolated, I couldn't get in touch with the joy. The holidays aren't about inner peace. They're about goodwill toward all. Until I was willing to venture out of my comfort zone, it was likely none of my feelings were going to change. The best way to feel good about myself would be to do something for others."

"Geez, just who is your chiropractor? T. D. Jakes?"

"Close." Tyson let out a hearty laugh before adding, "Turns out he was right. That kid, his story, and a tree saved me that Christmas. The whole episode stayed with me, made me realize just how blessed I truly am. And that I had a responsibility to pay it forward. I kept running into the kid, whose name was Adam, and when the following Christmas rolled around and he reminded me about how much fun he'd had the year before, I got the idea about inviting other kids to spend the afternoon with me and be able to participate in the tradition without having to worry about the expense. Then I branched it out to include their families. Nobody ever spread the word because that would create a mob scene. I think they knew if word got out, I'd have to shut it down. It wouldn't feel the same if I had to do it somewhere else."

He didn't tell Dani that each kid left with a big bag of goodies and gift cards that were waiting for them in the chiropractor's office.

Within four years, the parking lot tree decoration project grew from the lone tree into a celebration for Tyson and his "little brother" Adam, who had since moved to El Paso with his mom and was now thriving in high school. Sometimes as many as twenty families were invited, and all the trees surrounding the strip mall were adorned with some sort of festive flair.

Tyson also supplied a cleanup crew that showed up the day after New Year's. First thing on January 2· they arrived to remove all the decorations and chase down any that tried to make a break for it. But many families came back and cleaned up their own trees in the interim, taking mementos away with them from the year they decorated a tree with the Austin Mavericks all-star quarterback on the sly. And they were encouraged to do so.

"Tyson," Dani said slowly. "I feel awful that this was exposed without your permission. If you want me to, I can see to it the footage meets with an unfortunate accident."

"Thanks for offering, but it's really okay. Maybe it's time for it to come out. Maybe it will make someone else reach out and pay it forward."

The more time she spent with Tyson, the more aware she became of all the mistakes she had made. Yet she had no choice but to continue making them.

"And what about you, Dani Carr, on this first holiday season away from your comfort zone? How are you going to find the joy?"

The way he was looking at her had the potential to melt her quicker than the Texas sun. In an effort to keep him from seeing he was turning her into a puddle, she said, "I'll be hanging around with Marcus, of course."

She knew she didn't sound the least bit convincing. He smiled at her and made a face. "No, you won't. You spend about as much time with Marcus as I do. And that ain't much."

"Come on, you saw what the gossip columns said." The disdain in her voice was offset by her knowing grin.

"Darlin', if I thought for one minute you were really with Marcus, I would lose my mind. Besides, you told me you don't mix business with pleasure, and I know you're a woman of your word."

One of the families came up to them to thank Tyson and, for the moment, broke up their conversation.

A loophole, Dani thought as she watched Tyson share a minute with his parting guests, giving her a break in the action. A justification that would make it okay for when she finally told him about Brendon. She wasn't a liar. She just hadn't yet told him the truth. And she would tell him. The way she would have if he hadn't turned his back on her that night.

"I hope you realize when you smile like that, it only makes me more interested."

He had busted her again. But this time, she was perfectly all right with him teasing her about it.

"I think I caught some of your Christmas spirit."

"Then my work here is done," Tyson said. His phone went off, interrupting them again.

"Excuse me," he said, reaching into his back pocket to retrieve it. "My pants are vibrating."

"Maybe they're just happy to see me." Ba-dum-bum. Corny, yes, but that didn't mean she could resist saying it.

He looked up from unlocking his phone to get to the text message he'd received long enough to wiggle both his eyebrows. "That too. Now what were we talking about?"

"Christmas cheer and comfort zones," she reminded him. She wasn't sure if he was paying attention. He was busy reading the text on his phone. She watched his face break out in a broad smile. "Good news?"

"The best news," he said, looking back up and refocusing on her. "And it sort of relates to our conversation. So tell me, Dani Carr, just how willing are you to take a step out of your comfort zone?"

Maybe it was the holiday vibe that was in the air. Maybe it was just being with him when he was relaxed and happy. But at that moment, she would've agreed to step out onto the moon without a spacesuit. "You should know by now, I'm all about taking risks."

"Just what I wanted to hear. What are you doing New Year's Eve?"

"I'll be home in Pennsylvania for New Year's. I leave right after the game on the twenty-eighth."

But Tyson didn't look daunted. If anything, his smile broadened. "Well, would you look at that? Turns out, I need a date to a wedding in New Jersey."

She probably should've said no, he was starting to get dangerously close to home . . . and Brendon. But now the only thought running through her mind was how much she wanted him to see her in a little black dress. She smiled back at him. "Is that an invitation?"

"It's a Christmas miracle!" Tyson felt like bear-hugging the next person he came in contact with. Dani smiled and tried not to blush . . . or worry.

CHAPTER 13

DANI CIRCLED AROUND Terminal B at Newark Airport for the third time, weaving her rented Mercedes in and out of the traffic, competing for some space at the curb. She'd already been chased away by the police once for idling too long. After telling the cop she was there to pick up Tyson Palmer, she was met with a sarcastic "That's great. He just flew in with the First Lady. Move out!" Maybe he was a Jets fan. *Happy New Year to you too, bub.*

The third time she got lucky. Just as she slowed the car down, ready to double-park if she had to, the last set of the sliding glass doors parted like the Red Sea and Tyson emerged, simultaneously managing to walk, carry his bag, and sign an autograph for a teenager. He handed the magazine he signed back, the two quickly put their heads together, and the kid snapped a picture with his phone. When Tyson looked up,

Dani beeped her horn lightly, and with a quick wave to the kid, Tyson trotted the few steps over to her. Dani steadied herself as her heart gave a quick flutter.

"Sorry about that," he apologized, tossing a garment bag into the backseat and sliding into the passenger's side. "I got a little side-tracked."

"Not a problem," Dani replied, pulling back into traffic. If she concentrated on the road, she could slowly acclimate to his sexy without getting too flustered. "Those are some pretty smooth moves you've got going on there. I like the way you're able to carry a bag, sign your name, and walk, without tripping."

"You missed the show inside the terminal. You would've really been impressed. I tangoed with a ticket agent pushing a luggage cart while eating a Cinnabon."

"Were you still holding the garment bag?"

"What do I look like, some kind of amateur?"

"Forgive my ignorance. I should've known better."

"Fortunately for us, that kid was the only one who could keep up once I started beating feet. It was like a built-in opportunity to work on my game."

"I don't think you could fine-tune your game any more."

"That's really nice of you to say, darlin'. So was your offer to pick me up here. You didn't need to do that."

Yeah, I did, Dani thought. His plan to fly into Philly and pick her up at her house made her break out in hives. If there was any bullet she needed to dodge, it was that one. It was hard enough to explain the car rental to her family, who thought it was a waste when she had a perfectly good car to use back home: a patriotic American-made Ford Taurus with plenty of trunk space. It was equipped with all the latest and best safety features . . . and a baby-turned-booster seat in the back. She wasn't willing to risk taking it out and sticking it in the trunk, lest he discover it by accident. Trying to leave it home wasn't an option; that was sure to raise suspicion. Her parents easily bought into her excuse that the New Jersey Turnpike was riddled with potholes and if she had to have a car damaged, she'd rather it not be hers. There was certainly an element of truth to that. As it was, they were already thrilled that she was going to a New Year's Eve wedding with Tyson Palmer. In their eyes, his past transgressions were just that, his past. Who knew her family's faith in the Resurrection could be so problematic?

"I just figured with all the traveling you already do, it'd be nice to drop you closest to our final destination," she told him, finally feeling ready to venture a look. "Where to now?"

"Turnpike south to the Garden State Parkway. I've made reservations at the DoubleTree right off our exit, which is one-oh-five." He thought he detected her knuckles grip the steering wheel tighter and added. "Two rooms."

Dani didn't know if it was better to be grateful or disappointed. He clearly wasn't taking anything for granted.

"Is that where the wedding is?" she asked, to seem like she wasn't affected one way or the other.

"There's a reception there after the ceremony. The wedding itself is at a state park somewhere close by."

Dani was glad Tyson couldn't see her rolling her eyes. This was the price to pay for not asking questions, but from working for Marcus, she had gotten used to it. Now it was beginning to resemble a bad habit. But seriously, who gets married in a park in the middle of winter? Then she remembered just how quickly this wedding was thrown together. Her focus turned to hoping the ground would already be frozen enough to support the ridiculously high heels she had brought. They probably wouldn't seem so high once she started sinking three-inch divots with every step. On the bright side, as long as she didn't walk out of them, the shoes would be like little anchors, tethering her to the ground.

"That's pretty original." She tried not to grumble. "Not many people I know would choose a park in December to take their vows, at least not in New Jersey. I'm glad I brought a heavy coat."

Tyson raised an eyebrow and grinned. "Dani, do you think we're all going to be standing around in the woods? There's a chapel there."

"Oh!" she exclaimed, now feeling embarrassed.

"But if anyone was going to do something like that," Tyson added cheerfully, "it would be these two."

"And these are good friends of yours?"

"The best kind of friends. Logan was my athletic trainer when I got out of rehab. The man was my shadow for six months. I think he's been with Holly forever. I'm so stoked about them taking the plunge. Sorry . . . I probably could've done better filling in the details."

"I noticed you're not big on the texting."

"I try not to get too attached to my phone. Gotta keep the thumbs nimble," he joked before taking a more thoughtful tone. "I read texts. But I'm terrible at responding. It's hard to connect to people that way, too much room for misreading tone. I don't have that many friends now anyway. Funny how once the party ended, so did most of the calls. When people really need me, they manage to get in touch."

So, he wasn't playing the indifferent game, he just wasn't a slave to his iPhone. Dani was surprised she had never really noticed it before. When she first heard the rumors about how much he had changed, she figured it was just publicity. When she joined up with the Mavericks, she was too busy thinking he was a jerk.

"So you're like Kung Fu? Destined to wander the earth alone, seeking out those needing life lessons and filling people with wisdom?" she teased.

"I'm not all that wise. It's all I can do to keep my own head above water. But if someone can learn from my mistakes, I'm glad I could help. And spending the rest of my life alone sounds horrible. Wasn't Kung Fu married?"

"I think he was a monk."

"Well, I'm certainly not one of those." Tyson started to laugh.

"No. No, you're not." She didn't laugh along. She'd known he dated but wasn't linked to anyone specific, not that it made her feel any better about it.

He stopped the snickering and cast a quick look in her direction, watching her drive. When it came to Dani, it was hard to move forward without occasionally looking back. He had always felt attraction, but she was so different now. Maybe it was those old feelings combined with her newfound sass that made him want to open up to her more.

"Sometimes I don't know what was harder, straightening out my head or my heart."

Dani's thumping pulse slowed down to a dull thud at his admission. He sounded so melancholy, a marked difference from his usual playfulness.

"Did you ever figure that one out?" she said, striving for casual.

"Some days are better than others. I'll probably never chase out that demon until I forgive my father. But I don't see that happening anytime soon."

Douglas Palmer, a man almost as memorable as his famous son, for all the wrong reasons. She would see him around campus, always in attendance whenever Tyson was on the field or receiving an award.

Even back then, he had a creepy aura. He was the kind of guy who loved to watch a girl walk away, especially the ones half his age.

"I heard that he took all the money you paid him, went to Vegas, put it all on one hand of blackjack, and won," she said, thinking that when it came to Palmer senior, it would be best to stick with what she thought was common knowledge.

Even with her eyes on the road, Dani could feel his gaze searing into her from across the car.

"I wouldn't know. I was busy trying to save my life at the time. But I had heard it was playing double zero on a roulette wheel. I think I like your version better. It's a little less insulting."

Dani mentally landed a face-palm to her forehead. The new Tyson didn't run away from his problems. He put on his brave face and dealt with them. At this point she decided it would be best to stop with attempts at being witty and just be sincere.

"I'm really sorry, Tyson," she said. "I know he's a touchy subject. You're in such a different place now, but it sounds like your father has 'unfinished business' written all over him."

He tried to go back to jovial, but it was a wasted effort. "Oh, that business is definitely finished. Five years later it's still the same old same old with him. I know he shows up to a game every now and then. I'm so ashamed every time I look at him, now I just don't look. He'd never have the courage to actually approach me."

"But if he did?"

He didn't miss a beat before answering. This was an issue that had been well thought out. "I guess for the sake of my mother, I would try to be civil. She was able to bounce back, and I wouldn't want her to ever go through that sort of humiliation again. I've brought enough disgrace to her door."

"I think you're being a bit too hard on yourself. Moms don't work like that. I'm sure she's so proud of you she's ready to pop!" Dani borrowed one of her mother's favorite lines, a quote she used herself to entertain and encourage Brendon: I'm so proud of you I'm ready to POP!

Tyson didn't want the conversation to turn into a therapy session, even if part of him really did want to confess that most of the disgrace he spoke about was all tied up in how he enabled Douglas Palmer's worst demons. After all, if it wasn't for him, good old Doug would still be white-collar middle management, and his parents would still be together. When he looked at his father now, all he saw was his mother's anguish. This was supposed to be a happy time, full of new beginnings and adventures. Not just for Logan and Holly, but for him as well. He gave Dani a smile, the kind meant to assure her that he was all right.

"Thanks, Dani," he told her, adding off the cuff, "You know what? If you ever have a mind to, I bet you'll make a great mother someday."

If he wanted to end the conversation, he couldn't have chosen a better way to do it. Dani instantly shut up. After several minutes of uncomfortable silence, the remainder of their travel talk switched to football and focused solely on who the Mavericks were facing in the first round of the play-offs.

CHAPTER 14

DANI STOOD STARING in front of the full-length mirror that doubled as the closet door. She was showered and her hair already blown dry, flowing and waving just the way she wanted it. Her makeup was applied to perfection. Then there was the dress, a gorgeous form-fitting black number she had picked up at Nordstrom while finishing her Christmas shopping. It had tiny sleeves, a surplice neckline that made the most of her cleavage, and a deep V back. One look at her in this outfit and the most memorable gift her father got this Christmas would've been a stroke. She pulled at the tags under her arm and caught sight of the designer—Tart Collections. Never was a garment so aptly named. She turned and looked over her shoulder, trying to get a view of the back, and debated whether or not she should switch it out for the more modest and dependable Calvin Klein she had brought along as a backup. She was interrupted by a slight tapping on her hotel room door.

She stole one more glance at her reflection, tossed the tags in a nearby wastebasket, and said, "If the dress fits, wear it."

Dani slipped on her black patent leather spiky six-inch heels, steadied herself, and opened the door. Well now. A Perry Ellis black pin dot suit never looked so good. The only way this picture was getting any better was if the wearer was going to attend this wedding buck naked and carrying a strategically placed tray of chocolate-covered strawberries. She couldn't identify his cologne, but if she had to name it, she would've called it Aphrodisiac.

His first thought was to ask her if those legs went all the way up, but he liked to believe he had permanently risen above the usual locker room boorishness.

"Ms. Carr, you look absolutely stunning," Tyson said in full appreciation. "Ready to go?"

He folded her coat over one arm and crooked the other in her direction. She happily took it. It was too early in the evening to break an ankle.

They got back on the Garden State Parkway, this time with him driving. He wore a small grin that seemed to grow the farther south they headed, but he was mostly silent until she finally asked, "Penny for your thoughts?"

"I've made this drive many times. It was a big part of my salvation. I was just taking a few minutes to thank my higher power for every day since then."

Dani swallowed the lump in her throat and gently placed her hand over his, which was resting on the gearshift. He turned his hand over to get a better grip on hers and moved them both down to rest on his leg. Then she left him to his thoughts. She refused to think of anything herself. It would only ruin the moment.

She knew they had reached their destination when he turned onto a driveway and the car's headlights lit up the sign welcoming them to THE HISTORIC VILLAGE AT ALLAIRE. He found a space to park and got out, coming around to her side of the car to open her door. He consciously slowed his pace while walking so that she'd have no problem keeping up.

The grounds were dark, but lanterns glowed along the path to the chapel. Dani was able to make out the buildings that housed a general store and a museum. They passed a sign pointing the way to the Pine Creek Railroad, an old-style historic train that offered rides around the park.

Several people stood guard along the path, ready to lend assistance if needed. They were dressed up in period clothes from the 1800s. They all nodded politely as the couple walked by. Some of them wished them Happy New Year.

"I think this park is closed," Dani mused.

Tyson gave her hand in the crook of his arm a little squeeze and replied, "The best man is good at getting whatever he wants. And the bride is crazy nuts for this place."

They continued to stroll on the illuminated path until the chapel came into clear view. It was a pristine white square building with a window on each side of the front door and two fan-shaped windows on either side of a big center window set into the triangle-shaped roof. Soft light flickered from within. There was a clock tower for a steeple. By the time the chamber music reached her ears, Dani was utterly enchanted. The best man took up the majority of the small single door to the chapel, greeting the guests.

Dani was so caught up in the atmosphere that she didn't recognize him until he was shaking her hand and Tyson began an unnecessary introduction.

"Dani, I'd like you to meet—"

"Chase Walker," Dani finished for him with widening eyes, hoping it was dark enough so Tyson couldn't see her blush. The Golden Boy of baseball had a notorious reputation for making women take leave of their senses. But she was a professional sports reporter. Fangirling was in poor taste.

"Dani Carr. It's a pleasure to meet you." Chase smiled and released her hand, then gave Tyson a friendly clap on the shoulder, adding what she could only define as a subtle wink, discreet but suggestive. She took it as verification that the two were at least casual friends. "Happy New Year, Ty."

"You could've warned me about that," she admonished him as they moved away from Chase and the door.

"And ruin the surprise? No fun in that," Tyson replied.

They stepped into the small chapel. There were maybe two dozen rows of matching wooden pews where other guests were seated. The music was live, supplied by a string trio in a corner. There were so many blossoms and garlands that it looked like a flower shop had exploded down the main aisle. A blue wooden cross was mounted above the altar where the minister was in conversation with a man whom Dani presumed was the groom. His back was turned to them as she and Tyson took a seat in the fourth row. All she could make out was his jet-black hair and athletic body.

Then he turned around and Dani swore she could hear her jaw hit the floor.

Tyson was the only man who would ever lay claim to her heart. And she could understand why she might get a momentary case of the giddies around Chase Walker, since she would always appreciate a legendary jock. Over the years, she'd been flirted with by some of the prettiest boys in football.

But this guy was disgustingly, over-the-top handsome, and it wasn't just because of the well-fitted black tuxedo. This stud muffin was some sort of movie-star-handsome genetic freak. It was impossible not to stare. When she finally tore her eyes away, she looked at Tyson to see if he noticed her gawking and flushed again to find him not only studying her, but grinning. He leaned over to whisper in her ear, "I know. Don't worry, you get used to it. That's Logan Montgomery. He's the groom."

Dani spent the next ten minutes continuing to steal peeks at Logan and pondering just what sort of supermodel would soon be coming down the aisle. Maybe some hybrid of several supermodels, designed in a lab. Was there such a thing as a super-duper model? By the time Chase joined Logan at the front of the chapel and the music switched to Bach, she was ready to burst with curiosity.

First there was only the maid of honor, and it was little surprise when Amanda Walker stepped down the aisle. She was beautiful and radiant, her fuller figure and raven hair a good combination for showing off a rose-colored tea-length silk dress. Dani snuck a final look in Logan's direction and caught Chase beaming while watching his wife. So, those rumors were true, Dani thought. The Walkers were the great American love story, with a twenty-first-century spin. Amanda took her place at the altar and the music paused before starting up again.

Dani looked to the back of the church, blinked, and then blinked again as the bride started making her way, alone, toward her groom.

Holly wore a lovely pink gown, not too frilly. It was classic, off the shoulder with a slightly flared skirt, no train or veil. But she was not a long, lean debutante or starlet with a flowing mane of flaxen hair. Holly was shorter, a little bottom heavy, with red hair in a small French twist and a round cherub-like face. As she got closer, Dani couldn't even be sure she was wearing makeup.

Holly caught sight of Tyson as she passed and give him a smile and a wink before taking her last few steps to meet Logan at the altar. The music stopped, and she handed her bouquet of pink and red roses over to Amanda. The chaplain cleared his throat and the short ceremony began.

Dani didn't hear most of it. We are gathered here together, yadda yadda. She already knew the drill, mostly from being in the bridal party at her oldest brother's nuptials. She was busy admonishing herself for making assumptions about the bride. By the time she was finished, the chaplain was announcing, "The bride and groom have written their own vows and at this time would like to share them."

Holly and Logan turned to face each other and joined hands. Holly looked up into his face, then searched it and gave him a tender smile.

"Logan, I met you during the darkest days of my life. Convinced I would never know joy, I was lost in a sea of despair, too weak to swim, more than willing to drown. God sent you to me disguised as a friend, so that I might slowly make my way back into the light. Even then I wasn't willing to believe. But you believed in me when I refused to believe in myself, until I regained my strength. And then I gained so much more, because that cherished friendship had turned into love. And as I got stronger, so did my love for you, until there was nothing else. As we stand here tonight, I know tomorrow that love will be stronger still. Only when the sun rises and a new year begins, I will have the honor of calling you my husband. I will thank God every day from this day forward for giving me such a precious gift. For giving me love, for giving me you."

By the time Holly was finished, Logan had lowered his head, his gaze fixed on the ground and his shoes. Seconds dragged on and silence lingered. Dani held her breath. She looked quickly to Tyson for direction on what to do, but he was still watching the ceremony, his face tranquil.

Then Logan raised his beautiful head, and Dani felt her own eyes tearing up.

Logan Montgomery wasn't abandoning his bride at the altar. He was completely overcome with emotion. His expressive chocolate eyes were glassy. His perfect lips were drawn tightly together and his chiseled chin was all scrunched up in the attempt to hold it back to no avail. He blinked hard and shook his head slightly in the effort to get a grip and compose himself.

Then Holly took her hand out of his and cupped his face, her thumb stroking over a cheekbone most women would sell their souls for. For them, in that moment, they were alone in the room. He took her hand and kissed her palm before settling it back into his. He took a deep, centering breath and squeezed her hands tight in his. With a shaky but deep voice that was in keeping with his overall excellence, he spoke.

"Holly, you came into my world and completely rocked it. Since I met you, I've become a better man, a more worthy human. You are the bravest, most beautiful woman I have ever known. All the best parts of me can be traced back to you. There isn't one single part of my day, or life for that matter, that isn't better just by having you in it. Today I have the privilege of giving you my name. But I also give you my heart, knowing that it's safe, because of the way you have already enriched my soul. If I live forever, I will never love another the way I do you."

By the time he was finished, there wasn't a dry female eye in the house. Even some of the men's eyes were shiny, including those of the best man and Dani's own date.

Except for Holly's. Hers were dry but bright as the candles that flickered all around them, shining with love and affection.

There was the exchange of rings, the final announcement, and Logan leaned over to thoroughly kiss the new Mrs. Montgomery.

Tyson introduced Dani to the wedding party at the back of the church. Logan was just as superb up close, and Holly was positively tickled that Tyson had brought along a date. Chase Walker gave her a wink this time. His wife gave Dani's hand an extra squeeze.

By the time they walked back to the car, Dani's right foot had started feeling that uncomfortable little twinge of tightness. Right on the back of her heel, nothing that sitting for a while wouldn't cure, she hoped.

By the time they got back to the hotel and she took those first few steps out of the car, Dani could feel the rub becoming more intense, the worst of all possible signs. She didn't dare try to take the shoe off, afraid that her foot would refuse to fit back into it. She had done too much walking and not nearly enough sitting. She could tell with one look that her foot had started to swell. It was beginning to look like bread dough, puffing up over the top of her shoe. But this was not the sort of crowd where Dani felt comfortable ditching the shoes and dancing around barefoot. It was time for drastic measures, and that meant walking as little as possible and sitting as much as she could. She bit back a wince as they headed toward the banquet-hall entrance and tried to walk normally. They caught sight of the sign indicating the Montgomery wedding and she headed right for the bar. A drink would ease the pain. Just one shot, maybe a quick chaser.

"I'm going to go drop my coat off in my room," Tyson said.

Her swollen foot pulsated at the thought of walking to the elevator, much less the hallway of their floor. Just as Dani tried to think of a good excuse to keep from accompanying him, Holly appeared to save her. The bride rushed over to them, giving Tyson a big hug.

"Happy New Year, handsome!" she exclaimed while he wrapped his arms around her and lifted her off the ground. "I can't tell you how great it is to see you."

"Like I would miss this?" Tyson said before setting her down and stepping back while still holding on to her hands to get a better view. "You clean up nice."

"Take a good look. I can't wait to get out of this thing! I don't think I'm the fairy princess type."

Dani liked Holly already, even after sneaking a look at Holly's shoes and seeing the bride was smart enough to have worn ballet flats.

Tyson reintroduced Dani and then offered to take her coat up to his room as well. What a relief. It would give her a few minutes to get her cocktails in, not wanting to toss them back in front of a date who didn't drink.

"I'll keep her company," Holly told him, anxious to get a few moments alone with Dani.

Saints be praised.

As soon as Tyson left, Dani motioned over to the bartender.

"I'll take a shot. What do you recommend?" Dani asked.

"All the cool kids are drinking Fireball these days," was the bartender's enthusiastic response as he put two shot glasses on the bar and grabbed the bottle.

"I'm okay for right now," Holly began to stop him from pouring.

"That's okay," Dani interjected after downing hers and pointing to

Holly's glass. It tasted like a syrupy Red Hots candy. Good choice. "I'll do them both. I'm not a lush or anything. My feet are just killing me."

"I get it." Holly laughed. "Now I'm not quite so jealous. I can't even count all the bones I would break in shoes like that. I tried a pair of high heels once and face-planted right in the shoe department at Macy's."

"I also wanted to get them out of the way before Tyson got back," Dani said after the second shot of cinnamon burned its way down. "I don't want him to feel uncomfortable."

Holly gave Dani a genuine smile. "I get that too. I'm so glad you take his lifestyle into consideration. But with shoes like that, a girl's gotta do what a girl's gotta do. You look gorgeous, let's keep it going."

Amanda floated up behind them. She took a quick look around to make sure that Logan and Chase were still on the opposite side of the room. "Holly, I need you to do me a huge favor tonight."

"Amanda, this is Dani Carr. She's here with Tyson." Holly bobbed her head in Dani's direction and cleared her throat, to remind her that they weren't alone.

"Hi again, I'm sorry to interrupt, but I don't have much time," Amanda said in a rush while picking up Dani's empty glass and calling out to the bartender. "Give me three shots of whatever was in this glass."

The bartender quickly lined up three more glasses and poured more Fireball.

"What in heaven's name is wrong?" Holly asked.

"I need you to drink yours. And then mine," Amanda insisted while smiling brightly and holding her shot up in a salute, checking to make sure Chase was watching. She blew him a little kiss and pretended to put the glass to her lips.

"Slow down," Holly said. "What are you up to?"

Amanda turned her back on her husband and put her still full glass back on the bar. Holly and Dani followed suit.

"As soon as he finds out I'm not drinking anything, the whole night will be ruined!" Amanda said in desperation.

"What are you talking about?" Holly said with a slight shake of her head.

"I'm pregnant," Amanda whispered. As soon as Holly's face registered joy at the news, Amanda quickly grabbed hold of Holly's hand to keep her from saying anything or moving away from the bar where now two shots remained untouched. Dani had tipped hers right after the fake toast. The pain in her foot had been reduced considerably. She felt warm and wonderful. She had just found out the juiciest bit of gossip, not that she was going to do anything about it. Fireball must really be what the cool kids were drinking, because she was feeling pretty cool.

"Amanda, that's wonderful! Congratulations!" Holly said, then her brow furrowed. "You shouldn't be drinking."

"I know that." Amanda gave an exasperated sigh, pointing at the drinks. "That's why I need you to drink this. Chase doesn't know yet."

"What?" Holly admonished her. "Why not?"

Amanda's forehead began to wrinkle with the face she made. "I'm going to tell him tomorrow. I have a wonderful New Year's surprise all lined up for him. Do I really need to remind you about the false alarm last year? He practically followed me around with a pillow and built a shrine."

"Yeah," Holly acquiesced. "He did go a little overboard with that."

"I didn't want to ruin your wedding with his foolishness. And I really wanted one more night to get some action. Damn him, every time he puts on a tux, my libido soars off the scale. Once he finds out about this baby, he'll be treating me like one of those Fabergé eggs! If he thinks I've been doing a few shots with you, he won't keep asking me to do any with him."

Holly worried her lower lip. "What is going to happen when he thinks you've been doing shots while pregnant?"

Amanda gave her a mischievous grin and placed her lips near Holly's ear. "If I'm lucky, I'll get one more trip over his knee before the drought." Then Amanda stood back up and resumed her normal voice. "I'm going to come clean. Eventually. Now drink up."

"Amanda, you know what a lightweight I am. I hadn't planned on spending my wedding night passed out," Holly said slowly, wanting to help her friend but aware of the repercussions in doing so.

As Holly and Amanda deliberated, Dani reached over and quickly did both the remaining shots. If her presence was going to force Amanda Walker to make her privy to a very private conversation, she might as well make herself useful.

"There you go," Dani said cheerfully. "Problem solved."

Both Holly and Amanda looked at Dani with wide eyes.

"You're my hero," Amanda said, unaware of Dani's previous consumption. "Bless you."

"Dani, are you going to be all right?" Holly asked with a touch of alarm. "You just pounded enough Fireball to take down a frat boy."

"Of course," Dani reassured them as her heart suddenly began to swell with all the love she had for just about everyone in the world. "I feel fine. I'm Italian. I've been sipping wine since I was five."

"I really owe you one," Amanda said and added, "can you keep this to yourself until tomorrow? Please? He'd be devastated to think he was the last to know."

If there's one thing I'm good at, it's keeping baby secrets, Dani thought before nodding her head half a dozen times. "You can count on me."

Then she saw Tyson step back into the room, and all she could think of was the crisp white tailored shirt clinging to broad shoulders and bulging biceps. If he turned around and walked backward toward her, she was sure she would faint.

Tyson could tell from one overanimated wave across the room upon his return that she was tipsy, if not on the fast track to inebriation. Keeping one eye on her, he met up with Logan and Chase on the dance floor.

"Congrats again, my friend." Tyson shook Logan's hand a second time and they pulled each other close for a quick chest-bumping bro hug. "You looked a little shaky there for a minute. Good job."

"I spent the night memorizing my vows." Logan shook his head and tsked. "I think she made hers up on the spot. She really knows how to gut punch a guy."

The trio made their way over to their ladies at the bar.

"Can you imagine what a wreck he'd have been if they had taken the time to really think about this thing?" Chase commented as he reached his wife and kissed her before wrapping a protective arm around her. "Hi, ladies."

"I'd been asking Holly once a month for the last three years. When she actually said yes, I knew I had to act quickly. I didn't want to run the risk of her changing her mind, right, Mrs. Montgomery?" Logan smiled at Holly.

"Worried I might turn fickle on you?" Holly remarked, slipping her hand into Logan's.

"Not anymore," Logan stated proudly. "Now if you'll excuse us, we have guests to mingle with before the DJ makes us do all the corny stuff and my mother cries all over your dress. It's bad enough she thinks we've ruined it for her by not taking five thousand pictures and doing a receiving line."

Holly took one more apprehensive look at Dani and let her new husband lead her away. "Make sure you eat."

Chase took Amanda's hand to lead her to the dance floor as soon as the music started playing. Amanda turned her head and mouthed "Thank you" to Dani over her shoulder.

"Want to tell me what that was all about?" Tyson asked, then ordered a club soda, taking note of all the empty shot glasses as the bartender removed them from the bar.

"I was telling them how beautiful they looked and what a wonderful wedding it was. We just did a shot in celebration," Dani told him.

"Dani, you don't have to hide it from me. In case you didn't know, I'm the perfect designated driver." Tyson stopped the server who was carrying trays of tiny quiches and took a plate, then loaded it up. He held one out to her and when she opened her mouth, he popped it in.

"We're staying here," Dani said after taking a swig of his club soda to wash down the mouthful of delicious flaky crust filled with egg, cheese, and broccoli. The more delicate, not to mention sexy, move would've been to bite the quiche in half, but to hell with that, she was starving.

"That lobby gets pretty congested," he commented while ordering himself another club soda and one for her as well.

The Montgomery wedding turned out to be both classy and casual. There were no place cards or a sit-down dinner, just enough appetizer stations and tray-carrying servers to end the hunger problem in the third world. All the tables had been elegantly set for whoever chose to sit at one, complete with glasses of expensive champagne. There were about fifty guests in attendance, due to the short notice and the holiday, most of whom were Logan's family. Dani found it curious that nobody was there representing Holly's side. She had already started to become bolder and pointedly asked.

"She's estranged from her family," Tyson explained tersely. "And most of her friends live across the country or in Canada."

I guess when you get a Logan, you pretty much have all you need, Dani thought. She was starting to feel the effects of the shots. Before she could delve deeper into what was an interesting topic, the DJ announced the bride and groom's official first dance. Logan led Holly to the dance floor and took her into his arms.

When "All I Ask of You" from *The Phantom of the Opera* started to play, Dani began to choke up. Every emotion she had was intensified courtesy of her new still unacknowledged buzz. They had chosen the very song that Dani had used in every imaginary wedding she envisioned, the groom in her dreams always remaining the same. With that first arching crescendo about sharing one love and one lifetime, she began double fisting the quiches off Tyson's plate to keep from bawling. She was starting to feel dizzy and was sure it had nothing to do with alcohol. She stopped another server, this time with mini salmon cakes and devoured six of them while they watched the happy couple sway and spin. Her feet had gone numb.

It was so depressing. Tyson was attentive and charming, always considerate of just how deep her feelings for him had run at one time. How deep they still were. And they were here, together. To start their New Year off with his friends who welcomed her right into their lives, taking her into their confidences as if she were already one of them.

By the time the song ended, Dani had made a decision. She was going to tell him. She was going to tell him tonight. He deserved to start his New Year off as happy as his friends. She would drive him right back to Philly, introduce him to Brendon, and they could live happily ever after.

They sat down at a nearby table and Tyson left to get them more food. He came back with a vast array of choices, and they shared off the same plate. It was so romantic. Dani took a minute to get caught up and fully enjoy it, secure in the knowledge that it was only going to get better. At one point, she leaned over to give Tyson a kiss on his cheek. He didn't protest, but it put him on alert that she was starting to act a little out of character.

Chase made the toast, and during it, Tyson lifted his champagne flute, but when it came time to drink, he switched it out for his club soda. Dani caught Amanda putting hers to her lips but was sure Amanda didn't swallow any of it. And that was a lead she should've followed. But instead, Dani drank hers in one gulp.

And if she really knew anything about drinking, she would've known that once she added the champagne to the mix, things were going to go rapidly downhill.

The music started up again and Tyson rose, holding out a hand to her. "Dani, would you like to dance?"

She didn't care if her feet were nothing more than bloody stumps when it was over, this was one dance she had no intention of missing. She placed her hand in his.

Once she was on her feet, he moved his hand to the small of her back to guide her past other couples to an open spot on the dance floor. Fingertips that lightly aligned with her vertebrae sent jolt after electrifying jolt up her spine. He could've easily led her off a cliff. He really did have magic hands. And all she could think about was them roaming all over her.

They got to the dance floor, and with the magic hand still on her back she turned to face him and placed her hand into his free one. The fingertips gently guided her closer to him and then they tightened ever so slightly as they began to dance, slowly.

"Are you having a nice time?" Tyson asked, looking down at her.

"A wonderful time." She sighed giddily, and he pulled her even closer, his pinky a respectable inch away from what would be considered her backside.

"Good. I'm glad. I think both Holly and Amanda have taken a real shine to you."

"I had no idea you were such good friends with Chase Walker," Dani commented, her words starting to sound much more spirited. And why wouldn't they? She was secure in the arms of the only man she would ever love and he was gushing all over her. She felt free and ecstatic.

"We have a lot in common," Tyson said.

"You do?" Dani couldn't hold back the laughter.

Tyson caught on a few moments later and gave her a smile before clarifying. "We both rose above scandals that tested us."

Dani kept laughing, glancing over at the Walkers, who were also still on the dance floor. "That's *very* interesting."

"Dani Carr, just how much have you been drinking?"

"Just a bit," she replied, leaning into him. "Why do you ask?"

"Because you're getting very cheeky," he whispered into her ear.

"Cheeky." This time her laugh had a snort-like quality to it. "That's so appropriate, considering what Chase is known for."

Tyson rolled his eyes but his grin got wider. She never ceased to amaze him. "I had no idea you were so fascinated by Chase Walker's extracurricular activities."

"And what if I was?"

"Then I would know you were drunk," Tyson replied with his eyebrows disappearing into his hairline.

"Maybe I am. And I think such a serious infraction deserves a good spanking," she retorted, and his hand on her back went lower to rest perfectly on the center of her bottom. Not so respectable anymore, but all the more electrifying.

"I sometimes hit people for a living, darlin'," he drawled. His lips brushed against her temple and his hand steadied her when he felt her knees wobble. "I'm not into doing it for pleasure. You'd pretty much have to throw yourself over my lap and demand it."

Dani took her hand out of his and wrapped both her arms around his neck and pulled his lips to hers. She kissed him right in the middle of the dance floor. Her lips were soft and sweet, just as he knew they would be. His arms crept around her waist, and he lifted her to her tiptoes. He opened his mouth to steal the air right out of her lungs. But he could taste it. The alcohol was heavy on her breath. Whatever was happening between them was going to have to be put on hold. He pulled away and set her back on her feet, looking at her with a mixture of disappointment and longing.

"Let's get out of here. I have something very important to tell you," she proclaimed a little too loudly. And her words were beginning to run together, another sure sign that her sobriety clock was now ticking.

"More important than your sudden spanking fetish?" he teased while taking her hand to help her off the dance floor.

"Much." She nodded at him, already forgetting what they were talking about as she watched his face come in and out of focus.

With his hand securely at her elbow to steady her, he made their good-byes to the wedding party, taking special interest in the way Holly was studying Dani. The look on her face was clearly one of concern as Dani gave everyone a firm handshake followed by an overly affectionate hug. She thanked each one of them for inviting her.

"No matter how it looks right now, I think she's a keeper," Holly told him as she hugged Tyson good night. She averted her eyes after being met with Tyson's narrow-eyed stare. Amanda didn't seem too shocked by Dani's behavior either. That gave him a small sense of relief. Whatever his date was up to, the girls appeared to have been in it together, although he never would've pegged Dani Carr as someone who succumbed to peer pressure. Chase merely smiled and shook his head.

"Why don't you come back down, after you put her to bed," Logan said knowingly.

Tyson walked Dani slowly to the elevator, with her snickering quietly at every stumble she took. Not only did he not want to let her go, he knew if he did, there was a good chance she might fall flat on her face. She hadn't actually made a scene, but he wondered if that was only the luck of the draw. He watched her in the elevator as she held on to the rail for dear life once it started ascending.

Even drunk she was enchanting. They got off on their floor and started down the long hall.

After wobbling on her stilettos and nearly falling for the second time, Tyson forced her to give up on the walking. He crouched down, wrapping his arm around her thighs, just above her hemline. He lifted, than tossed her over his shoulder.

Dani didn't protest, giggling instead at the view presented to her. Her gaze drifted down to settle on his tight round buttocks that flexed as he strode with her down the hall.

"Lower me farther down your back. I want to bite your butt," she gurgled, then giggled again. Her arms flailed trying to grab it.

Little did she know, he was appreciating a similar view. Only his was much better, eye level to be exact. But he was sober and too much of a gentleman to take advantage of her suggestion, at least in public.

But oh, how tempted he was.

Tyson set her down in front of her door and waited patiently while she continued to twitter and fumble in her tiny handbag for her room key. After a failed attempt on her part to get the key to swipe in the lock, he took it from her and opened the door. She stepped in and kicked off her shoes. One flew through the air, knocking over the desk lamp on the other side of the room. Dani went over and painstakingly stood the lamp back up before retrieving the shoe from the desk where it had landed and reprimanded it.

"Stupid shoe, thanks for the blister." She tossed it again. This time it came to rest perfectly inside her small suitcase, which was open on the ottoman in front of the room's armchair.

"She shoots, she scores!" Dani quickly raised both her arms high in victory and her dress hiked up. The only thing standing between Tyson and a peep show was the sheer black control top of her panty hose.

And as much as it pained him to do so, Tyson remained in his spot just inside the entrance to her room and chivalrously concentrated on the curtains. He crossed his arms over his chest and let out a cough-laugh combo to remind her he was still in the room at the same time she felt the cool breeze between her legs.

She was too sloshed to be self-conscious. The only thought running through her mind was that the love of her life was standing in her room looking every bit as hot as she felt.

"Like what ya see?"

"Always have," he confirmed, checking to see if her dress was pulled back down. Not quite far enough, but it would have to do.

"So what are you going to do about it?"

"Tonight? Absolutely nothing."

Dani blew him some raspberries and stumbled her way over to her suitcase. She fished around and pulled out the lacy lavender teddy she had packed just in case the occasion arose. It had been part of a very different plan. She held it up by its spaghetti straps and dangled it, then swished it from side to side to make it look like it was dancing in front of him. "Oh yeah? What do you think about *this*?"

"I think it's very sexy." That was his monotone reaction as he finally moved away from his post near the door. He picked up her other discarded shoe on the way over to her and dropped it into her suitcase, followed by the teddy he had no trouble taking out of her hands. "Got any pajamas in there?"

Dani searched around the suitcase again and this time came up with her only slightly less erection-inducing baby-doll nightgown. "I've got this?" She threw it on the bed and began swaying provocatively to some imaginary music, her dress still showing more than it was covering.

"Well, it's a start." He sighed right before she presented her back and started vigorously twerking.

Damn, even three sheets to the wind, she was good at it.

He looked away and ran a hand through his hair as she took off the dress and slipped the nightgown over her head. As torturous as it was, he took it as a good sign that he was at least getting a step closer to the end of this episode.

And then she touched him, brazenly running her hand up the front of his pants, stopping just short of his zipper.

There is only so much a red-blooded man can stand. He took her hand and placed it firmly at her side before taking her by the shoulders and giving her a little shake. She went still.

"Look at me, Dani," he commanded and waited until she obeyed. "You're going to hate yourself in the morning as it is. And I made a promise to myself that the next time we shared a bed, the only high involved was going to be from a rush of endorphins. That applies to you too. I'm flattered, I really am. And I want you bad, but not like this. Do you understand?"

Dani stared at him through dilated pupils and blinked. Her head lolled back a little bit. Then she went ramrod stiff and clamped a hand over her mouth. She wrenched herself from his grip, making a quick albeit clumsy rush for the bathroom. She fell to her knees when she got there, all erotic notions left in the ether.

The next sounds Tyson heard were the night's festivities coming to a lurching, gut-twisting end. He shook his head in amusement while listening to her alternate between moaning and violently retching. He waited for a break in the action and the sound of the toilet flushing, then went into the bathroom to find Dani with her face hovering over the toilet, too afraid to move, waiting for the next round of protest from her stomach. He took a washcloth off the vanity and ran it under cold water.

"How much did you drink, Dani?" he asked, just to make sure she wasn't in danger of alcohol poisoning and in need of an ambulance.

"Five shots. No, wait. No, maybe six. And some champagne."

"Mixing is never advisable," he said amiably, confident he could handle the fallout without embarrassing her further. How had she managed to consume so much in so little time? He couldn't have been gone for more than ten minutes. But now wasn't the time to interrogate her.

"Fireball is so deceiving!" Her wail echoed from inside the commode.

"I know." He tried to commiserate but bit back a smile. He sat on the edge of the bathtub and began to pat her face with the cool damp cloth. Or at least, the side of her face that wasn't pressed up against the toilet seat. "That stuff is really whiskey. It likes to slam you out of nowhere. Of course, by anyone's standards, you were there to party."

"I'm a hot mess." She had begun to sound more like herself, but nowhere near back to normal. They both knew the worst was yet to come. And she couldn't explain the reasoning behind it. She had made a promise. "I'm so sorry. This isn't really me. It just sort of happened."

"That's okay. I got you. You owed me one."

"Yeah." She moaned, leaning back away from the toilet and onto her haunches. She began to wipe her own face with the washcloth. "Only when it was you, there wasn't the overwhelming stench of vomit-encrusted salmon in the air."

"Don't worry, darlin'. It stopped being food a while ago. Now you just sort of smell like warm cinnamon."

"That explains the burning in my nose."

She leaned over the toilet one more time, but there was no other sound except her painful dry heaves. Tyson left the bathroom, and after she was done, she fell away from the bowl and limply to the floor.

"These tiles are nice and cold," she said to no one in particular.

Dani didn't know how long Tyson left her there, but when she heard him speak, it sounded far away.

"I think you've slept here long enough," he said matter-of-factly before bending down to scoop her up into his strong capable arms. She weakly curled up within them and laid her head on his shoulder.

"You really are the total package, Tyson."

"You're not so bad yourself, sister," he replied as he carried her back into the bedroom. The sheets were already turned down and there were ten bottles of water lined up in rows on the nightstand. He gently placed her on the bed and opened one of the bottles before saying, "I know it's the last thing you want to do, but you need to drink as much of this as you can."

Being a good girl, she obediently sat up and tried to follow his instructions by taking several sips. Then she lay back down. A minute later, her eyes opened wide and she was back to moaning.

"I can't stop the room from spinning."

"Take one of your feet and put it on the floor. It'll make you feel grounded," he told her.

She planted a foot flat on the floor. Much to her relief it worked. It was completely awkward, but she was willing to stay in the ridiculous position all night if it kept the nausea to a minimum.

"Ha-ha. Grounded. That's what I should be. For like two weeks." She gave him one more giggle.

"I have a pretty good idea your day tomorrow will be punishment enough," he replied, letting himself enjoy the adorableness of it one last time.

"You know all the tricks," she murmured before passing out.

Tyson covered her up as best he could and tucked her in with a kiss to her forehead. He stood beside the bed and watched her, waiting a few minutes to make sure she was going to stay asleep. Before leaving to make his way back to the party he leaned over to kiss her one more time and said, "Except the one to get you outta my head."

CHAPTER 15

DANI'S EYES FELT like crusty, burning pits before she opened them. She kept them closed as she debated which was more debilitating, her pounding head or her queasy stomach. Her mouth felt like an army had marched through it and half the troops had wiped their boots on her tongue.

But her eyes shot open as soon as the memory of how she spent her New Year's Eve came flooding back. Dani quickly sat up, and with the movement her stomach took the lead in the "what's worse" contest.

With a slow and mortified turn of her head, she checked the other side of the bed and found it empty, with no indication that the covers had been moved in any way. Her panty hose and bra were still on under her nightgown.

Of course he went back to his own room, she thought miserably, carefully swinging both feet over the side of the bed and onto the floor. She placed her elbows on her knees and the heels of her palms on her eyes in an effort to stop the throbbing. *Not even Tiger Woods could get turned on by last night's display.*

She picked her head back up and spied all the bottles of water lined up on the nightstand. She also found the notepad with the DoubleTree heading and Tyson's neat, legible handwriting.

Happy New Year, Dani. Breakfast is 9 at Aqua. Checkout is noon.

He had the unmitigated gall to add a smiley face.

Dani covered one eye and glanced over at the digital clock at the opposite side of the bed: 9:45. Too late to join whoever else was downstairs in the hotel's restaurant. That was probably for the best. Not only was the mere thought of food revolting, but she also had no desire to do the walk of shame in front of Mr. God's-Gift-to-Women and his new bride. Or Chase Walker and his sassy wife, who hadn't touched a drop. She had embarrassed herself and Tyson enough.

"Tyson," Dani groaned out loud as a new wave of queasiness, this one mixed with a hearty dose of humiliation, washed over her. She fell back onto the bed praying another hour would be enough to sleep it off.

DANI AWOKE WITH A START an hour and a half later. She scrambled to take a quick shower and pack up, forced to temporarily put her suffering on hold. She didn't bother looking into the mirror after taking off what was left of last night's smeared makeup. Her face was sallow, and her eyes had circles around them dark enough to get the job as the cover model for *Raccoon Quarterly*. No amount of concealer or blush in her little bag of tricks would save her. The only thing that was going to help change how she looked was time and a whole lot of sleep. It was impossible for Dani to wrap her head around the fact that there were people who indulged in such behavior on a regular basis.

She sat on the bed after getting dressed, trying to stall until the last possible minute before going down to the lobby and facing him. At 11:55 there was a light knock on her door. Thinking it was housekeeping, she went to let them in. She opened the door to find Tyson instead.

"Morning, Dani," he said with a small telling smile as he walked into her room to get her suitcase. Without asking, he reached for her hand and placed two Advil in it. "How you feeling?"

"That question is rhetorical, right?" she groaned. Her fingers curled around the much-needed pain medication like they were diamonds.

"That good?" he continued, glancing over at the nightstand and the still untouched bottles of water. He took one and held it out to her. "I promise, the more of these you drink, the quicker you'll start feeling up to snuff. You have to hydrate. Your brain is banging all around in there from lack of water."

He pulled up the handle on her bag and began to roll it behind him. "We're all checked out. I made your good-byes to the Montgomerys and the Walkers. They asked me to tell you it was nice to meet you. And they hope you feel better."

Dani was still too muddled and fuzzy to tell if he was being sarcastic. She only knew one thing: she wasn't going to get a read by looking at him, since shame prevented her from meeting his eyes. And that was a real pity, because under normal circumstances, looking at him always made her top-ten list.

"I'm sorry I couldn't make it to say good-bye," she mumbled, contrite.

"It was only the Montgomerys this morning, all forty of them. The Walkers left last night. Chase was all hyped and yelling something about getting back to living the dream."

Dani kept her eyes on the floor. Right about now, Chase Walker was lavishing love and affection on his wife after finding out he was going to become a father.

Mercifully, Tyson led her out through a side door. Dani poured herself into the passenger's seat and let him drive them back to the air- port. They were quiet, but for different reasons she was sure. She was in twelve kinds of agony, and not all of them included the amber liquid that had turned her inside out. He was merely thoughtful. At first she didn't think much of it. Too many things were hurting her. And Tyson was good with comfortable silences. She had just worked up the nerve to start slipping in a few random glances at him when he spoke up.

"Dani," Tyson began slowly. "I think you may have been right in saying it was bad policy for us to be seeing each other. I think us going to this wedding together was a mistake."

"I'm sorry I embarrassed you," she said immediately.

"No, it's not that," he was quick to assure her. "But it is a stark reminder of just how different we really are. You got so blasted last night, but other than a wicked hangover, you don't have a problem. And by that I mean, you can go out socially, tie one on, suffer the con- sequences, and not drink for another six months without missing it. I'll never have that luxury. It's not fair for me to expect you to give up cocktails at a party or a beer at a game just because I have to. But it's also not fair *to* me to have to sit by and watch you do it. I make you so uncomfortable you didn't even feel like you could drink in front of me last night. I can't be responsible for something like that."

"I don't blame you if you don't believe me, but I swear this was a very, very rare occurrence. I don't know what came over me." She knew exactly why she did it, but how was she supposed to tell him any of her reasons now? Even the one about her shoes turning against her would just make her look reckless and stupid. She tried to make a small joke out of it. "It's another first I got to share with you."

Tyson continued like she hadn't spoken. He sounded resolved, although not actually sad. "There are just too many painful memories attached to it for me."

Dani knew in that one sentence he had already made up his mind. He wasn't lecturing her, and this wasn't about making her repent. He had thought about it rationally, then decided his course of action, what he thought was best for everyone involved. But for Dani, the disappointment was sudden, and crushing. Her response was to once again erect her wall of anger.

"You're probably right. We're not really a good fit," she told him curtly. She knew Tyson well enough to know there was really nothing else to say that would make any difference.

"If it's all right with you, I'd love to go back to being friends. I still think you're amazing. I'm just not the guy for you."

But his kindness was too little, too late. How nice of him to decide what was and was not right for her. She nodded, stone-faced, and he took her silence to mean she was still suffering and left her to nursing her hangover.

Nothing more was said for the rest of the ride, except that Tyson insisted that she keep drinking the bottles of water he brought along. Sometimes she took his advice, sometimes she didn't; all the while she intermittently stole glances at him. His face was unreadable.

"You going to be okay to drive home?" he asked politely as they got off the turnpike exit for the airport.

"Of course," she replied stiffly. *I'm used to you getting your jockstrap twisted in a bunch and discarding me.*

Tyson pulled the car in front of the terminal and they both got out. He went to grab his garment bag out of the trunk and she started making her way around the car to take the driver's seat. They met at the rear bumper, finally coming face-to-face. His look had softened and hers had turned to stone.

"I'll see you back in Austin?" he asked encouragingly.

"Unless you get me fired before then" was her ice-cold response.

Tyson shook his head and sighed. He hated the look on her face, and fought the urge to wrap his arms around her. He knew if he kissed her, all he had just put her through would be for naught. "Dani, it's not like that, and you know it."

Before he could say anything more, they heard the shrill yet familiar sounds of strangers shrieking, "Hey! It's Tyson Palmer. Over there!"

"Your public awaits," she said, her tone bland. Then she brushed past him to get back into the car. She looked over her shoulder as she opened the door. "Happy New Year, Tyson."

"Happy New Year, darlin'." Tyson watched the taillights of the Mercedes as she drove away.

Dani headed back to Ardmore and probably would've started to cry, but she was too dehydrated to produce any tears. There wasn't a single part of her body that didn't feel sick and sore. Now she could add her heart to the mix, the only part that wouldn't feel better over time and was already used to the ache. By the time she reached the rest area right before her exit to the Pennsylvania Turnpike, the water caught up to her and she made a pit stop. She dragged herself out of the car to the restroom, telling herself that she should be grateful and relieved. He had made it easy for her. She would never subject Brendon to someone as rigid and unyielding as Tyson. Her secret could forever remain just that. Hers.

She was so preoccupied with the stern self-lecture of all the things she would need to do moving forward, she never felt her iPhone slip out of her jacket pocket. It fell silently onto the bathroom stall floor, secure in its thin protective case.

By the time she realized it was missing she was already back home and had slept the day away, interrupted by occasional visits from Brendon to check on her by prying open her eyes with his fingers. It was only after her brothers reported getting some pretty outrageous texts that Dani starting manically searching for her phone. Then the Mavericks front office checked in to ask her why she was calling and hanging up on Tyson, Marcus, Cameraman Stan, and her boss. They also wanted to know just how many people she knew in Guatemala and why she would want to talk to them for nine hours.

Her cell phone carrier shut off the phone and the Mavericks office assured her a new phone and number would be waiting for her upon her return to Texas. All her contacts were lost in the mayhem. She would be denied the opportunity to tell Tyson to lose her number, assuming he had second thoughts and tried to reach out after dumping her. But she knew better than to think he might indulge in a late-night drunken text fest.

It may have been a new year, but Dani Carr couldn't think of much to look forward to. And there definitely was little to be happy about.

CHAPTER 16

DANI GOT OFF the elevator on the top floor and walked with purpose-ful strides down the hall, muttering most of the way. When the phone had rung in her room several minutes earlier, there was only heavy breathing and three words.

"I need you."

Romantic-sounding words, to be sure, but he hadn't called her with romance on his mind. At least if she was his girlfriend she would be taken out for dinner occasionally, maybe get some jewelry. At the very least, she'd have a random orgasm thrown in her direction.

She got to the end of the hall and rapped on the door to his hotel suite lightly three times.

Marcus opened it and Dani breezed in, taking a seat on his couch.

"I know, I know," she prattled, reaching for the remote to the television and fully expecting him to be out the door before she could finish the sentence, "don't ask, don't tell."

But Marcus said nothing. Dani looked up from where she was sitting to find him staring at her. His blue eyes regarded her warily, the expression on his face bemused. If she didn't know him better, she would've said he looked rattled. But Marcus was an expert at holding his cards close and rarely showed nervousness about anything.

"You know I love you, baby girl."

"That sounds like a slick come-on. Asking me to do something sketchy usually follows."

"Did anyone see you?" Marcus asked, ignoring her quip, which wasn't anything new. What was unusual was the edgy tone of his voice. Marcus was always anticipating the next danger. It was clear he was feeling threatened now.

"No. I don't know. Maybe." Dani shook her head, mostly to clear it. She had been so wrapped up in her own thoughts, she honestly couldn't remember if she had passed anyone or not. "Why?"

Marcus sighed loudly, aggravated that her observation skills weren't as keen as his. "There's a journalist that's getting too close. He's been following me for days. Dude actually went so far as to get a room here. He's already tried to gain access to this suite by posing as housekeeping."

"Marcus, we leave in two days for New Orleans. Need I remind you that this *is* the Super Bowl we're talking about here? The guy is probably just trying to get a jump on press week. Slam the door in his face if he shows up again and just go about your business."

He wasn't interested in explanations or justifications. "I need you to do me a favor, Carr. I need you to give up your two days off and stay here."

"Say what?"

Marcus took a quick look around the room and spying an ice bucket, went over to it and picked it up. "If I'm not back in five minutes, I need you to stay here. If anyone knocks on the door, and I mean anyone, I want you to muss up your hair and your clothes, put on your sexy face, and answer the door. Then you're going to tell them I'm in the shower."

"Are you insane?"

"You're right, that won't work. Put on one of the robes instead. The hotel gave me like three of them. They're in the closet. And every now and then, order lots of room service. Get two of everything and always shut the bedroom and bathroom doors when they deliver. Yeah, that'll make it look really legit." Marcus and the ice bucket began making a beeline for the door.

"That's not what I mean, Marcus! What the hell is going on?"

He stopped short and turned back to her. "I don't have time for this right now, Dani. I promise it's the last time I'll ask you for anything. I really need you to do this for me. Please?"

Dani gave an exasperated sigh, but before she could agree he was gone and all that was left was the sound of the door slamming shut, leaving her alone in a fictitious den of iniquity.

If this isn't an adventure, I don't know what is, she thought. She wished he had left directions for what to do if one of those knocks was from the police, since surely he was up to something nefarious. Why else would he concoct such an elaborate plan? There was no point in staying angry. Marcus was just being Marcus.

In the month since returning to Austin after New Year's, Dani was the walking definition of manic-depressive. As the Mavericks systematically obliterated their play-off matchups, the excitement in the locker room and team offices was palpable. So was the desolation she felt watching Tyson from the sidelines.

True to his word, Tyson had kept her at arm's length, but he had stretched the truth when he had claimed that he wanted them to be friends. Now it was his turn to play the avoidance game. They were back to the days when he was waving to her from across campus. Only now, instead of looking forward to them, she was filled with such an ache by the chance encounters that she had forgotten what it had felt like to be happy in his presence. Then the team would score another win, and the cycle would start over again.

Having an excuse to stay locked away was ultimately a welcome reprieve. She was tired of moping around her own suite.

Dani put her feet up on the coffee table and got ready to turn on the television but halted when she heard something. It was a gentle tone, then a buzz. She ignored it, but it when it happened again, she got up to investigate. Like a game of Marco Polo, the sound would go off and she'd move toward it. She won when she found the source.

On top of the small refrigerator that accompanied the honor bar was Marcus LaRue's cell phone. She brought it to the coffee table so that she could hand it over when he came back for it, which she assumed he would when he realized he'd left it behind.

The problem was, after two hours, Marcus had not returned.

Every time the phone began to hum and vibrate, it pushed Dani one step closer to the brink of insanity. She'd stare at it and another bead of sweat would erupt on her upper lip. There was no point in touching it. Without his thumbprint, she couldn't unlock the shiny black screen. What if it was his "meeting" trying to get in touch and his lack of response was going to alert suspicion and set off a chain of events beyond her control? Worse yet, what if it was someone from the front office calling and they realized one of their star players was AWOL? Dani hated to admit it, but she needed to call in reinforcements. She pulled out her own phone and dialed the number of the only person she knew could help. It coincidentally was also one of the few numbers that she had committed to memory.

"Dani, what's up?"

The question was met with brief silence as Dani quickly tried to regroup. She had been busy thinking of the message she would or would not try to fumble through when he didn't pick up. But he had picked up, and even more disconcerting, he sounded concerned.

"Dani?" Tyson repeated.

"I can't find Marcus," she said in a rush.

"Is he supposed to be someplace?" Tyson asked calmly.

"I don't think so," she replied, kicking herself for not having thought out her explanation. Answering too many questions would end up revealing his ruse. "But he left behind his phone. He never does that. And it's beeping like crazy."

"Can you answer it? See who it is?"

Dani snorted. "You're kidding, right? This is Marcus we're talking about. It's locked up."

There was a long pause, this time on Tyson's end.

"Meet me in front of the hotel in twenty minutes. Bring the phone with you," he instructed.

"What are you going to do?" she asked the dead air before realizing he had already hung up. Dani grabbed the phone and her jacket and went out in front of the hotel to wait. She was already trying to tamp down the dread she felt. But with that came a rush of endorphins, the kind reporters get that causes an altogether different type of buzz.

She was going to be alone with Tyson Palmer, very alone and in very close quarters. Dani knew what happened when their quarters got too close. She shook herself. *I can only handle one crisis at a time*. The first was the missing Marcus.

Tyson pulled up and Dani got into his car. She sank into the expensive leather and buckled her seat belt, trying to ignore how sexy he looked behind the wheel. She was already losing the battle to ignore how fresh he smelled, like he'd just showered. The hair peeking out from underneath his wool skullcap looked damp. Together they drove out of Austin and well beyond the city limits. They continued southeast into hill country. The feeling of dread intensified with every mile.

"Do you know where we're going?" Dani asked, staring straight ahead in the vain attempt to create some imaginary distance between them.

"Pretty much," was his only response.

"Do you know where he is?" she persisted, a knot beginning to grow tight in her stomach.

"Yes."

Dani turned her head to stare at him. Why didn't he just tell her? Dani swallowed hard as the realization ran her over like a train. All along she had been made to feel like she was the only person Marcus came close to trusting. Clearly this was not the case.

"How do you know?" She kept her voice level, though she wanted to begin screeching.

Tyson cast a quick glance in her direction. "It's probably best if you wait for Marcus to explain."

Dani crossed her arms over her chest and bit her tongue. She silently fumed. Once again, she was getting a shining example of how she was really living in a man's world. A world she'd always be shut out of. *Bros before hos*. She had sacrificed so much for Marcus LaRue. She'd been separated from Brendon, she'd been forced to call a hotel room home for more than six months for the "chance of a lifetime," which was really nothing more than a publicity stunt. She'd covered for him by letting people believe they were having an affair when everyone in the league knew he was gay. She did it all without complaint. And how did he return that favor? By making Tyson Palmer of all people his confidant. And Tyson was only willing to risk betraying that trust because whoever was trying to reach Marcus was probably more important than the three of them put together. It was a complete slap in the face. Dani was certain if she opened her mouth, the end result would be one long shriek after another. Wherever they ended up when this drive was over, the next stop would be back in Pennsylvania, with her beloved son in the next room and her mom in the kitchen, no matter what it cost to get there. She could begin making up for all the lost time. She was done, with all of it.

They drove about an hour before Tyson turned off the highway, entering a sleepy little town. He began to slow down. Dani was able to decipher from the name of the post office and a school that they were in Cedar Creek. Marcus was here? It seemed illogical if not impossible. Tyson took a series of turns before pulling into a driveway in front of a tidy, modest beige ranch-style house that looked like it might have once been a double-wide trailer. While the property sat on several acres, small brown rocks made up the front lawn that surrounded the house, likely thanks to someone who had finally given up trying to grow grass in the inhospitable dusty soil. A lovely little porch with an awning had been added on, and two rocking chairs sat pointed toward the sunset. If her nerves weren't strung so tight, she might have labeled it inviting. Tyson cut the engine.

"We're here," he said with a chuckle after noting her confused stare.

Together they made their way up the path to the front door and Tyson gave it a knock. A minute later it was answered by a middle-aged man dressed in slacks and a plain white button-down shirt with a dark green sweater vest, holding a book. He was tall and thin and what was left of his hair was peppered with gray. He partially opened the door and regarded them curiously, lowering his chin to get a good look at them from above the frames of his wire-rim reading glasses.

"Can I help you?" the man said politely.

"We'd like to speak with Marcus, if he's available," Tyson replied respectfully. Dani began to feel dizzy.

"Certainly, please come in." The man opened the door wider. Tyson stood back, letting Dani go in first.

"Thank you, Pastor," Tyson said, and as far as Dani was concerned, she had just been invited into the Twilight Zone. She nodded a greeting, still speechless, and stepped inside.

The interior of the home was clean and neat. Dani could tell the high-traffic areas by worn-out spots in the carpet. Pictures of serene nature scenes adorned the walls and the scent of baking was in the air. Bread maybe? Pie? The Twilight Zone meets Norman Rockwell, Dani mused, still too confounded to say anything and now grateful that Tyson was there to keep her from feeling totally out of her depth. A moment later they were joined by a woman who was presumably the pastor's wife. She was also tall and slender, sporting a pixie haircut that was more gray than blond. She looked like a female version of her husband and breezed into the living room wiping her hands on her apron. She gave them a bright smile, as if strangers popping into her living room was no big surprise.

"Hello!" she sang out warmly. "Please have a seat. Can I get you something to drink?"

"No thank you, Mrs. Green." Tyson smiled. Dani followed his lead and shook her head politely.

"They're here to see Marcus, Lila," Pastor Green told his wife, and her smile faded. Not completely gone, but now wary.

"Of course," Lila Green said graciously, still very much the pastor's wife. She took a few steps toward the entrance to a hallway and called down it in what could only be described as a motherly fashion. "Marcus! You've got company."

"We're, uh, bringing him his phone," Dani bumbled in an attempt to waylay the woman's fears. She pulled the phone out of her pocket and held it up, feeling like she needed to prove it.

There was a thumping of multiple pairs of feet coming down the hall. It was accompanied by laughter, unfamiliar, almost childlike laughter. All of which abruptly came to an end when Marcus appeared and saw them. Beside him was the cutest, most fresh-faced girl Dani had ever seen. She looked barely out of her teens and was dressed in jeans and a sweatshirt, her long brown hair pulled away from her face by a chaste-looking headband. She had big brown eyes that grew wide when she saw Dani and Tyson, like she knew some sort of jig was up.

Apparently it was. The scowl on Marcus's face confirmed it. He looked from Dani to Tyson, then quickly back to the pastor and his wife, then finally to the young woman. The glare then settled on Dani, accompanied by a cold "What are you doing here?"

The question broke Dani out of her stupor. It was too much. She'd spent all day, nay, the last six months worrying about where he was, what he was doing, and if he was in trouble. She had missed her own son's fifth birthday to sit alone in a hotel room waiting for a half-hour phone call with Marcus. She had made up excuses for him that nobody believed. And all the while he was deep in the heart of Texas in some bizarre version of *Leave It to Beaver*. She walked up to Marcus, thrusting his phone in his direction. She didn't care about decorum or politeness or even if there was a reasonable explanation. As far as she was concerned, if she never saw any of them again, it would be too soon.

"I might ask you the same question," she hissed at him. "You forgot this. It's been ringing all day. You're welcome. I quit."

With that, Dani walked out the door.

Her dramatic exit lost some of its effect when she realized that she was stuck until Tyson followed her out. After all, he was her ride and the car keys were in his pocket. She paced back and forth by the car, mentally writing a list of the things she needed to do, which consisted mainly of booking a flight home and putting in an application at the local Starbucks once she got there. Maybe she could try her hand at teaching. Thanks to her master's degree, someone had to be willing to hire her for something that wasn't sports broadcasting. She was through with football and the backbiting, judgmental world of television, where every time she put a piece of chocolate in her mouth, she'd have to measure the circumference of her upper arm to make sure it wasn't too fat. Because for a female broadcaster, the most important thing in broadcasting was lady arm fat, even when wearing a coat in the dead of winter standing next to a football player twice your size. At the time she thought she was doing what she had to, to win some imaginary game. The dyed hair, the contact lenses, and the push-up bra—all to stand out and get noticed. Now she felt like nothing more than a puppet, one she herself wouldn't want to play with. She stopped and took a deep breath, then another. If anyone was watching from inside the house, she must've looked like a raving lunatic.

Dani leaned up against Tyson's Bentley, which looked ridiculously out of place parked next to a ten-year-old basic minivan and a rusted-out pickup truck. She laid her hand against her forehead, pinching at the bridge of her nose with her thumb and middle finger, trying to push her brain's reset buttons. Who was she kidding? What had driven her all along was the hope her career would help bring her back to Tyson. How did it turn out that getting everything she wanted was the worst thing ever? It was time she got her head on straight.

"Dani?"

She dropped her hand and looked up, expecting to see Tyson. But it was Marcus who was now standing beside her. She glowered at him, not trusting herself to speak.

"Walk with me?" he asked, already taking a step in the direction across the lawn of rocks. It sounded like a plea. She might have refused, but curiosity won out, and she followed. She thought about picking up one of the landscaping rocks and beaning him with it, but a very healthy-looking red tabby cat dashed from around the back of the house to join them. The cat ran to catch up and tried to brush against him as he walked. Marcus stopped, reaching down to give it an absent-minded pat. The cat rubbed up against one of Marcus's legs and then the other as he stroked it, then plopped down on the ground in front of him, meowing when Marcus straightened back up and went back to walking. The cat gave Dani a disgruntled glance, its tail slapping against the dust hard enough to create a small cloud as Dani passed it.

They walked around the back of the house and across the property to an octagonal wooden gazebo by a large pond. Beneath its canopy were several picnic tables. Marcus took a seat on one of the long benches and patted the space beside him in invitation. Dani sat down next to him. It was serene and lovely, rich with the sounds of the wildlife around them. She could see the top of a white steeple from above the tree line in the distance. The pastor's church. Her anger began to ebb, and she could feel a difference in Marcus as well. All his edginess was gone, replaced with a demeanor she had never witnessed before. Tranquility maybe? Or vulnerability?

"I thought football would be fun." Marcus sighed wistfully.

Dani couldn't help laughing. "So did I."

Marcus grinned, before spreading his legs apart and hunching over, resting his elbows on his knees. He looked down at his hands as if they held the right words and then gave up. "We were so damn poor. I went to bed hungry a lot. And alone, I was always alone. I had to grow up fast."

Dani could feel her chest beginning to tighten. She had wanted Marcus to explain himself, but now that he was actually doing it, she wasn't sure she wanted to hear the story. With each word he spoke, the more vulnerable he looked. He picked his head up and gazed out over the pond in a way that suggested he was still searching for words.

"I thought I was so smart, you know? The more people started to suck up to me, the cockier I got. By the time I was all buttoned up with the Blitz, it was already too late. . . ." His voice trailed off.

"Too late for what?" Dani probed gently. She wanted to stay angry with him, but seeing him so defenseless brought out all her motherly instincts.

"All I saw were the dollar signs. It never dawned on me, all the debauchery and mess that came with it. I thought the streets of New Orleans were bad, but at least when I was getting attacked there, it was up close and over fast. I learned how to fight for survival, and when it was over, I knew I had lived to fight another day. I got good at honing my instincts. But now, it's all about back-slapping fools who grin as they feed off me. Before the first shovelful of dirt was thrown into the hole where they dropped my mother's coffin, they were telling me I should get back to business. I was terrified they would grind me down until there was nothing left."

Dani knew who "they" were. Not only the paparazzi, but also the master manipulators like Clinton Barrow, whose only focus was the bottom line and winning seasons. She had been their victim as well. But that still didn't explain why she currently found herself in Cedar Creek.

"Marcus, none of that gets me any closer to why you're here. And I think I've earned the right to hear the whole story."

He took a deep breath, sat back up, and for the first time since she met him, did exactly what she told him.

"I met Beth and her family at the hospital after they thought I dislocated my shoulder in that game with Houston during preseason the year before last. Her grandfather was dying, and they had been there for days. They all looked at me with the kindest eyes. None of them had a clue who I was. She told me she would pray for me. Before I knew it, I was asking her to have coffee with me. Her parents said they didn't think it was a good idea for her to go out with a stranger, so I ended up inviting all three of them. I was so sure they would be impressed once they found out I was a rich and famous football player, because heck, isn't everybody?"

He chuckled at his own sarcasm.

"Aren't you supposed to be gay?" she said.

"Gay? I never said I was gay. Y'all were the ones who said I was gay. I just didn't bother correcting anyone. " He chuckled again but the pained look returned and he continued with his confession.

"Not only was her dad not impressed, the man was downright disapproving, especially after he found out I had never set foot inside a church. After he thanked me for the coffee, which he insisted on paying for, he said it was probably for the best if I didn't try to contact his daughter again. I was a nice kid and he would keep me in his prayers, but they were simple, godly people and he didn't want his only child falling in with hotshot athletes like me. He said it as we all sat at the same table, so it wasn't like he did it behind my back. And Beth looked like she agreed. For the first time in my life, I was truly ashamed. I told all of them I would do anything they asked to change their minds. I think the pastor saw me as a soul that needed saving and he couldn't turn his back on that. I walked away from that meeting with an open invitation to join them at their house whenever I wanted to, and I used it to get my foot in the door."

Dani couldn't help but smile. She had firsthand experience of the power of persistence.

"I knew I wouldn't be able to wow them by trying to bring them into my world, at least not at first. I was already behind with my Sundays dedicated to football. So I joined their church. I had to do it without anyone finding out and blowing my cover. If the media found its way to their door, it'd be all over. I was already good at being sneaky. I started spending all my free time there, which was hard to do when I was with Boston. I'd fly in and ditch anyone who happened to notice and try to follow me. Then take a cab, sometimes the bus. Nobody's looking for a football star on a crappy bus rolling through small towns, even if this is the middle of football country. If anyone did recognize me, I'd just hop off the bus or ditch the cab, jog a few miles, and try again."

"That's why you wanted to sign with the Mavericks," Dani said slowly as the pieces came together. It was awe inspiring. "You did all this to date a girl?"

"I know it sounds crazy, and looking back when I started it I was probably just doing it to be stubborn. But I love this girl. When she looks at me, I get all hot and cold inside."

And with that quietly spoken declaration, Marcus LaRue, the coolest, most aloof character Dani had ever met, willingly reduced himself to a puddle of lovestruck mush. His eyes were still as blue, but the ice had melted from his stare. For the first time since she'd met him, the cold, jaded look was gone and Marcus looked his age.

"It looks like you succeeded in winning them over," Dani remarked sarcastically, if not bitterly. In the end, he had sealed the deal. All in the name of love no less, a feat she couldn't manage to accomplish.

"It wasn't easy. At first the pastor really made me earn it. They wouldn't even let me sleep in the house and set up a little room for me in the barn. He made me go fishing and sit around in nature, picking berries and stuff. He was really good at getting me to tell him about where I came from. Sometimes he'd put his arm across my shoulders as I did, like he was trying to hold me up and support me. I could tell he felt bad for me too. This place became my sanctuary. The more time I spent with them, the more it turned from wanting to get them on board with my way of living to this desperate need to keep them shielded from it. The longer it continued, the higher the odds got that someone was going to find out."

"So you used me to run interference." Dani sighed. She looked at him with more empathetic eyes now. He hadn't singled her out. He had used everyone and everything to his advantage. She began to realize just how much they had in common. Dani had also been living within enormous lies and ulterior motives. But he hadn't trusted her completely. Someone else had gotten full disclosure. "But you let Tyson in on what you were up to."

Marcus gave a shrug. "The deeper I got into it, the more I realized

I would eventually have to trust someone on the team. Tyson gets me. He knew what I was feeling."

Dani shook her head. More proof she would never see the inside of the boys' club. "That's what cuts the deepest."

Marcus put his hand on her knee. "Look, Dani, I didn't know my dad. My mom was sunk in her addictions before I got out of grade school and everyone in the league knows what happened once she had money to burn. Tyson has a lot of experience with addiction. I knew from the time I was little that I wanted what the rich folks have. But it's nothing if I have no one to thank for it or share it with. These people have become my family, the family I never had. I'd do anything to protect them. I'm really sorry you got caught up in that, baby girl."

Dani could've chosen not to forgive him, but that thought never crossed her mind. She could only imagine where Marcus was coming from. She knew nothing of dysfunctional families or addiction. Her tight-knit clan had rallied around her without judgment whenever she needed them—no questions asked. They wanted her to pursue her dream, even if it was completely misguided. Besides, her grudges had already weighed her down for a long time.

"Apology accepted. So what's next?" she asked.

Hearing her words of forgiveness, he visibly relaxed. Shades of the Marcus she knew returned with his insolent grin. "For me, I'm going to finish out this year with the Mavericks, hopefully win the Super Bowl. Then I'll cash my check, walk away, marry Beth, and give her parents all the grandkids they can handle. I'm through leading a double life. The Greens are tougher than I ever gave them credit for. They've wanted me to stop living in this mess for a while now. What's next for you? You going to keep running?"

Dani sucked in and held her breath, the hairs on the back of her neck rising in the same way they did every time he got too close to her truth.

"I'm not running from anything," she protested.

His grin got wider. "You know, I never expected you to take it all so seriously. All my instincts told me you just loved the publicity. I thought I was just going to be making it easier for you to work your own agenda. I really got that one wrong."

He wasn't talking about her aspirations in broadcasting. The conversation had just been flipped on its head. He was giving her a new sort of grin. There were times his intuitiveness was fascinating. But most of the time it was a real pain in the ass. At the moment, it was a whole lot of both.

"You're not as smart as you think you are," she said, making one more valiant effort to ward off his knowing look. "And my only agenda is to make it to the top."

"Getting fired is really going to put a damper on that."

"You didn't fire me." She was flustered. "I quit."

"Oh yeah," he said slowly, and started to rise from the picnic table. "Then I guess you better make this last car ride count."

Dani watched him make his way out of the gazebo and start heading back across the field. After a few steps he turned back around. He stuck his hands into the front pockets of his jeans, his thumbs sticking out. If he had a cowboy hat on and a cigarette dangling from his mouth, she'd have sworn he was the Marlboro Man. For the first time since he'd come onto the scene, he looked truly comfortable in his own skin. "You coming?"

He waited for her to catch up and she fell in step beside him. They strolled leisurely together in silence for a bit. Dani had a lot to process. Marcus was really an enigma. And his story was nothing short of remarkable. As they passed the barn behind the Greens' house, she smirked, picturing him sleeping inside it, on a cot next to some hay, surrounded by the lingering smells of the animals that had once lived inside it. He chose to forsake his twenty-four-hour concierge service to win over not only a girl, but also her entire family. And he was completely at peace with having done so, all because he had broken free of his deception.

"Were there rats in there?" she asked, pointing to it.

"Not that I saw. Plenty of mice though. But Tigger and Meowsy are good at earning their keep. Why, you looking for a place to stay?"

"I don't think so." She gave a half laugh. "Not a fan of vermin in general."

"Oh yeah, that's right." He chuckled along, another trait he had picked up that suited him. "I thought it was just insects that bothered you. Remember when that wasp wouldn't leave you alone in Philly? You were jumping around like you were being Tasered."

"Excuse me, but those things are nasty. For crying out loud, they build their nests out of their own spit." She shuddered at the recollection.

"And let's not forget about the fly," Marcus mentioned casually.

How could she ever forget the infamous suicidal fly? Its death had launched her wild ride. Dani couldn't tell if he was just making conversation or trying to prove a point. The house was starting to come into view. So were the Bentley and the minivan in the driveway. And leaning up against the beautiful car with his long muscular legs crossed at the ankles was its equally attractive owner, who never seemed to look out of place anywhere anymore. He hadn't noticed them yet, busy studying his phone. Her heart began to speed up at the sight of him. She wanted to fill the air with something, anything to cover up the sound of it, afraid of it beating so loud that Marcus would hear it and it would blow her flimsy objection to his observation.

"I won't really quit if you don't really fire me."

"I would never fire my partner in crime. It would be bad karma. I know you're not a quitter. In another couple of weeks, it won't make any difference."

She knew what he meant. If he had spoken the truth, which Dani knew in her heart he had, he wouldn't have the need for any reporters. She wanted to be the first to congratulate him if by chance they won it all. And she wanted one more opportunity to watch Tyson from the sidelines, doing what he did best. Well, second best, in her personal opinion. The three of them had come so far in the course of the season, with her fighting at least one of them most of the way. They were a strange triad that had been guided by fate and perseverance and maybe something more.

"Marcus? At least tell me who was calling you all day?"

He stopped walking, gave it a moment of thought, and then broke out into a smile that stretched from ear to ear.

"It was Palmer. And just for the record, I didn't willingly tell him what I was up to. He followed me after practice one day and I couldn't shake him. It's funny. He was the only person I couldn't outrun."

She wasn't sure if he was kidding or serious. But either way, this time it took all her will to not reach for two rocks. She'd be aiming to hit one and then the other, right between the eyes.

CHAPTER 17

TYSON LOOKED UP from what he was doing as soon as he heard the crunch of feet on gravel. His gaze met briefly with Marcus's.

"We all good?" he asked.

Marcus nodded. "Yup. See you on the field." He proceeded to make his way into the house without looking back.

Tyson's look tempered as he settled it on Dani. She attempted to meet it head-on but failed and looked at the ground instead. He opened her car door.

"I made our good-byes, spitfire. I'm getting pretty good at that. The Greens asked me to tell you that it was nice to meet you." He gave her a little wink when she caught his eye and then he closed the door before she could fire off any retort. He couldn't tell if her blush was courtesy of her talk with Marcus or the memory of her tantrum in front of the pastor and his family, but he adored it either way. Once again, he had her alone. With every fiber of his being, he was going to make sure that this time it wasn't going to end with either of them getting away.

Within minutes they were back on the road, each of them lost in their own thoughts, his about the right words to convince her to give them a chance, hers about how it was time for her to stop living in lies. It wasn't until they reached the highway that she finally spoke up.

"Tyson, how did you know it was me when I called? I got a new phone number after New Year's."

"Marcus gave me your new number," he told her.

"As part of this jacked-up conspiracy?" she asked with a false sense of righteous anger to keep herself ahead of the mounting guilt and attraction.

"Nope." He grinned, his eyes shifting briefly off the road, to give her a palpitation-inducing once-over. "Just 'cause I wanted it."

"So you've been keeping tabs on me?"

"Guilty as charged." Tyson didn't take his eyes off the road, but Dani could tell by his profile there wasn't an ounce of remorse in his expression. He turned to look out his window in a failing attempt to hide the grin. "Marcus taught me the basics. It's not like I was sleeping under your bedroom window."

Tyson wished he wasn't driving. Having to keep his eyes on the road prevented him from being able to fully appreciate her blush again. But he could wait. If he had his way, he was going to make sure she blushed for him every day for the rest of their lives. If he had his way, her next one would be occurring within the hour.

"You know what else I want?" Tyson asked her.

"What?"

"To take you home."

She felt a rush of giddiness bubbling up. His voice was warm and sincere and she remembered it all too well. She felt nineteen again, only instead of being in a dorm room, she was in a car. In his car, with him sitting next to her and his sexy voice was not asking this time, but telling her what he wanted. Reality could wait a little longer while she wrapped herself up one last time in this wonderful fantasy.

"Whose home?" she teased.

"My home, your home, our home, wherever you lead, I'll follow," he said without reservation. Her eyes began to get glassy. She had waited for so long for him to say such words, for her to hear them, to believe them, and it didn't disappoint.

When she didn't answer, he took another quick look at her. After noting her pensive expression and watery eyes, he gently placed a hand on her knee. "Look, I know I'm doing a complete one-eighty from what I said after New Year's. Holly told me how you helped Amanda with her scheme. I jumped to all the wrong conclusions and I'm sorry about that. You're under no obligation."

It was all too much, too much to hope for. But he was here, saying and doing all the right things. And his hand on her leg burned like a branding iron.

"Your home," she murmured and watched his hand as it gave her knee a little squeeze, then slowly began to move back and forth up to her thigh as he sped up to get them there.

She wasn't sure where they were going or what to expect when they got there. It was strange to think about how she had spent years obsessed with him but really knew so little about him. If his car was any indication, she imagined their destination would be some sort of outlandish mansion. And she wasn't entirely wrong.

They ended up in the exclusive Northwest Hills, but his contemporary two-story house was far from the most ostentatious on the block. There was no other flashy car vying for attention in the garage, but there was a golf cart.

"We're home," Tyson announced with a grin, and Dani felt another rush, this time of pure adrenaline.

The house with its open floor plan was neat and spotless, courtesy of a maid service, if she had to guess. But there wasn't much by way of decorating. Most of the walls were bare, with the exception of a large flat-screen TV in the family room. There was also a sectional couch and two recliners with a coffee table in the family room, but the formal living room was barren. So was the dining room. The kitchen had a table and a set of four chairs that looked like they'd never been pulled out, much less used. On the counters sat nothing more than a toaster, a coffeemaker, and a worn old football of all things. But all the wide windows presented spectacular views and provided great natural lighting.

"You're really an exhibitionist." She noted the lack of curtains. "Ever heard of window treatments?"

He gave a laugh. "When I was getting back into shape after rehabbing, I didn't see all that much daylight. After a while it got to me. I don't think I ever fully recovered."

She wandered over to the door leading to the backyard. A wide cobblestone patio fed a path over to the enormous pool with a high cascading waterfall and what had to be a fifteen-foot slide built into the side. The water was crystal clear and the landscaping meticulously maintained. And there was a single piece of furniture, an oversize round lounger, big enough to act as a bed, complete with cushioned pillows. It was as if he lived here, but didn't.

"Can I get you something to drink?" he asked her from across the room. "I'd give you the tour, but there's not much to see. I don't entertain much anymore."

"You host events all the time."

"Not here. This is my inner sanctum."

So that explained it. She kicked herself for not thinking of it on her own. His wasted days were behind him. And in exchange for peace of mind, he really had forced himself to become a loner.

"I pretty much bought it as an investment," he added. "For when I start a family. It needs a woman's touch for sure."

Dani began to worry her lower lip. He already had a family, at least the beginning of one, and because of her, he didn't even know it. What seemed reasonable and justified at the time now felt the ultimate in selfish. She didn't want to think about it now. One more night wasn't going to matter.

"But . . . but the pool looks great," she stammered to get them off the subject. "That slide see any action?"

"Yeah, in rehab I really developed this thing for water. Would you like to go for a swim?" he asked with the beginnings of a most devilish grin.

"I didn't bring a bathing suit," she saucily replied.

His eyebrows rose in invitation and he took a step in her direction. "This place is pretty private. I never wear one."

"Maybe later." She took a step toward him as well. "I can think of better reasons for taking off my clothes."

"Are we really going to do this?" He took his turn with another step, his look beginning to smolder.

"What's the matter, you afraid you're going to get called for a false start?" Dani teased as she took her step.

"Hmm. You're worried that I might start before the snap. But in case you hadn't heard, I have remarkable stats with third-down conversions." Even when it was at his expense, he loved her wordplay. He drew closer. "I don't like to have to turn over the ball."

"I think if anything, you may go down by contact," she sassed from nearly an arm's length away.

"This may be the only time in history a roughing the passer call gets declined." He grabbed her around her waist and pulled her in until she was stopped by the wall that was his chest. Dani stuck her hands in his back pockets and gave his butt a squeeze. His lips brushed hers, once, then twice, and his tongue coaxed her mouth open. It was soft, it was warm, and then he delved inside.

"If you call time-out, I'm going to face-mask you." She giggled when they came up for air. She pulled the skully off his head and tossed it on the counter.

"You should be way more concerned about holding." He took her hand and led her purposefully through the house to the staircase. He graciously bowed, allowing her to go first. Then he playfully spanked her all the way up the stairs in an effort to get her moving faster, with her squealing, "Excessive celebration!" When they reached the top and after one more opened-mouth kiss, he scooped her up into his brawny arms, eager to get to the really fun part, which included watching her face as she came undone.

He effortlessly carried her down the hallway, past three empty bedrooms and into his own before setting her down. He drew her into his arms again and took several steps backward to get them closer to the bed, with each step giving her another kiss, his lips sliding soft and warm over hers. They stopped at the foot of the bed and he wove his hands into her hair, tilting her head up to look into his eyes.

"I've waited so long for this," he breathed, his mouth sweeping along her jawline. "A lifetime."

She grabbed him by the collar of his shirt in the effort to bring him closer. "Me too. It's always been you."

They separated long enough for him to unbutton her blouse, which he accomplished with little deft flicks of his fingers. He peeled it off her shoulders, bunching up the material as he did so, until it reached her wrists and pinned her elbows to her sides. Feathery kisses that started at her throat moved leisurely down to the tops of her breasts, which were heaving within her bra. He took a minute to nuzzle her until he felt her begin to pull against the restraint with fervent frenzy. He released her and she pulled her arms free of her shirt while he quickly removed his own. Together they reached for his pants and with his hand over hers they undid his buckle and pulled his belt free of its loops and tossed it aside. She reached for him and unbuttoned his jeans and he grabbed her hands again to stay her, pulling them up to place them on his chest. He let them go, and she wrapped them around his neck as he whispered, "Not so fast this time, gorgeous. I want to get it right."

He slowly finishing disrobing her, so gentle with his touch this time; the difference in it brought tears to her eyes. He was unhurried, savoring every caress and inch after inch of her already feverish skin until she was bare. Then he lifted her, and as she wrapped her now-naked limbs around him, he sat down on the edge of the bed, settling her on his lap. He looked into her eyes like he was recommitting them to memory. He brushed the back of his hand across her cheek. She broke the stare with a blink, then took his hand and kissed the tip of every finger, deliberately, to satisfy his call for them to pace themselves.

He held up his hand and she did the same until their palms met. He slowly closed his fingers, webbing them into hers. Then he pulled her to him again, and the light smattering of chest hair created exquisite friction against her already taut nipples. She couldn't hold back the moan or the involuntary wiggle-like grinding of her sex against his still denim-covered prominent and increasing bulge. He groaned at the sensation and each of their hands tightened while holding the other's.

He lifted her again and deposited her on the bed, then quickly ran into his bathroom to retrieve a condom. He returned with a corner of the condom wrapper between his teeth, unzipped his pants, and finished removing them. He was better than she ever remembered. From the top of his head to the soles of his feet was pure excellence. He was toned and ripped and magnificent.

"Wait," she squeaked.

He halted, dropped the condom into his hand, and his face instantly fell. She had changed her mind. His heart pounded in his ears.

"I want to look at you," she said in full appreciation, and suddenly he regretted insisting they take their time. He could feel himself throbbing while he indulged her with several flexing poses. He heard her exaggerated sigh and joined her on the bed.

"You're so beautiful," he breathed in her ear, and his lips nipped at her neck.

She had called him beautiful once, a long time ago, and through the buzz of her arousal, she recalled it. She lost all equilibrium, stuck between the past and present. But this time the roles were reversed. He was the one in complete control and she was the one wishing they could turn back the clock. But the words he spoke sounded as heartfelt as when she had said them, as was the look.

"Please," Dani whispered feverishly.

"Please, what?" Tyson leaned on an elbow and looked down upon her as his fingers began a sensual tracing in the cavern between her breasts. Back and forth he stroked and coaxed. "Tell me what you want, Dani."

I want you to love me. I want you to not hate me for the secret I'm keeping from you.

"Touch me, Tyson," she murmured, blinking away building tears, "everywhere."

Even the way he fondled her was perfection. His hand cupped her breast with the same execution and precision as he gave his game, only there was no rush to let anything go. When he did release them, it was to move down her belly. By the time he reached her pulsating core, she was sure her skin was sizzling. He shifted and bent her knees, settling between her legs, and he spread them farther apart.

His scruff teased the inside of her thighs. That alone was enough to send her back arching. And then he kissed her, dead center. His tongue repeatedly brushed over the bud that stood guard to the entrance of her soul and she was soon dripping with nectar. She could hear his words of encouragement to give in and let go. It was too much, emotionally as well as physically, and she couldn't stop the surge of passion and love from building until she cried out his name repeatedly and squirmed in rhythm with him. He held fast onto her legs as she convulsed against his mouth. He felt her finally go limp and he kissed his way back up her now-glistening body. He left her momentarily. In a daze, she heard the ripping of foil and through dilated eyes watched him roll the condom over his solid erection, barely able to lift now-languid arms to beckon him back. All her words were nothing more than breathless pants and mews.

"I hate to sound selfish, but I wanna see if I can make you do that again," he said huskily as he took her back into his warm embrace. She weakly placed her arms around his neck and pulled him to her kiss as he sheathed himself to his hilt inside her.

ONCE ALL THEIR PENT-UP DESIRE was finally sated, Dani fell asleep cradled in his arms. A few hours later, long after the sun had set, she awoke to the sound of snoring. At first she believed she was having just another one of her recurring daydreams. His deep heavy breathing nearly lulled her back to sleep. But then he rolled over, taking her with him, an arm still wrapped around her, and her eyes flew open wide.

She was in bed with Tyson. Not in some sleazy motel, but his bed. And this time, by the way he still held her tight, neither one of them was making an escape. Her dreams and reality had finally merged, and she was still reeling (although maybe that was thanks to her first, well several, orgasms that had nothing to do with batteries). Now Dani fully understood what all the fuss was about. The only man she'd ever been with had been well worth the wait. Dani untangled herself and leaned on an elbow to watch him as he slept.

He was absolute perfection, even in the half-dark. Better than the untamed college boy ever was, because now he had so much life experience. She couldn't decide if he really looked better with his eyes opened or closed. In sleep, he appeared adorably innocent, but she was well aware of the royal blue glimmer safely tucked away behind his eyelids. Even the way he snored was endearing. His lips were slightly parted and she fought back the urge to lean over and kiss them, for fear of waking him and breaking the spell. She wasn't done admiring him, free of having to worry that he might catch her. She didn't think she would ever get enough. But once he joined her in the waking world, she would once again be faced with what she had done.

This hadn't been about mindless sex or making up for lost time. Not for him. It had been about pleasure and connection and caring. It showed in every stroke of his hand and brush of his lips. By the time he was done she knew the true meaning of making love. She felt an overwhelming wave of guilt and remorse wash over her. She thought she had done everything right, but she couldn't have been more wrong. It wasn't like she lived a separate life. After he had tossed her to the curb and she began to raise Brendon without him, she'd been justified in keeping him away. During most of her pregnancy she hadn't even been able to find him. She had thought about trying to at first. But he had fallen off the grid entirely. She remembered waiting with bated breath for the news of his demise, certain that he would eventually self-destruct. But she could tell in a glance once he returned that he had broken free of the vices she'd held against him, no matter how she tried to convince herself otherwise. Not even a shadow of the man she had been with that night remained. And she'd been afforded every opportunity to do the right thing.

Who was she kidding? From the moment she heard his name at homecoming she had begun to weave her web of deceit. It disgusted her with just how well she had adapted to it, persuaded by people around her who had no problem lying. *Do what you have to when clawing your way to the top*—that had been the mantra of many of those who, much like herself, were determined to succeed. She had assuaged her conscience by believing that's what was necessary to get ahead, until she got reacquainted with the gentleman who had done it through honesty, generosity, and hard work, after having hit rock bottom no less.

As Tyson actively pursued her and began to piece it all together, Dani had no choice but to keep digging the hole deeper. And now, when she should be savoring the ultimate happy ending, she would lose it all. If she didn't act quickly, Brendon would soon be old enough to understand that she had robbed him as well. That thought was more than she could bear.

Tyson began to stir, his arm blindly reaching out for her. She scooted over and cuddled up next to him, not wanting him to wake fully and see the tears in her eyes. His arm wrapped around her again and he exhaled.

"Bella," he murmured drowsily, his hand drifting down to settle on her bottom, giving it a pat. She wondered fleetingly if he was dreaming he had scored a touchdown.

If she was going to stop the lies she would have to start with herself. That college nickname had never slipped from his lips except for once, when he confronted her with the knowledge that he knew who she was. He never used it again, respecting her wish to be called Dani, the name she had switched to as part of her grand plan.

The hand on her behind began wandering gently, up and down her back at first. She watched in captivation as the blanket that covered them began to slowly rise just below his waist. She reached beneath the blanket and tentatively stroked, then wrapped her hand around him. He groaned and shuddered and throbbed from inside her closed fingers, filling her hand with the lusty mixture of silk and steel. He pulled her up to meet his sleepy kiss and she released him to bring her own arms around his neck, now clinging to him in both passion and desperation, silently praying the night would never end, before the need overtook her.

Adding to the long list of bad decisions, she returned to the scene of the crime and her original sin. She made uninhibited and unprotected love with a very groggy Tyson Palmer.

CHAPTER 18

THE NEXT TIME Dani woke up, she was alone. The sun was up and it was the makings of what would be the fourth consecutive day of unseasonably warm weather for winter. The temperatures had been in the eighties all week, and this day looked like it wasn't going to be an exception. It was already bright, also one of the things she liked best about her time in Austin. Back at home, February was usually nothing but snowy, dreary, or cold, often all three. But she'd better get used to it, because she would soon be heading back, this time to stay.

Dani sat up in bed, all her mixed feelings rising once again to the surface. She took a minute to scold herself. She'd made a mistake, okay, lots of them. That was going to end today. She owed it to Brendon and Tyson and her family. But mostly she owed it to herself. At first she was going to wait until after one last game day. It would be unfair to come clean and distract him with such an explosive revelation when he was getting ready to play the biggest game of his career. But if she was taking anything away from what she learned from Marcus, it was that nobody deserved to live in chaos. What Tyson had taught her was that whatever followed after she came clean, she could handle it as long as she took it one day at a time and walked a path of truth and honor.

Of course that sounded easy without having to look into Tyson's beautiful blue eyes as she did it.

"Doesn't matter," she chided herself again. "Your dishonesty ends today."

Her now-wrinkled blouse, jeans, and lingerie were sitting folded up neatly on the end of the bed. Just seeing them made her tingle; oh how wonderful it had been as they were taken off. She put on her panties, but it was his button-down shirt from the day before that she was wearing when she padded barefoot down the hallway in search of him. When she passed by one of the bedrooms she at first thought was empty, she saw a treadmill and some free weights. His only other sign of life was invested in physical exertion, as if she needed the reminder.

She went downstairs and checked the den. But he wasn't there either. She opened the door to the garage. Both his car and the golf cart were there. Maybe he went for a run. She went into the kitchen, ready to search the cupboards for the K-cups to his Keurig machine, and glancing out the patio door she found him.

He was lounging shirtless on the round oversize love seat. His back high against the cushions, he was tossing a football up into the air and catching it. She checked to see if the one she saw on the counter was still there, but the space was bare. Tyson looked relaxed but focused, like he was deep in thought. He had his jeans on, and it all combined to be the single sexiest sight she'd ever witnessed. She watched until it became too much and then went out near the pool to join him.

"Nice outfit." He smiled as soon as he noticed her approaching in his shirt.

Nice everything, she thought as Tyson slid over to make room for her to sit beside him. He tossed the football into the air again. Maybe the better plan would be to wait until after the Super Bowl to tell him.

"You thinking about the game?" she asked.

"I'm thinking about a lot of stuff," he replied, tossing the ball one more time before setting it down to deal with what was occupying his mind. "I did a bad thing."

Dani frowned. Was he talking about their hookup? Was this the gentleman's version of wham-bam-thank-you-ma'am? Was he getting ready to break it to her gently? And if he was, she couldn't decide if that would make what she needed to tell him easier or more difficult, or if it would keep her silent.

"That's a pretty rough opening line, considering last night." She looked down at her feet and pretended to study her pedicure, so he wouldn't see the hurt in her eyes. Maybe she wouldn't have to tell him after all.

He didn't say anything. The silence lingered. Finally came a stern "I'm not going to continue until you look at me and join the conversation. I've got all day."

If anyone else had spoken to her like that, her head would've snapped right up, ready to dole out a piece of her mind. She timidly looked up to meet his gaze, and what she saw was all warmth and affection.

"That wasn't what I was talking about, darlin'. Not completely anyway. I meant getting all freaky without protection."

That was another thing about leaders. They took responsibility for their actions, sometimes for things that weren't their fault. They were equally responsible. If it came down to the nitty-gritty, she was more so. Her first instinct was to tell him she was on the pill, but it simply wasn't true. She wouldn't tell him one more fib. She tried instead to follow his lead, but her head was starting to pound with dread

"I was there too, you know. It wasn't like I tried to apply the brakes."

"True." His face lit up with her favorite smile, the adorable mischievous one from the old days, when he saw her from across the courtyard. "And I don't think we swapped diseases. You look pretty safe. I get tested for everything under the sun on a regular basis. And my partners are a short list. I'm totally safe disease-wise."

"That's good to know."

"I made a huge mistake New Year's Day. When I told you it would be best if we didn't see each other anymore. I haven't been able to get you out of my head since. And when I woke up this morning and saw you curled up next to me, I decided I needed to remedy that, pronto."

He paused, as if to stop from getting ahead of himself. Then he smiled again.

"But, truth be told, I woke up excited by the prospect that I may have knocked you up."

Dani's mouth dropped open and every hair on her body stood on end. He had mentioned children. "I would never try to trap you like that."

She was blushing again, and he took a moment to enjoy it. "Of course you wouldn't. If anything, it's me that's trying to corner you."

Now she needed to sit down. She perched on the end of a lounger in case she needed to jump up to get away. He moved to join her. They sat side by side, their legs touching. "I don't know if you know this, Dani, but my next game is also going to be my last. Win or lose, my playing days are over."

"I knew that." She didn't want to admit that it was another reason she loathed him, back when hating him was fashionable. "I had heard you'd been originally offered my dream job with the network. I was trying to get in the running when I was told I'd be working for Marcus."

Tyson was momentarily shocked by her disclosure. "That's interesting. It was Marcus who was the catalyst for my playing one more year. Did you know that?"

It was her turn to look stunned. They stared at each other as they came to the realization that for better or worse, they had Marcus LaRue to thank for bringing them back together.

"I've been thinking about you for a very long time," Tyson said, breaking the silence. "Sure, in the beginning it was because I wanted to strangle you when the chicken thing stuck. But even then I didn't want to take my eyes off you. Once I found out you were really my Ella Bella and I came to terms with what I'd done to you that night at homecoming, it practically sealed the deal. You're gutsy and snarky and beautiful and you'll keep me in line. I've been telling myself for a while that I thought we were destined to be together. Now that I know about the LaRue connection, I'm sure of it."

She tried to draw a breath without gasping, both terrified and delighted by his declaration. She nodded in her struggle to find her voice, which seemed to enchant him all the more. He took her hand.

"I'm not sure what your plans were for the future, but I was thinking, if you weren't busy, maybe you'd like to live with me, here or anywhere you'd like. We'll make babies. Have a good life."

It was that *B* word again. Dani felt ill.

"I know my track record is sketchy, but I also know what's truly important now. I can be a good husband. And I love you. Maybe I always have. Maybe you've been in my heart forever," he continued earnestly.

How she had longed to hear those words come from him. When she told him what she had to, he was going to take it all back. Dani put a shaking hand up to her mouth and shook her head.

"I understand," he told her sadly, standing up. "I figured it might be too soon but I wanted to try. If you want to get dressed I'll take you back to the hotel."

He started to make his way back into the house and stopped, turning back around and added, "I'm not sorry about last night. If it turns out that you are pregnant, I'll support whatever you want to do. But I promise I can be a good father. You can change your mind. We can take it slow. Whatever."

He turned back to continue on to the house but was stopped again, this time by the rush of air that preceded the cry she could no longer hold back. Despite all her efforts to hold them in, the floodgates opened and she began a series of heart-wrenching sobs. They came one after the other, stealing the breath straight out of her lungs until there were no other sounds beside them.

Tyson rushed back to her, pulling her to her feet, then into his arms and still-bare well-built chest, dismayed by her overwrought weeping. She let him because she knew it would be the last time. He gently rocked her back and forth, trying to calm her, and rubbed her back until she was all cried out and there was nothing left but her ragged breathing and sniffling.

"Was it something I said?" he asked teasingly, still shaken by such an onslaught of raw emotion.

"You weren't supposed to be so nice," she babbled. "You weren't supposed to try so hard. I didn't want to love you again."

Tyson hugged her tighter, smiling into her hair. She loved him. "I'm so sorry I blew your trust. And I'm guessing your mind."

Dani forcefully tore away from his embrace, desperate for some distance from his all-encompassing sweetness. She didn't want to get used to the safety or the comfort, because as soon as she came clean with what she had done, chances were he would turn his back on her again. If he didn't walk away with actual custody of Brendon, she would still have to face him on a regular basis. And each time she did, it would be a painful reminder of all the things she had done wrong. He would never smile at her again, or look at her with devotion in his eyes, or tell her he loved her. But for Brendon's sake she had to do the right thing. Dani drew a shaky breath. "I've loved you since the day I met you."

"That long?" He smiled. "Sorry I came late to the game."

"Stop it!" Dani exclaimed, filled with guilt. "Stop teasing and apologizing and letting me off the hook!"

He was momentarily taken aback by her now-angry outburst. Clearly one of them had done something wrong, only now he wasn't sure which one of them it was. "Okay then, how about I forgive you? Whatever sin you think you've committed, you can stop beating yourself up."

"You don't know what you're saying, Tyson. The things I've done are unforgivable."

His look softened. "No, Dani, you're wrong. Take it from one who knows. We're all worthy of forgiveness."

She shook her head and struggled to get the words past what felt like a permanent lump in her throat. "Not me. Not for this."

He reached out to gently stroke her cheek with the back of his hand, a gesture so tender, new tears from red-rimmed eyes spilled over her already wet lashes. He cradled her head in his large hands and swiped at them with his thumbs. He tilted her head up to meet his adoring gaze. "Yes, you. For everything. Try me."

He led her by the hand back to the big round love seat and sat her down, and took his place beside her. He held her hand and patiently waited while she took some time to regain her composure.

There is no way out now, Dani thought. She stared into his handsome compassionate face one more time and tucked it away in her memory bank. By the time this conversation was over he'd never look that same way at her again.

"That night, at homecoming, I did seek you out, but for all my good intentions, I really only made things worse, for both of us," she began.

"Well, you're really in luck then," he openly confessed. "There isn't much I remember about that night, other than I was a really bad boy who earned the vengeance of a scorned woman."

She tried to drown out what he was saying, all his tolerance was making it that much harder.

"It was so painful to see you like that. I was sure if you would just let me, I could make you feel safe and loved and you wouldn't feel the need to keep slowly killing yourself."

"That was a losing proposition, Dani. I fed off the bottom for a long time."

"I just kept telling myself that if you knew you had somebody on your side, it would make all the difference. I had this ridiculous notion that if I could get you to tell me your story, it would be like therapy. Chances were, you were losing your job anyway. You'd have nothing to do and all the time in the world to do it. I would've done anything to be near you."

Tyson could feel his shoulders and neck beginning to tighten. Ella was one of those loose ends from his past he just couldn't tie up. She was a different person who masqueraded her way past being listed as one of those "people, places, and things." It was hard to be reminded of those days, and even meditation sometimes couldn't stop that reaction. He didn't think she had no reason for going that far back in time to rehash something they'd previously discussed. But what she was doing was likely going to trigger a flashback, something he thought he was long past and wanted to be prepared for.

"I remember," he said quietly.

She took a deep breath; now it was time for the hard part. "But the truth is, I didn't want to miss another chance to be with you."

He began to grin and told her reassuringly, "Sweetheart, that's nothing. I've seen girls do all sort of outlandish things to try and get me into bed. I'm guilty of a few myself. If you recall, one of my favorite games when you were my tutor was making you blush. It still is."

Why did he have to make this so difficult? Because he wanted to believe all the good things he thought about her. "After you left school, I realized that I had made a terrible mistake. I'd been saving myself for the boy I thought was perfect and I'd let him get away. I swore if you ever asked me again, I was going to change my answer."

His neurons fired and for a quick second he was back at the Bunker and reliving the first time he felt the surge of anger at her, the one before the fury. He shook his head to dislodge it but vividly remembered what caused it. "I know. I really didn't deserve to make the cut."

All hints of good humor vaporized. It wasn't the fact that he was her first; last night had started a new chapter. It was that if she was telling him now, it was because it was leading up to something. Something big. Life-altering big. So big, that he would fail in his attempt to reconcile it and things would never be the same again, for either of them.

"That's all right, Dani, I'm sorry I wasn't able to make it special. But that's not it, is it?"

Her chin began to tremble and she shook her head.

He stood up abruptly, could feel all his control starting to slip. He took several steps toward the house and quickly turned back around. His hands settled on his hips and his face began to register the look she feared and had seen before. But that look now paled in comparison. His blue eyes appeared demonic and she wouldn't have been surprised if his head started to spin all the way around.

"Say it!" He shouted so loud and fiercely, she flinched and the tears were back in her eyes with a blink.

"Tyson," she said sorrowfully, "I had a baby."

The rage that engulfed him was all-consuming. It burned through him and it felt as if his brain might turn to cinder. He turned and began to walk forcefully to the house. After several steps, he stopped short but didn't turn back around, unable to bring himself to look at her. He said with cold indifference, "I'll call you a cab. Make sure you're gone when I get back."

Dani sat alone on the patio and wrapped her arms around herself and began to shake. It was worse than she could've imagined. Not only was he not going to forgive her, he was going to turn his back on his own child. He didn't even stick around long enough to find out whether he had a son or a daughter. She was wrong again. The truth hadn't brought her a single ounce of relief. Dani didn't think she had any tears left, even as they began to roll down her face.

CHAPTER 19

TYSON'S ONLY REGRET about having left in such a hurry was forgetting to take his reliable old football with him. Since Logan gave it to him, all those years ago, he had never needed it more. That tired piece of pigskin really did have the power to calm him. But he couldn't go back and get it with Dani still out there.

He switched to automatic pilot and went right into his closet to do the next best thing. He changed into his running gear. As he sat down on the bed to tie his sneakers, he caught sight of her clothes still piled on the bed. He forced out of his mind the image of her in his shirt. He went back downstairs and called a cab. He should've made her do it herself, but since getting sober, he always tried to be a gentleman. Plus she really did need to be gone, and soon. It had been a long time since he'd thought about doing something he would actually regret. Then Tyson hustled out the front door.

And he ran. He waited for the rhythmic pounding of his feet to catch up to his furiously pumping heart, washing away some of his angst. It took longer than he expected, but he knew it wouldn't fail.

At first his inner dialogue was harsh, to match his anger. He tried in vain to conjure up the memory of that night, but it was futile. So was trying to get the time back. Precious moments with a child that would have enriched his soul and healed the scars of his past. No matter what he had done wrong, it didn't warrant the sentence he, and subsequently an innocent child, had received. His child.

Dani Carr had withheld information, the most important information of all the whole time she had taunted him and teased him. She'd had ample opportunity to tell him he had a child. In this miserable world, children deserved unconditional love by anyone who was willing to provide it, and he could have given that love, and received it.

And then he remembered something Logan had told him as he trained to get back in the game. Perspective is perception. At first he had blown it off as just another one of Logan's inspirational phrases. But as Tyson looked back over how he'd conducted his life, he began to wonder just how much of it applied.

He'd been passive for way too long. Barrow, Logan, Marcus, all had managed to get into his head and manipulate him. And he let them, at times willingly. Was it because they were men? As soon as he thought Dani was doing it, he was full of righteous indignation . . . but was that fair?

He was momentarily sick inside, thinking of the possibility that he had drunkenly fathered children all across the country. But the women from that part of his past were the type who would've stood front and center, demanding he claim responsibility and pay up. They never would have kept such news a secret.

But Dani Carr was not that kind of woman. She never had been. When she told him she loved him, she had meant it. Then, after he broke her heart, she transferred that devotion to someone who carried a piece of him.

Tyson realized he knew what he could expect from men. But women were very different creatures. They needed a different set of survival skills. One more time he was compelled to take his own inventory. First he had put women on pedestals, starting with his mother. Then came a time when he looked at them as toys. Eventually, when they tried to play his game, he began to view them as villains. And Dani was the only woman who had the honor of being all three.

As the sweat poured off him, Tyson's head began to clear. He started walking back in the direction of home. He was fatigued, drained both mentally and physically. Tyson knew Dani wouldn't be there when he got back. They were both well versed in the fight-or-flight response. What a pair they made. He stumbled when his knees nearly buckled with the realization: despite everything, he really did love her. And you can't love someone on your terms, only theirs. Marcus was living proof of that, and once again, Marcus had been right.

He took a shower and went back out to the pool, where his football was waiting. He sat down on the chair and resumed tossing it up in the air. And then he held it. Without realizing it, Tyson cradled it in his arms like he would a newborn, thinking of the time he couldn't get back.

Tyson had a choice to make. There was no way he would go back to living his life the way he had before he found out. He wouldn't be an absentee father. He could continue to waste more time and make his child's life a battleground or he could man up and move his family forward. He could be the kind of father that his own father wasn't, and start to heal that betrayal as well. Now the thought of having a child filled him with a sense of pride and belonging. Within an hour, he was in his car speeding to the hotel.

Once again, he needed to find Dani Carr.

He blew into the hotel lobby, determined to get her room number, even if it meant shameless flirting, deceit, or strong-arm tactics. Before he could reach the front desk, he felt a hand on his shoulder, practically spinning him around.

"What did you do?" Marcus barked. To Tyson's surprise, there was panic written on Marcus's face.

"It's going to be okay. I'm going to clear this up right now," Tyson said quickly, breaking away from the grip. "I'll explain later."

"Dani's not here," Marcus replied, watching Tyson's face fall. "She sent me a text and was gone before I could get back."

They were too late. There was no point trying to call her; they both knew she wouldn't answer. If he left right away maybe he could make it to the airport in time.

"What the hell is wrong with you, man?" Marcus growled.

"What did she tell you?"

Marcus shook his head in disgust. "She didn't tell me anything other than she was finished and it was nice working with me. But when I left her in your capable hands, she seemed pretty optimistic. Looks like you saw to that."

Tyson stared at Marcus, dumbfounded.

"She worked for you, Marcus, or should I say ran your interference. I know you know her address. Where did she go?"

Marcus continued to shake his head. "She never volunteered that information, and I never asked. Whatever you did, it must be a real deal breaker."

"She had my baby and never said a damn word to me!"

"Well, duh, you just figured that out now?"

"You mean you knew? She told you?" Tyson could feel his blood pressure reaching blastoff.

"Of course I knew, but she didn't tell me. She didn't have to. I mean, I knew she had a kid because her boss let it slip, but think about it: what single twentysomething with her sort of celebrity status sits all alone in a hotel room night after night after being transferred to one of the hippest, most happening cities in the country? She could have been painting the town red with any guy, but she was pining for you. Damn, for someone who claims to be so enlightened, you really are dumb as a bucket of rocks."

"Don't you dare lecture me, Marcus. No one watched your back more than I did. Now we can either stand here swapping insults or we can try to track her down."

Marcus may have found religion, but he still had all the street smarts of his childhood: "Come on. I know the best place to start."

They drove together to the Mavericks' front office and proceeded to tag-team Clinton Barrow's secretary for Dani's address, even after she politely told them she couldn't give out that sort of information.

"Mr. Palmer," she said, trying to reason with them, "I'd lose my job for that. It would be like giving out your address to some fan."

"It's nothing like that," Marcus scoffed. "We all have the same employer."

"Not anymore you don't." A voice came from behind them. Both men whirled around to the sound of it. It was Clinton Barrow, who for the first time, looked rattled. "Dani Carr no longer works for this organization."

What Barrow didn't share were Dani's parting words in the e-mail she sent to him along with copies to everyone on her command chain. It told him in no uncertain terms what exactly she thought of him and his organization, and suggested a few profane things he could do with his team and then to himself. The audacity of being addressed in such a fashion and having it exposed to so many had left him steaming. *Cheap Yankee trash,* he thought. In the throes of press week before the Super Bowl, he didn't want to risk bad publicity, so he had put her on the back burner to be appropriately dealt with later. He would start by making sure she'd never work in broadcasting again. Although he was fairly certain that had been her plan all along, or she never would have sent that e-mail. The thought of being unable to punish an underling by destroying her career only infuriated him even more.

"We know that," Tyson said. "We want her home address."

"What in tarnation for?" Barrow asked suspiciously, and then attempted to redirect the conversation. "Never mind that now. You boys have a plane to catch, a press week to get ready for, and a game to play. We've already lined up another reporter to cover Marcus."

"I don't want anyone else," Marcus protested.

"And I'm not leaving until you tell this lady to give me Dani's address, Clint," Tyson reiterated.

Barrow could feel his nerves beginning to fray.

"Look, boys, I don't know what's going on here, but y'all seem to have your priorities backward. Does this woman have something on either of you that I need to worry about?"

"No," both men said in unison. Marcus because he had never told Clinton Barrow anything in the past, and there was no reason to start telling him anything now. Tyson because for the first time in more than five years, he viewed Barrow as an adversary and not a savior.

"Great. There'll be plenty of time for you to worry about your love lives after the game. Now let's get a move on. Saddle up!" Barrow clapped his hands together and turned to leave.

"I don't think you understand, Clint," Tyson told his boss's back. "If I don't get what I'm looking for here, there isn't going to be any game. Not for me."

All Tyson meant was that he would never be able to get into the proper head space to play until he talked to Dani. But Clinton Barrow stopped cold in his tracks. He turned slowly back around to face Tyson and Marcus. His eyes narrowed and his cheeks started to take on some color through his bronze permatan. It was probably the first time the polished billionaire had received an ultimatum.

"Are you threatening me, Palmer?" Barrow's voice was silky smooth and laced with venom.

It was in that moment that Tyson realized just how one-sided the loyalty in their relationship had truly been. As long as he toed Barrow's line, he'd been in his good graces. Now he knew how quickly he could fall out of favor.

"All I thought I was doing was trying to get an address. I'm not threatening you." His face hardened. "So don't threaten me."

Barrow looked like he was trying to figure out if Tyson was capable of calling a bluff.

"This is how you repay me? After everything I've done for you? You'd be dead or in a gutter somewhere if it weren't for me."

"And I've repaid that debt, several times over. Today it's my turn to set some rules."

"If you don't show up and play, I swear I'll see you bankrupt for breach of contract."

"Oh, I'll show up all right. And I'll take the sack for every down."

"You'll spend the greatest game of your life sitting on the bench!" Clint bellowed.

"I guess that's where I'll come in," said Marcus in the same insolent monotone that they all knew, completely unaffected by the threats and the yelling. "I will come down with the worst case of slippery hands that the league has ever seen. I might even set some new records for dropsies."

Barrow's upper lip began to curl up with the snarl. "You gutless wonder, since when did you start giving a shit about anyone other than yourself?"

"Probably around the same time I realized I'd always have to keep one up my sleeve when it came to folks like you. Now I'm just looking at a grown-ass man throwing a temper tantrum."

Theo and Sal could be seen swiftly coming down the hall in response to Barrow's shouting. Marcus pointed at shiny-headed Sal with his finger before they got too close. "Stay right where you are, Baldylocks, this isn't your fight."

The two men waited for some sort of direction from Barrow, but Clint did nothing more than give a slight single shake of his head without looking at them.

Satisfied that both men were going to keep a safe distance, Marcus turned his attention back to Barrow. "So what's it gonna be, boss? You gonna sit your two star players or you gonna play ball?"

Clinton Barrow's white-hot glare went from one man's determined stare to the other's. And then he began to grin. In the next moment, his toothy smile emerged, one that didn't reach his eyes. It was the smile he usually wore for publicity's sake.

"Well, it looks like Tyson told you all about my fondness for challenges. A strange, not to mention inconvenient, time to open negotiations, but let's get down to it."

And in the spirit of a last hoorah, Marcus once again persuaded Tyson to enter into a most unholy alliance.

TYSON AND MARCUS ARRIVED TOGETHER to meet the Mavericks chartered flight to New Orleans. They sat alone, huddled with their heads together for most of the trip, quietly talking and making sure that no one else was privy to the conversation. By the time they landed, Tyson was feeling confident, about some things more than others, but confident nonetheless.

As they waited to check in, Tyson heard someone call his name. It was a familiar, warm voice that he loved and he automatically turned to it.

"Hi, Mom." Tyson wrapped her in a bear hug. "I'm glad you made it early. I'm not sure how much free time I'm going to get, but I could really use a pep talk."

After all she had been through, Karen Palmer never left the house until her full face of makeup was flawless and her purse always matched her sensible shoes. She never had a hair out of place, even after those first few strands of gray started to appear. The only time she had shown no interest in her meticulous daily routine was when she initially had to come to grips with her husband leaving her. For days she'd barely been able to get out of bed, much less do her hair. That period of grieving had been short-lived, but even when Tyson was in the thick of battle with his demons, remembering how his mom had looked back then had haunted him.

Karen hooked her arm in his and began to move him away from the rest of the team toward the lobby door. "Of course, sweetheart, I'll be here following you around all week. This place is a madhouse. I'm so excited for you, and proud, so proud."

They made small talk about how much she was looking forward to seeing the French Quarter, and her plans to take a bayou tour and eat at Commander's Palace. Tyson carried her bags in from the parking lot. But just before he could tell her what was really on his mind, another person came into view, stalking out from behind a large SUV. It was

Douglas Palmer. As soon as he recognized him, Tyson froze, refusing to budge from his spot.

"What is he doing here?" Tyson asked his mother, moving protectively to stand between them.

"I brought him," Karen told him with a smile. "You did send me two tickets. I don't recall you giving me any restrictions with them."

When Tyson sent the tickets, it was with the intention that she bring one of the more upstanding men she occasionally dated. She had told him years ago it was unlikely she would ever marry again.

"But Mom . . . *him?*" Tyson asked with wide, incredulous eyes. He took a quick look over his shoulder to make sure Douglas Palmer wasn't getting any closer. With all his recent revelations, this was bordering on becoming just too much. He didn't need any more bombshells in his life right now.

"Don't worry, Ty, this isn't a reconciliation, if that's what you're thinking. Did you know he spent a fortune on buying a ring for that floozy, and within a week she pawned it and took off?" Karen shot a sidelong glance at her ex-husband. "Guess she got wind that the money was running out. I actually feel sorry for him. I really don't want to take your father back, but I'd be flat-out lying if I said him tripping all over himself to be nice to me isn't pretty damn gratifying."

Not only did Karen Palmer sound positively elated delivering the news, but it was also the first time in all his life Tyson had ever heard her even close to cussing. The closest she had ever come was a rousing *H-E*-double hockey sticks.

"He really wanted to be here," she added as she took him by the arm to gently turn him back around. "And I think he should be. He's your father, Tyson, and he loves you."

Tyson gritted his teeth and took a good look as they made their way over to the spot along the SUV where his father was deep in concentration, shuffling his feet to kick a small rock from side to side. He still wore an expensive suit, but it looked worn and faded, as did he. The bald spot on the top of his head had gotten bigger, and he had forsaken the cheap rug he had purchased to hide it. His skin looked blotchy and burned from all the time he spent in tanning booths in the desperate attempt to recapture his youth. As they neared him, Tyson could see the deep lines in his face. His eyes were red and glassy. His father wasn't drunk but was more in a state of having a never-ending hangover. Tyson knew that look all too well. He had gotten his comeuppance and then some, but it brought Tyson no joy.

"Hi, Dad," Tyson said, trying to sound casual. He refrained from calling him Doug because even now, he knew his mother would see it as disrespectful and wouldn't approve.

"Tyson." Douglas managed a half-smile while swiping at some bug that had tried to land on his cheek. "You're looking strong. Big game coming up, hope you're ready. You likely won't get another chance."

Tyson tilted his head and looked at his father with new eyes. The words tumbled forth without any effort.

"I forgive you, Dad."

Douglas Palmer's face turned ruddy. Whether it was from embarrassment or rage, Tyson would never be sure. It was probably a combination of both.

"Forgive me? Forgive me for what?" He scowled. "Dedicating my life to you and your career? You never would have got that first deal if it wasn't for me."

In that moment, Tyson understood. He finally got it. His father might never understand, but the words would set him free. As he said them, he meant them.

"No, Dad, I forgive you for me. I know you did the best you could. Thank you for that."

"You and all your self-help bullshit," Douglas Palmer mumbled.

"Douglas," came a low yet sharp warning from Karen. "Why don't you go wait in the car while I talk to our son."

It wasn't a request, and after kicking at another rock Douglas Palmer skulked off and disappeared to the driver's side of the SUV, looking over his shoulder to grumble a parting "Good luck on Sunday."

Karen watched him with an eye-rolling little shake of her head before turning back to the momentarily stunned Tyson with a wide smile.

"He knows that if he takes one step out of line, he can find his own way back home. Don't pay him any mind, baby. He's still letting his pride do most of his talking, but I really think he's doing better. Now you go back to the hotel and rest up. I'm going to take your father to get a new suit and a haircut. I can't have him looking like a washed-up degenerate on your big day. Call me if you have any free time, we'll grab a bite to eat."

Tyson took a deep breath. His chest had begun to feel tight. Telling her she was now a grandmother could wait; she already had her hands full. She reached out to give him an encouraging squeeze on his arm that turned into Tyson pulling her to him in a life-affirming hug.

"I love you, Mom. Thanks for making this sacrifice. Thanks for making all of them."

Karen Palmer hugged her six-foot-three-inch baby tight and rubbed his back before pulling away and reaching up to brush a lock of hair off his forehead and into place. Even when Tyson was a kid, she was way too classy to make use of the spit hairspray technique.

"Sweetheart, I would sit with Satan and present a united front if it helped you. That's just what mothers do."

CHAPTER 20

THE AUSTIN MAVERICKS did win their championship rings, but neither Tyson nor Marcus had much to do with it. Both men, while not exactly sloppy, were a bit off kilter. But the defense stepped up and scored twenty-one points to beat the Boston Blitz 31–14.

Once the ring was on his finger, Marcus actually decided to stay on with the Mavericks. After all the threats, Clinton Barrow offered him another deal. Tyson wasn't really surprised; it just reinforced what he'd already figured out: it was always about the bottom line. Barrow couldn't risk Marcus going to another team, and now that the trophy greeted Barrow every time he entered the stadium, he found it easier to be forgiving. It was the Greens of all people who encouraged Marcus to change his mind. The pastor figured that God-given talent like the kind Marcus possessed shouldn't be wasted. By now he felt confident that Marcus was savvy enough to keep from being drawn into the dark side of fame and fortune. Money wasn't the root of all evil, greed was. The pastor was willing to lend his guidance in helping Marcus put his millions to good use, starting with a lovely spacious house Marcus started building a little ways down from the church where Pastor Green preached . . . and officiated at his daughter's wedding.

DANI PULLED HER CAR UP around the back of the house and cut the engine but took a minute before going inside. To say the last week had been tumultuous would be an understatement. After fleeing Austin and heading home, she was faced with the long overdue task of coming clean with her family. Once again she had to sit her parents down and tearfully tell them the truth about why and how she left her job. But this time it was the whole truth. The sadness and confusion in their eyes was piercing. The only thing worse was the genuine worry on their faces that followed.

"If this man wants to fight us for custody, he probably has the resources to completely annihilate us." Danza looked with panic-stricken eyes at her husband.

"Relax, Ma," Dani murmured with her head still hanging in shame. "He didn't stick around long enough to find out whether he had a son or a daughter. I don't think he's interested in fatherhood."

She couldn't even blame Tyson anymore. In the end, she mentally declared it a no-win situation and thought it best to try and move on. She couldn't live in fear of what Tyson might do. And he wasn't going to do anything, it seemed.

Her parents didn't stay angry with her for long, but after a few days it wouldn't have mattered anyway. The depression that followed her return to Ardmore overrode everything else. All her misery was brought on by her own actions. She had no right subjecting anyone else to it. Dani managed to drag herself out of bed every day. She forced herself to smile and laugh and take Brendon to the park, but it was all a facade.

That year was the first time in Carrino history that no one watched the Super Bowl. The television stayed on Nickelodeon the whole day. It was as if by their ignoring the reality, it would go away.

Dani entered the house through the back door and walked into the kitchen. Her mother was there, bustling about with her usual happy hum. The steam from her various boiling pots competed with the cold water humidifier she insisted prevented them all from getting nose-bleeds in the winter.

"What's cooking, Abbondanza?" Dani asked, lifting a lid and finding the stewed prunes that Brendon enjoyed. She looked into another pot and found minestrone. The humming had stopped, but her mother didn't say anything. She glanced over to find her mother staring at her, looking incredibly pleased.

"How was your job interview?" Danza asked.

Dani couldn't decide if the job interview went well or not. On the one hand, the office manager at the accounting firm in Philly thought the famed chicken girl would make a nifty little surprise to any client walking through the door. On the other, she would be spending day after day answering phones and filing. It was all she could do to keep from yawning during the conversation.

Dani shrugged. The house was quiet. "Who knows? Is Brendon napping?"

"No."

"He go somewhere with Dad?"

"Sort of." She continued to stare and added a hint of a smile. "Dad's here. They're in the den."

Dani grabbed a cookie out of the jar on the counter and headed in the direction of the sounds coming from the television set in the den. She had just caught sight of her father's slippers sticking out from his favorite Barcalounger when she heard it, the whooshing sound of Brendon's Little Tikes cars, followed by the sound of Brendon's happy squeal.

That was followed by more laughter. But this laugh was deep and robust. It made her hair stand on end and her heart flutter.

Dani tiptoed down the hallway on feet that felt weighed down by lead, until she was standing in the doorway of the room.

Brendon didn't notice her arrival. He was too busy pushing his car across the carpet.

And sprawled on the floor next to him, with a car of his own following closely behind, was Tyson Palmer.

Dani's sharp intake of breath alerted them both to her arrival. Two pairs of striking blue eyes. Then Brendon added his cheerful smile. "Hi, Mommy."

Tyson presented more of a smirk with a thoroughly raised eyebrow.

"Hi, baby," Dani managed weakly.

"And I thought I was good at running," Tyson said with a wink before standing up. He crouched down until he was eye level with Brendon and rumpled his hair. "I'm going to go have a little chat with your mom. But don't forget, you promised to show me all your Transformers later."

"I'll go line them up in a row! I've got lots!" Brendon broke away and started sprinting down the hall, nearly knocking Dani over to race up the stairs.

"I see you still have your coat on, so why don't we take this out-side?" Tyson suggested, not smiling anymore but still congenial.

Dani led Tyson through the house but not before catching her father squinting at them with one eye open as he lay back in his recliner. He gave her a little smile and closed both eyes to resume his nap.

When they reached the kitchen door, Danza looked up from the apples she was paring for applesauce.

"I hope you stay for dinner, Tyson. It's lasagna night."

"Wouldn't want to miss it," Tyson replied before placing a hand on each of her shoulders and whispering into Danza's ear, "We'll see how it goes. Wish me luck."

Dani had only been gone for a few hours, but it seemed that was more than adequate time for him to win them all over.

It was sunny in Ardmore that day, but the winter chill was still in the air, and the ground was frozen with patches of ice. The crisp cold-ness outdoors felt good on Dani's suddenly flushed face. Tyson waited patiently with his hands in his pockets as she struggled to find the right words. Or any words.

"Does he know?" she managed to rasp out, glancing back toward the house.

"If you mean did I storm in here and force a five-year-old to start calling a complete stranger 'Daddy,' the answer is definitely no. For one thing, your mother would have hit me upside the head with one of those pots."

A small laugh bubbled out of her, and Dani finally found the cour-age to meet his gaze. Without Brendon acting as a buffer, she fully expected to be met with anger, but all she could read on his face was determination.

"Why didn't you tell me?"

"At first . . . at first I didn't know what to do," she stammered haplessly.

The words sounded ridiculous, even to her. He must have agreed, because he threw his hands in the air with disgust.

"Damn it, Dani! You were supposed to do what all Americans do! You were supposed to file for child support and at least make sure our kid gets what he deserves!" he shouted before lowering his voice. "And what about me? You were supposed to give me my chance to do the right thing."

"Not at the expense of our son. What if you really hadn't changed?" she answered sadly, preferring to get right to the point. "I didn't need you financially to make a nice life for Brendon. I knew he would get strong male role models without you. My dad and brothers adore him. Plus you did get your shot. That first time I approached you and you didn't recognize me."

"Everything about you had changed."

"I did what I thought I had to . . ." Her voice trailed off. There were no more lame excuses for her to offer.

"Even if I didn't recognize you at first . . . what about later? You had no right to keep it from me, especially after it was clear where we were headed."

"I know. I know!" Tears stung her eyes. "I messed up bad. First I let all my anger get in the way. Then after the fly thing happened I was embarrassed and scared to death that you'd be hell-bent on revenge. By the time I realized that wasn't the case, you were already saying and doing all the right things, and I . . . I didn't want that to end."

She knew she was dancing all around the real issue, so she squared her shoulders and took a deep breath.

"I wanted you to love me the way I loved you, before Brendon.

When I finally started getting my wish, I was afraid that once you found out, everything would change. I know now all my choices were the wrong ones. I have no right to ask you for forgiveness."

"Don't you think it's up to me to decide if I can forgive you?"

"I got the impression you had made that decision the minute you called me a cab. Are you trying to tell me you've had a change of heart?"

"I am."

"Why?"

"Because, Dani, there are some things that are too big to stay mad over. Or in this particular case, too little, like that beautiful little boy in there. We've already lost too much time."

Dani knew she should've been relieved. This was the best of all possible outcomes. He was there, once again saying and doing all the right things. But now that all the drama was over, all that was left was the cleanup. She stared down at her feet, so emotionally drained it was hard to even look up at him.

"Of course, I don't recall you once saying you were sorry." He faked a pout.

She tried to look him in the eye but was afraid if she did so, she would crumble and he'd feel the obligation to make it better. "I'm so sorry, Tyson. I wish I could go back and do things differently."

"You know, they say you're supposed to forgive people for your own sake, not for theirs. But I can honestly say I've never met someone who needed forgiveness more than you. It's written all over your face. I accept your apology, Dani. Now I really want you to let it all go. We have a son to raise, he deserves the best his parents can give him."

"We're going to have to tell him." She pulled her coat around her to ward off the chill that was now invading not only her body, but also her soul.

"Nope, not we. You. But right after you do, I'm going to ask his permission to marry you."

For almost a decade she had daydreamed that Tyson would propose to her. True, there were times when the dream included ruthlessly shooting him down and making him beg. But now she sadly shook her head and swallowed another round of unshed tears. "I can't marry you, Tyson. Not now. It would be for all the wrong reasons. I know you're only stepping up because you think you're supposed to. We don't need to subject each other to that. I don't want to keep you from Brendon. Lots of couples make custody work. We'll be good at it. We have a common goal."

Tyson was having none of it and swiftly closed the distance between them. He took her head in both of his hands and tenderly lifted her face up until she was looking into his.

"For way too long now, I've kept my distance from people. Not because I didn't think they were worthy, but because I didn't think I was. Of all the gifts I got to make me whole, the biggest one was presented to me on a night I didn't remember. I don't want to spend one more day without you. I started to ask you before I knew about Brendon. Finding out about him is just God's way of telling me that it's the right call. Darlin', if it's all right with you, I'd like to spend the rest of my life swinging from your heartstrings."

How was she supposed to argue with that kind of logic? He lifted her off her feet, kissing her until all her worries began to melt away. By the time he set her back down, she didn't want to debate him on anything.

"I guess I can take that as a yes?" he asked while she caught her breath.

She nodded, and he pulled her back to kiss her again. Then he held up her hand. "I didn't come with a ring because I didn't want to pressure you. I thought it'd be nice if we picked one out together."

"I don't need a ring," she told him, unconcerned now about the tears running down her cheeks.

"Don't be ridiculous. If anyone has earned a flashy ring, it's you. Let's make it the gaudiest one we can find."

They heard the storm door slam and turned to see Brendon, his winter coat, hat, and mittens on, standing on the back porch.

"Danza told me to tell you that dinner is in twenty minutes," Brendon announced with a call across the yard. "And I can't find Optimus Prime!"

Dani and Tyson looked briefly at each other and smiled. Their new journey had officially begun.

"Coming!" Dani called, slipping her hand into Tyson's, and together they made their way back to the house.

"How long did it take Marcus to find out my address?" Dani asked as they walked.

"Longer than you'd expect," Tyson replied, giving her hand a squeeze. "We had to resort to drastic measures, mainly shaking down Clinton Barrow."

She laughed. "Yeah, that sounds like Marcus's style. He likes to rock the boat more than he'd ever admit. So what did you guys do, put a gun to Barrow's head?" She was only half joking.

"Close. I told him if he didn't me tell how to find you, I wouldn't make a single throw in our last game. Marcus was more than willing to back me up. Barrow's counteroffer was that he would tell us, but only if we won."

"That's the worst wager ever. What if you lost?"

Tyson rolled his eyes before snickering. "Come on. We weren't losing. And I knew he was going to tell me either way. He just wanted to give us all a little time to let the dust settle and get his trophy."

"And if he called your bluff?"

"Then I guess I was going to spend the entire day getting sacked. I figured it was a win-win. If you weren't moved by the sight of me taking that kind of beating, then we probably didn't belong together."

"I didn't watch the game at all," Dani said with a smidge of guilt.

"I think it's on tape somewhere if you really care," Tyson replied with a laugh, wrapping his arm around her.

CHAPTER 21

IT WAS A rare quiet May evening in the Northwest Hills of Austin, a Sunday oddly enough. But the whole weekend had been a tad on the strange side. Dani Carr had been in a writing frenzy the entire time. And why wouldn't she be? She'd been asked to tell a story. About a football team that was willing to throw away a winning season, and then won it all for no good reason. The publisher that approached her with the offer of a ghostwriter was quickly rebuffed. There was nobody who could tell the whole story better than Dani herself, she told them. And she was mildly surprised when they agreed to let her have a shot at it.

Tyson was so proud of her, even if he did grumble about having to share his precious off-time with her new obsession. On July 1, he'd be starting his new job with the league's own broadcasting channel, a contract Tyson was sure was proffered based on his own merits and not because it was part of anyone else's grand plan. Another bonus—he'd be doing the play-by-play for Philadelphia. It was the only thing that kept him in Danza's good graces. Home games guaranteed he would arrive to work with his family in tow.

But none of that meant anything to Brendon, who had spent the better part of Saturday and all of Sunday getting various nods and absentminded hugs, but no meaningful attention from his preoccupied mother. Take-out containers from their dinner were still gathered near the kitchen sink.

"What's the matter, Bren?" Tyson asked as soon as he saw the youngster sulking and loitering near the arm of the sofa where he was stretched out watching the NFL draft.

"Mommy's mad at me. And I miss Danza," was the forlorn answer.

"Want to go in the pool?" Tyson offered in consolation, but Brendon just shook his head and made a face.

"Can't. I already took a bath and Mommy said it's almost bedtime." He gave the leg of the couch a tiny kick in protest.

"She's right," Tyson said, standing up and walking over to the kitchen counter to the spot where he kept not only his worn football, but also a smaller, softer Nerf version. "Let's play with footballs."

He brought both balls back to the couch, handing Brendon his while he sat back down.

"She looks so mad." He looked like he might start to cry, and Tyson could feel his heart once again start to melt.

Tyson started tossing the football in his hand, spinning it into midair, where it would stay suspended for a few seconds, spiraling the whole time, before dropping back down into his large hand. It was a motion Brendon imitated with his smaller football. He tried to duplicate his father's skill, but it was still much more fun to watch. With his miniature football tight in his hand, Brendon cuddled up alongside Tyson on the couch.

"That look isn't for us, partner," Tyson said low and conspiratorially, wrapping an arm around his son to pull him in close, the other launching the football into the air in front of them again, much to the young boy's delight. "That look is definitely for the computer. Mom wants to make sure she gets every word about Marcus right."

The five-year-old was satisfied with that explanation, and he began to yawn. It was exhausting going to a new kindergarten and running around football fields with your dad. Not to mention swimming and going down the pool slide until he was wrinkled as a prune. Within a matter of minutes all Tyson could hear was Brendon's deep even breathing.

"Hey, lady," Tyson called in a hushed tone across the room. "What's a guy in this house have to do to get a little attention?"

Dani looked up to the sight she was sure she would never get tired of seeing.

"Are my boys feeling neglected?" she asked with a hint of a grin, glancing over at the clock on the microwave.

"I can't speak for our son, but I could sure use a few of your smiles. Maybe your naughty one."

That was all the motivation she needed. She closed the lid on her laptop.

There were so many things that made Tyson a good father and husband. One of the best things was his ability to carry a sleeping future quarterback up a flight of stairs with no effort.

"I'm so glad I kept you around," Dani remarked after noting once more just how tall Brendon was growing by how far his once tiny legs dangled from Tyson's arms. "He's getting so big."

"I'm so glad your brother and sister-in-law decided to tell your mother they were having a baby before you moved down here. The looks she was giving me were starting to get scary."

"That's only going to hold her off for so long. God help us if we decide to have another kid. We'll have to buy another house up there."

"I can do that," Tyson said. "In fact, I look forward to it. Just think how much they'll enjoy winters in Austin."

They tucked the barely stirring Brendon safely into bed and went to their own room, where Tyson wasted no time in pulling her close, knowing he only had a few minutes before some idea sent her flying back downstairs to quickly type it out.

"I really do love you, you know," he told her with sincerity as he helped pull the shirt over her head. His lips grazed over the now-exposed skin and with a quick flick of his fingers her bra began to come apart. "I think I always have. You are the best thing that ever happened to me."

"You are such a smooth talker." She pulled at the belt buckle that held up his jeans and leaned into him as his mouth descended on her now-uncovered breast.

"It's easy when you speak the truth," he murmured, and the race to disrobe was on.

ACKNOWLEDGMENTS

I fell in love with Austin, Texas, after being invited to give a talk at the Lake Austin Spa Resort. Granted, it's hard to hate on a gorgeous spa resort, but from the moment I landed in Austin I was enchanted. Thank you, Robbie Hudson and the rest of the staff, for your generous hospitality, not once but twice! I thought of you all often as I wrote *The Total Package*. I hope I get to see you again soon.

This probably isn't a very good sign in a writer, but it's hard to find the words to express my gratitude to my editor, Rachel Kahan. Thank you for your love of words, attention to detail, and appreciation of a good corny joke. I can't even picture being on this journey without you.

I'm also extremely grateful to the team at William Morrow including, but not limited to—Heidi Richter, Dianna Garcia, Kathy Gordon, Kaitlin Harri, Trish Daly, Jennifer Hart, Angela Dong, Doug Jones, Shelby Meizlik, Virginia Stanley, Lynn Grady, Shawn Nicholls, Lisa Sharkey, and Michael Morrison. I know there are so many others whose names I've missed, but I do know this much: it takes a village to publish a book and my village rocks! Special thanks to Liate Stehlik, whom I don't see nearly enough, but who makes me smile every time I do.

Diane Short La Rue, Alison Skap, Stacy Schlanger Alesi, Melissa Amster, Anita LeBeau, Kristin Thorvaldsen, and Tamara Welch— thank you so much for allowing me into your blog-o-spheres and then giving me the precious gift of your friendships.

Thank you, Ron Block, for being all that and a delicious bag of chips. (Hold the quail eggs.)

Sandra Bunino, my writing friend, what can I say? You're amazing. Thank you for always being an enthusiastic sounding board, your general wisdom, and the unique ability to turn any stressful situation into an all-out laugh-fest.

And no blessing count would be complete without saying thank you to my readers, for your encouragement and support. Without you, I would be in a cubicle maze, crunching numbers. Because of you, I still pinch myself on a daily basis. Because of you, a dream came true. I wish there were words bigger than THANK YOU.

ABOUT THE AUTHOR

Stephanie Evanovich is a full-fledged Jersey girl from Asbury Park who began writing fiction while waiting for her cues during countless community theater projects. She attended the New York Conservatory for Dramatic Arts and acted in several improv troupes and a couple of B movies, all in preparation for the greatest job she ever had: raising her two sons. A full-time writer now, she's also an avid sports fan who holds a black belt in tae kwon do.